Ian Taylor is an award-winning director of numerous television documentaries and documentary series, together with contributions to *Newsnight, Panorama* and *Dispatches.* In a distinguished career he has seen his work broadcast on all the British terrestrial channels and rebroadcast around the world. His stories have taken him to over sixty countries. It is from that wealth of first-hand experience that the story in this novel is drawn.

To Anis
with best wishes
Ian Taylor

THE
BIG
STORY

a novel by

Ian Taylor

Matador
9 De Montfort Mews
Leicester LE1 7FW, UK
Tel: (+44) 116 255 9311 / 9312
Email: books@troubador.co.uk
Web: www.troubador.co.uk/matador

ISBN 978-1906221-294

Typeset in 11pt Bembo by Troubador Publishing Ltd, Leicester, UK
Printed in the UK by The Cromwell Press Ltd, Trowbridge, Wilts, UK

Matador is an imprint of Troubador Publishing Ltd

In remembrance of Rosemary

Believe it or not...
The least plausible aspects of this story are closely based on real events, witnessed by the author.

FOR THE BACKGROUND there was a mountain. Along its slopes dense, green vegetation climbed to an awesome cloudbase. Here and there memorials to a rain forest stood erect, tall trunks, giant dandelion stalks, headless, dead and white. The nearest and most prominent of these was framed to the left.

In the middle distance an odd assortment of men stood in some sort of formation, ill-dressed, some barefoot, each one carrying a weapon – a rifle with a long, wooden stock, a bow and arrow, one Kalashnikov.

And in the foreground.......a man was combing his hair.

The man combing his hair studied his reflection in the lens of a camera. Behind the camera other characters formed a complementary group: the cameraman stooped to the eyepiece; his soundman, the one with the earphones, standing as far from the camera as his umbilical cord would allow (the better, he liked to think, to emphasise his individual professionalism); and further still two more – one of these a tall, ill-at-ease young man in wire-frame glasses. From time to time this anxious young man removed his glasses, polished them nervously on his shirt, then replaced them. He appeared uncomfortable in the presence of his companion. They were both, in their different ways, in command of events but the other, with his black moustache and his camouflage fatigues and his rocket-propelled grenade launcher, was also in control.

A short exchange was taking place between the cameraman and his reporter. This was overheard but not understood by the ragged combatants who presumed it to be technical. "I know you think it's thirty-five grands worth of dressing table," the cameraman was saying, "but to me, Peter, it happens to be my camera..."

Peter returned the comb to the breast pocket of his pressed safari shirt and stared through the lens with just the slightest flaring of his attractive nostrils: "We're only interested in the same thing, you know, Dave. We're all trying to make the best film we can".

Short on repartee, Dave mouthed a silent 'bollocks'.

The worried-looking young man hurried forward to keep the peace. This was his responsibility. He was responsible for the present tension and would be responsible for its appeasement. He was responsible, he thought, for far too much; he was responsible to his military host, the commander of the guerrilla forces, who was growing visibly impatient. He would have liked to have explained his problem to the commander but to do so would have been to confess to a professional soldier the true cause of the poor morale amongst his own troops: that this was nothing more than the mutinous discontent of men forced, against their will, to endure three successive nights without en suite bathroom.

"It's just not very professional," Dave was saying. "You tell him. You're the director."

"Professionalism is the last refuge of the mediocre," said Peter. "People only ever say 'he's very *professional*,' when they can't find any actual talent to praise. It means 'he's dull but conscientious. He turns up on time and hits his marks. He does his job."

"I'd settle for that in your case. What take are we on?"

"Can we just do it?" said the young director, "turn over."

"*I'm* running."

The reporter grudgingly slipped his hands, thumbs outside, into the waist pockets of his safari shirt then turned to look over one shoulder at the guerrilla platoon. As he began to speak he swung a quizzical gaze back towards the camera.....

"*But the problems for the Armed forces of the Philippines, the AFP, don't end with the New People's Army or NPA, the military wing of the communist-led National Democratic Front, the NDF. Here in the mountains of Mindanao the MNLF, or Moro Islamic Liberation Front and a splinter group the MILF...*"

"Cut!"

"Sod it, what is it now?"

"Sorry, Peter.... *National.*"

"National?"

"It's the Moro *National* Liberation Front. The M.N.L.F."

"That's what I said."

"Well, you said M.N.L.F. but you called them Islamic. That's the M.I.L.F."

"I thought they were both Islamic."

"They are. But only one of them's called it."

"You think anyone's going to notice?"

"We have to get it right Peter. Turn over!"

"Running."

A sigh then: *"But the problems for the Armed Forces of the Philippines, the AFP, don't end with the New People's Army or NPA, the military wing of the communist-led National Democratic Front, the NDF. Here in the mountains of Mindanao the Moro National Liberation Front, the MNLF and a splinter group the MILF, the Moro <u>Islamic</u> Liberation Front, have been waging a guerrilla war now for three decades. Despite previous settlements and ceasefires, a recent spate of kidnappings…"*

"Cut!"

"What do you mean *cut!*. I was getting it right, every sodding acronym. I was getting it right and you say cut. Who are you to say cut, Jonathan?"

"It wasn't me," the director said, "it was Andy."

The soundman was removing his earphones slowly. He did this the better to hear himself speak. He had something to say. "Helicopter," he said.

Peter rolled his eyes upward. "Andy, so you can hear a helicopter. There's a fucking war on. You hear helicopters."

"Only doing my job."

"Ok let's do it again....."

A gunshot exploded nearby and echoed five or six times through distant valleys. Then silence. The commander lowered an arm and replaced his smoking revolver in its leather holster, re-buttoning the flap. "You have finished now," he said, "no more filming."

"Well, not quite," the director said, "we just need to do it one more time. You see the helicopter...." but his words were engulfed in a throb of rotor blades. With a synchronous crescendo the helicopter rose into view, entomic above the treetops, strobing the sunlight. It circled once, then began a slow, wobbly descent into the gathering whirlwind.

"Now we go," said the commander.

"Where? You want us to go too?"

"Just you."

"He wants me to go alone," Peter shouted to the others through a hail of flying grass, "It's probably an off-the-record briefing. We'll meet up back in Koronadal."

The commander shook his head. "You are to be our guest," he shouted above the throb of the turbine, holding his beret down with one hand, "we do not know how long you will be staying."

"Very hospitable of you, commandante, but there's still more filming for us to do."

The commander shook his head a second time and pointed to the helicopter. Two of the armed men came forward and stood one at each of Peter's shoulders. The helicopter's pulse was becoming oppressive, numbing, excluding thought. Debris swirled all around. The director screwed up his eyes. "I don't like to say this Peter," he screamed, close into the reporter's ear, "but has it crossed your mind that he might mean 'guest' like we say 'guest of her majesty', you know, 'at her majesty's pleasure'?"

A slow recognition crossed Peter's face. His mouth shaped a silent, vulgar monosyllable; his eyes made frantic voiceless appeals to the others. He turned to the commander. "Look....you do realise who we are don't you? We're the BBC, the British Broadcasting... I mean you can't just....."

The commander's smile was broad but not benign. "This-is-Lun-dun," he intoned with mock solemnity, "rum tiddy tum, ti rum tiddy tum...."

"For God's sake, you don't understand. You don't imagine they'll pay you anything for me." Peter's voice strained against the noise. "It's not even their money, it comes from the licence fee....."

The commander looked puzzled.

"The licence fee. It's a mechanism for keeping the broadcasters free from state.......Oh for God's sake, this is bloody ridiculous. I'm trying to explain a free press to a terrorist who wants to kidnap me. Nation shall speak peace unto nation huh? Look, you want money? I've got money. He fumbled in his pocket and pulled out a wallet. "Here, credit cards; some of them are gold......" But the two armed men had already seized him by the arms and were bundling him towards the hovering helicopter. Only Andy the soundman protested.

"Just a minute," he screamed above the noise, "you can't do that."

The guards hesitated and, in the momentary confusion, Andy knelt down, unplugged the wire trailing from the reporter's trouser leg, then deftly unpinned the tiny microphone from inside his shirt front. "Thanks," he said, "nearly lost that."

As the helicopter wobbled momentarily, adjusting to the added weight, then lifted and began to crab over the treetops, the remainder of the Moro Islamic Liberation Front slipped unseen into the jungle background. The throb of the rotors gave way to the buzz of cicadas.

Dave was the first to speak. "Got it. Great."

"What do you mean, great? He's been kidnapped, for Christ sake."

"Well, I got it, didn't I?"

"Got what?"

"The whole thing. Peter being taken hostage. When that bloke said no more filming I just pressed the tit and held the camera under my arm. You always do when they tell you not to. It's all right. Not the best of angles but it's on the wide end. It'll all be in frame."

No-one spoke.

The cameraman shrugged and began to collapse his tripod. "Okay, please yourself. Just doing my job. I mean anyone would think you didn't *want* to win an award?"

THIRTEEN MONTHS LATER

The dining rooms of the Hotel Octyabrina opened one onto another, high-ceilinged, ornate with *fin-de-siècle* pomp, faded red plush curtains, gilded plaster and one of the best views in Moscow across the parade ground of tarmac, which is the Manezh Square, to the floodlit walls of the Kremlin. At the circular tables Russians in shiny suits engaged in loud bonhomie with their western guests, encouraged by bottles of sweet red champagne and Azerbaidjani wine which tasted of sherry, and proposed repeated toasts to friendship between their countries, to their respective enterprises, to market forces, to their loved ones and, of course, to world peace. And at the end of the largest hall a balalaika band played *Moscow Nights* for the third time that evening, which, Gerry Harris calculated, was probably the sixteenth time that week and the forty-fourth time that month and who knows what multiple for the year. And they played it, as might be expected, languorously and colourlessly, which in no way mattered for that was the way it was meant to sound.

Gerry stood in the queue as the millionaire head-waiter strode past the line of beseeching guests, stopping only to take a proffered five dollar bill from the newest arrivals, whom he acknowledged with a nod and a shrug. And then he cast his eyes out across the great room counting the empty tables, balancing that mysterious equation, as only a Russian can, in which the number of empty tables must always exceed the number of guests waiting to sit at them. If the West could only crack this secret formula, Gerry liked to say, she would undoubtedly unlock the mystery of the Russian soul. And he might have said it again tonight, were it not that he had long since become irritable standing in this queue, that he knew, from past experience, that by the time they got a seat half the menu would have disappeared, that if they were unlucky enough only cold food would be left.

Part of Gerry had a nostalgia for the Octyabrina. This was the old Soviet Union unreconstructed, as so much of modern Russia still was. To a westerner the Octyabrina held the same combination of exotic charm and discomfort as does a Bedouin tent. Not for the Octyabrina the benefits of joint venture capital which had turned the nearby National into a Trust House Forte, with its well-mannered Swiss-trained staff who could say 'have a nice day' in a dozen languages. But the other part of Gerry was pissed off. This was a dinner he'd been looking forward to. He'd rehearsed a fund of good stories with which he proposed to impress the crew, stories from his own early days reporting the end of the cold war. They were of a generation young enough to have heard none of them before, unlike Felix, who would have been there most of the events related took place and so would interrupt the storytelling to contradict those little creative details which turned an account into an anecdote. But Felix was away bonking the researcher girl or whatever he was up to, so Gerry would be free to tell his cold war stories in the manner he chose, of KGB girls and confidences and concealed microphones. He would tell that one about the time he felt a bump under the carpet in his hotel room (this very hotel) and, rolling it back, had discovered a brass plate with four screws in it; how he removed the screws one by one with his Swiss army penknife and how, when the last screw was withdrawn, a chandelier crashed to the floor in the room beneath. He would tell it as his own story, even though it was really one of Freddie Downton's from the old days on *Panorama* but he didn't feel guilty because Freddie was long gone now and in any case he'd probably made it up.

But young Dave the cameraman and the other one, what was his name – Dave something too wasn't it? Anyway neither of the Daves looked like getting the star entertainment from Gerry Harris tonight. Gerry Harris was irritable. And getting worse.

"Sorry about this everybody," he said to them. He'd expected to enjoy himself, playing the old hand who knew his way around, showing the novices the ropes, showing off. But he was failing them and rapidly losing esteem. The head waiter passed again, not looking. Gerry reached out and stopped him with a hand. He reached into his pocket and held out a five dollar bill. The waiter took it. "Soon," he said.

"Now."

"Soon," said the waiter again and began to move away.

Gerry grabbed him by the sleeve. "No not bloody soon, bloody now." The waiter tried to remove the hand but Gerry gripped tighter. "That's the third bank note you've had from me in the last half-hour," he said, raising his voice. "Ok no big deal to us but that's hard currency, isn't it? Worth a few squillion roubles, right? You must be the richest bloody man in Russia. Now get me a table." Around the room several of the guests paused from their toasts and turned to look.

"Such talk will not help you to get a table," the waiter said quietly in perfect English.

"Well then," Gerry said, the pitch of his voice rising with the volume, "why don't I tell you something that *might* just help me get me a table. Do you know who I'm seeing tomorrow? Do you? Well let me tell you who I'm seeing tomorrow. I'm seeing your President. That's who I'm seeing. I'm interviewing the president of all the Russias, well one of them anyway, for the British Broadcasting Corporation. So how would you like me to ask him a few questions about the service at the Octyabrina? How would you like me to tell him there's a snotty-nosed waiter there who's extorting hard currency from the nation's guests for the courtesy of letting them eat....?"

Around the room the diners looked and looked away again, curiosity alternating with embarrassment. Gerry saw the turning heads and heard the room go quiet, save for *Moscow Nights* and whether it was his professional instinct to respond to an audience or just a final, uncontrollable urge to make a scene (in recounting the anecdote much later he would like to say 'I just saw red – no pun intended') he turned and addressed the entire dining room.

"You see this man," he shouted now above the residue of conversation and the balalaika band, "this man is corrupt. This man is an extortionist and a mafioso. This man is a crook."

Moscow Nights came to an end and the balalaika band shuffled quickly for a new number to play. In the momentary silence the Europeans and Americans among the guests tried to strike up spontaneous new conversations. The Russians for their part just watched, enjoying the novelty. What had *glasnost* been about after all, if not openness? Here was a man being open, telling everyone what everyone thought and nobody said.

"This man has just taken fifteen dollars off me," Gerry was saying, "not a lot of money but we all know what that's worth in roubles don't we? So how much did you all pay him? How much have all the people in this room paid him this evening for the privilege of sitting down? Come on, hands up all those....." Gerry stopped. A face had come between him and his audience. The face wore a peaked cap. "*Militsia*," it said solemnly.

In the anecdotal version of the incident, as subsequently told by Gerry himself, Gerry is said to have displayed exemplary quickness of thought, not to say some little wit, in seizing the initiative with the policeman. "Officer," he said, "thank goodness you've come. I want you to arrest this man." The two Daves, on the other hand, when pressed for their account, could not remember this line. "He kept shouting for the researcher girl to come and translate," they recalled, "he kept shrieking that she wasn't there so that the producer could get his leg over; she was there because she could speak Russian and most researchers would give their fucking eye teeth to come on a trip like this so why wasn't she here when she was needed...?" They also maintained that it was Gerry who struck the first blow.

Gerry never forgave them. It took two policemen in the end to bundle him to the door. His last glimpse of the restaurant, over the wide shoulder boards of their tunics, was of the two Daves, the one carrying his camera for safe keeping, being shown politely to a table by the head waiter.

Four floors above the dining rooms, Olivia Denning-Smith lay squashed in the single bed, staring across the room through a forest of soft-focus ginger hairs. The position of Felix's arm restricted her field of vision to the upper half of a varnished plywood wardrobe, on the door of which hung her own clothes, neatly folded. Felix's would be in a heap somewhere on the floor. She lifted the heavy arm and tried to push it out of the way but it fell back on her breasts then slid, once again, up around her neck. The ginger hairs tickled her nose. "Felix," she said, "you're crushing me," and she pushed the arm away once more. There was a moan from Felix who lifted the arm slowly and directed it in search of a whisky on the bedside table. But by the time his fingers had closed reflexively around the glass, he had thought better of it, relaxed his grip and let the arm drop down the side of the bed.

"God," he groaned, "the ceiling moved," and then, having thought about what he'd just said, added, "did the ceiling move for you?"

This line, given the intimate occasion of its utterance, was never to be immortalised. Indeed, given the events which were shortly to follow, it is unlikely that Olivia ever remembered his saying it. But if not exactly immortal, or even so much as famous, these were, without doubt, Felix Porter's last words.

"Felix," Olivia said, putting on her vulnerable, endearing voice, "Felix, I wanted to ask your advice on something. You know I've always admired your films. I think you're far and away the best producer on *Worldweek* and you and Gerry make a terrific team. I think your piece on Chechnya deserves an award, really I do, I mean that bit where they uncover the bodies....anyway what it's about is I've got this idea for a story and I'd really like the chance to make it myself, you know, produce and direct like you.....Felix?.... are you awake?....Felix are you listening to me...?"

A noise which sounded like "mmm..." came from Felix. Olivia went on: "...you see I want to make it myself but even if I get it past this new editor Boyle, he's just going to hand it over to someone experienced So what it is I'm suggesting is that if you were to put it forward, you know give it credibility, then perhaps when he's accepted it you could tell him it was my idea and....Felix?....are you awake?....Felix this is important.... you see it's about this refuge in Hackney for women from Africa and the Far East who come over here working for Arabs and....Felix?...."

Felix gave a snore followed by a strange snuffling noise. Olivia got up on one elbow. "I don't believe it," she said, "I do not believe it. Of all the bloody cheek...." She glowered at the sleeping Felix then fell back on the pillow deflating her lungs in a slow prolonged hiss. "Sod you," she said quietly in the direction of the ceiling, "just sod you Felix Porter." She took several deep breaths. Tears of frustration formed in the corners of her eyes. "I mean what the hell do you think I'm doing here Felix? I mean what exactly do you think I'm doing...?" Felix twitched and made another snuffling noise.

"....I mean can you think of any good reason why Olivia Denning-Smith, twenty-six, attractive, intelligent, fluent linguist, B.A.

oxon. etcetera, etcetera should be lying in bed with a boozy old slob biologically old enough to be her father....? Can you Felix? Well let me help you out. I'll give you one guess and, no, it's nothing to do with sexual chemistry...." She paused, listening to Felix's erratic breathing. "....I'm making my way in the world, Felix, or trying to, in one of the famous ways traditionally open to women. I'm whoring, Felix, sleeping my way up the greasy pole. Now there's a metaphor for you. I'm selling my beautiful body for prospects and all you can do is sodding fall asleep on me.....Felix?...." She dug an elbow hard into Felix's ribs. The snoring faltered, then became oddly irregular, more a kind of gargle in the throat. She saw Felix's right arm cross his chest and slowly clutch his left shoulder. She sat up and looked at him. His mouth drooped open. And then the gargling sound again, fainter this time. And then he became still, not just still but *really* still. And then the eyes popped open.

It was when his eyes popped open that Olivia screamed, not so much a blood–curdling scream of terror as a shriek of surprise. She backed out of the bed, covering her body with her hands, instinctively aware of the impropriety of being undressed in front of what looked very much like a corpse. Her first thought was to panic, although that was less of a thought than a reaction, like the scream. Her second thought was not to panic, though that was not nearly so easy. Just as the drowning man is said to see his life flash before him in moments, so Olivia saw, looking at the body in the bed, all the impossible, hopeless outcomes of all the impossibly hopeless courses of action she might take:

One: she could summon help. They would come to her room. *Why is this man in your bed Miss Denning-Smith?* He came to my room to discuss the programme, felt ill and lay down. *After taking off all his clothes, Miss Denning Smith?* Hopeless.

Two: she would have to dress him. Dress him! Felix must weigh fifteen stone... dead weight. (Why did she say that?) Impossible.

Three: she could get the crew to dress him, support him down the corridor to his own room. What was she saying? They were the last people she wanted to know. The embarrassment, the sniggers in the club. Unthinkable.

Four: she could leave the room, come back and discover him there. Scream, call for help. *So tell me Miss Denning-Smith how exactly did Mr. Porter come to be in your room....about your movements on the night of the sixteenth....* Suspicion... Homicide...Murder enquiry.... *Anyone vouch for your whereabouts?* Hopeless, impossible, all of it. She wanted to cry. She took control of herself. Deep breaths. A mirror. That's what you did. One thing at a time. Establish if the victim is actually dead. She found her handbag and rummaged inside for a mirror. She approached the bed, nervously. She bent over Felix and held the mirror close to his lips. No condensation. The victim was actually dead. The eyes stared right through her. She felt for a pulse but was unsure which side of the wrist the artery ran. She felt her own then tried Felix's again. Nothing. She let the arm drop. It fell in the lifeless way they do in films. The victim was actually dead.

And then Olivia had a thought. The thought somehow excited her yet made her feel guilty for having it, all at the same time. It wasn't anything which was going to get her out of her present predicament but it was more than ample compensation for any distress and embarrassment which might result. The thought was this: if Felix was dead then Felix couldn't direct the rest of the shoot. And if Felix couldn't direct the rest of the shoot then they'd have to find someone who could. And between now and 10.15 a.m. tomorrow when they were due at the Kremlin to interview the president (which was only 7.15 a.m. in London) who were they possibly going to find except the only available member of the production team, namely Olivia herself? Wow! Dead men's shoes, she said to herself and, looking at Felix, felt horribly guilty again. She bent over and covered his face with the bedsheet.

She began to think rationally now, promotion in the field heightening her sense of responsibility. She began to order priorities in her head. One: notify the hotel authorities of Felix's death and wait for the doctor. Two: phone London and inform Boyle that Felix was dead but that the production would go ahead. Three: find Gerry Harris and the crew....

There was a knock at the door. The cool rationality disintegrated into panic. "Who is it?" she said in a wavering high-pitched voice that belonged to someone else.

"Dave," said a voice.

Olivia cleared her throat and dropped a register. "Which one?"

"Well, both, actually. We're both here."

"What do you want?"

"We need to talk to you. Can we come in?"

"Er...no. Is it important?"

"Well it could be. It's about Gerry."

"What about Gerry?"

"Well I don't think he'll be doing the interview tomorrow. You see he's been arrested..."

From outside in the corridor the two Daves heard a shriek followed by a shuffling and then the key turning in the lock. The door opened a few inches.

"What did you say?" Olivia's face was white, her hair dishevelled. She was still tying the cord of a dressing gown. "What the hell did you say?"

"Arrested, Gerry's been arrested – for causing a commotion in the restaurant. Breach of the peace I suppose you'd call it. He was hoping you'd be able to translate."

"When was this?"

"About half an hour ago."

"And you haven't told us, I mean me, until now?"

"Well they gave us a table, you see, and if you don't accept it when it's offered then you never know when you'll get to eat?"

"Never know when you'll get to eat....!" Olivia's voice shot up a register again. "Do you realise what you've done? You've wasted half a sodding hour. If we don't get Gerry out tonight we'll miss the interview. You can't just book another one you know. Sorry Mr. President but can you make it Thursday? Christ....don't you realise this is my biggest...." and Olivia stopped herself in time, pressing the heels of her hands to her temples to regain her composure. But as she did this she unwittingly let go of the door handle so that the door swung ajar just sufficiently for the two Daves to make out Felix's shape beneath the sheet on the bed.

"Oh....er sorry, we disturbing you?"

Olivia closed her eyes, gave a sigh of defeat and kicked the door wide open for them both to see. "No," she said, fighting back sobs of self-pity and frustration, "I can honestly say that you're not disturbing Felix at all. Felix is not going to be disturbed by anyone....ever."

The Daves looked shocked.

"He's dead," she said, reasserting her self-possession, "heart attack. Not actually during the act of coitus, if that's what you're thinking.

13

Afterwards. I know it's a lot to ask of you two but if you could, you know, keep this to yourselves....."

"But you'll have to report it..."

"I didn't mean that," Olivia snapped, "I meant...." and she softened again, tears forming in her eyes, "I meant....back home....you know....it would be very...." and she was about to say 'embarrassing' but thought better of it and said instead "...distressing."

"Of course Olivia, of course. Wouldn't dream of it. Very distressing," the Daves said, meaning it.

"In fact," Olivia said, "it's all so distressing I really don't think I can cope with....you know....everything...." and she looked first at Felix then from one Dave to the other, her eyes moist and appealing.

"Anything we can do, Olivia, anything at all...."

Olivia took her clothes from the back of the wardrobe door. "You're terribly sweet, you really are. You see if you could just, well, take over from me here....." and she looked at Felix again, wiping the corners of her eyes with the back of her hand, "....I'll see if I can find out where they've taken poor old Gerry. He at least is in the land of the living," and with a brave, ever so slightly tragic smile she backed into the bathroom and closed the door.

Whilst the two Daves had been perfectly sincere in promising not to tell anyone the circumstances of Felix's death, each of them, as is usually the case with confidences, told just one other person with the promise-me-under-absolutely-no-circumstances-will-you-ever-tell anyone injunction, which is generally thought not to count as a betrayal, but which at the same time is taken, by the confidant, as a licence to do likewise. In this way it was only a matter of days before everyone in the club knew the truth in all its salacious, if frequently creative detail and not much longer before a whole repertory of jokes began to circulate, whose humour lay, as it was intended, not so much in their wit as in their tastelessness. Amongst the more original were:

Q: What's it like working with the Russian researcher?
A: The kiss of death
and
Q: What were Felix Porter's famous last words?

14

A:'Did the earth move for you darling?'

The author of the latter can have had little idea how close he had come to the truth.

The Grosvenor House Hotel in London's Park Lane resembled the Oktyabrina only in that they shared the common substantive *Hotel*. At precisely the moment when the two Daves had been sitting down to their cold sturgeon and tomato salad in the gloomy Moscow dining-room, the waiters in London were already serving cognac and cigars in the glittering grandeur of the Park Lane ballroom. At the precise moment when Olivia's taxi was speeding her to the police station, the celebrity presenter was taking the stage at the Grosvenor House for the annual BAFTA award ceremony. Only with hindsight would she see one day that the two events of that night were intricately, albeit distantly, connected. Only in retrospect could you see that this was where it had all begun.

The timing of the Philippine kidnapping had not helped towards the hoped-for award. The abduction had taken place in the January. The BAFTA's for that year had not been judged until the February of the following year, so that thirteen months had passed in which other events, disasters both natural and man-made, had left a more recent impression. But the gossip which circulated the ballroom that night went further. The panel of judges, they said, had been frankly incapable of concealing their collective dislike of Peter Neville. The professional assessment of his peers within the industry was that he was an egotistical prick who spent far too much time in front of the camera. Worse, they knew that the intensity of this dislike was in inverse proportion to the huge public esteem in which Neville had been held. It was their duty, therefore, as knowledgeable insiders, to see to it that such misguided popular acclaim should not be acknowledged by professional recognition. Instead the award went to an ITN reporter who stood bravely in front of the camera while the victims of that year's African war perished with nightly regularity somewhere over his left shoulder.

But the organisers of the event understood far better that the celebration of celebrity was today the backbone of broadcasting and felt a duty towards that very public – the Great British Public – whose taste the judges so disparaged. Peter Neville's disappearance from the nation's screens had been a loss to the broadcasting industry. The public would expect an acknowledgement of this. And so, in the absence of an appropriate award, the celebrity presenter asked the audience, both the 'glittering' one dining at the Grosvenor House and the one watching at home, to spare a moment to remember a colleague and friend held hostage 'in some corner of a foreign field'. (Half a minute's silence had been suggested but the idea quickly abandoned. This was a television event and the audience sat with the button in its hand; half a minute's silence would stretch its loyalty too far). As the waiters cleared the coffee cups they re-ran the soundless footage of the hostage-taking while the celebrity voiced-over someone else's script about the hopes and fears of everyone present with such skill and apparent sincerity that, for half a minute, half the dinner-dressed audience half-believed it cared.

Doug Boyle did care. Doug Boyle cared more than most. He cared for a start that he hadn't been invited to this penguin-suit do, that he was having to watch the broadcast like he was one of the Great British Public. He cared that this was one of *his* reporters who'd been shanghaied. He cared because no-one had *told* him this was one of *his* reporters. He cared because he was not in control. He switched the recording to *pause* and went to the door.

Outside in the production office a diminuendo spread through the room as, one by one, the researchers and assistant producers and production secretaries stopped their discussions and their arguments and their gossip and brought their telephone conversations to an end and turned to look fearfully at the new editor, standing in the open doorway of his office, remote control in hand. In a moment, if their worst fears were realised, he would point the control module at a victim and call a name and zap! – the victim would disappear into the office and the door would close and he or she would never be seen again. Vaporised. Kapow! In the lifetime of days which had elapsed since the arrival of Doug Boyle, the imagery of the strip cartoon and the ray gun had become a lingua franca, one of those shared jokes that brought people together, humour as a release for an oppressed people, humour as a defence against fear. Bill Neil had started it, quite unwittingly as it happened. Don't worry, he'd told them, taking them one by one into the viewing room for a confidential chat. Look I'm Deputy Editor, I'm Doug's Number Two and I should know. As far as I'm concerned your job's quite safe. Doug's not from another planet you know. He just wants to make a few changes and in my opinion its high time we had a few changes round here. And they'd all come out feeling buoyed up and morale was really quite good for the next eighteen hours until the man from another planet appeared in the doorway and summoned the deputy editor himself with his remote control and Zap! Kapow! the first change round here was made.

Boyle hadn't been around long enough to become conscious of the cartoon-speak, even less that it referred to himself. His own language usually drew its imagery from whatever production he'd last worked on. His current habit, by this token, was to address his subordinates as 'Citizen', an idiom derived from a triumphant mini-series back home, his co-production with the Koreans of 'A Tale of Two Cities'. In the new job it seemed appropriate. There were powdered aristos and bloody revolutionaries and, given the choice, he was going to be the one standing in the doorway calling the names for the tumbril. They were frightened of him, these people. They probably hated him, not so much for *what* he was doing but for *who* he was. They hated him because he was the vulgar little *Jacobin Citoyen*. They hated him because he had power without culture. They hated him because he was Australian.

And that hurt Doug Boyle. It hurt because he did have culture. Wasn't he was the only one back home who'd read the original of that Dickens show – Korean co-producers excepted that is? Trouble was your own countrymen sold you short over here. The only good Australian, according to one's compatriots in advertising, was the buffoon with corks hanging from his hat. Worse, that's what actually got you (himself included) hired by the Poms – head-hunted even. Dickens readers with culture were two a penny out there in the production office. The real jobs, the top jobs, went to a different breed, to people who were streetwise and insensitive, seriously philistine individuals who could take a show down market and up ratings without regard for any earlier reputation or for whatever they meant when they whinged on about public service broadcasting. In short they went to Australians. The Brits knew exactly what needed doing, they just didn't want to do it themselves. Like those companies who hire management consultants to tell them what they already know. Like hiring a contract killer. Zap! Kapow! Now where had he heard that kind of talk lately?

He scanned the anxious faces for sight of Julian Jenkin. Julian would know all about this Philippine thing. Julian knew everything. Julian was paid to know everything. He caught sight of him across the clutter of desks, shirtsleeved, a telephone wedged between shoulder and chin, typing with both index fingers. Julian was his best buy to date. Others in Boyle's position would have brought in their own people, surrounded themselves with like-minded friends, allies. But Boyle wanted team loyalty so Boyle had had a better idea – he bought one of *them*, one of the enemy. Julian was *their* friend, *their* ally and now Boyle owned him. And Boyle could scarcely remember such pleasure in ownership. Julian was young and bright and articulate and a formidable opponent had he persisted in his high-minded pronouncements on the intellectual independence of the BBC and the need to protect standards and the threat from the bum and tit brigade. But for no more than a promotion beyond the expectation of his years and a fistful of money, Julian had allowed himself to be bought and, once bought, had thrown himself with vigour and dedication into the spirit of the purchase.

Those who refused to believe in Julian's conversion underesti-mated the capacity of the human intellect for rationalisation. A man of Julian's integrity was unable to accept a job he didn't believe in. So, having accepted the job for the self-evident reasons of status and wealth, he set about believing in it. The process of self-justification was no different in kind from that of a salesman switching products, simply that the products, in this instance, were ideas. And he would have the advantage over his detractors, being able to sympathise with their point of view because, as he would like to say in that most patronising of arguments, it was a point of view he had once held himself. He knew their arguments and had his answers ready – challenging, radical, outra-geous: 'Thirty pieces of silver?' he would say, 'Rubbish, held out for three times that and then joined the Pharisees....(laughter)....not that

18

Doug would think of himself exactly as a Pharisee mind you....(more laughter)....' and the cautious amongst his audience in the club would laugh along with him. Then he'd go all serious and say that when you thought about it there was nothing actually wrong with American Television, no seriously, think about it – in the digital multi-channel environment you have to have a popular mix in current affairs programmes. Okay, so what exactly *is* wrong with a bit of tit now and then. Sorry girls but this is the post-feminist age, tits are a fact of life. It was a pre-emptive strike and it left the opposition disarmed and one by one they gave themselves up, leaving only outposts of sporadic underground activity – like the *samizdat* pages of an imaginary dictionary of Jenkinisms which began to appear illegally on noticeboards, translations of the euphemisms of the New Thinking:

> '*Facing up to the challenge for change*'...Some of you are going to be fired.
> '*Popular mix*'......Add some tit.
> '*Relevant*'........Add some pop music.
> '*Investigative*'....Find some tit.

And so on. Julian laughed at the notices. Humour as an outlet for an oppressed people, he was heard to say, humour as a defence against fear. And he laughed again but, even as he laughed, he inwardly plotted their author's dawn arrest. Julian was a very good buy indeed.

Boyle caught his eye across the room and Julian rose, collecting his jacket from the back of his chair. As he wove between the haphazardly arranged desks, adjusting his scarlet braces, muted conversations were resumed, telephones lifted, keyboards tapped. The pause button had been released. Julian disappeared into the glass-walled office.

Boyle sat on the edge of his desk and zapped the monitor with the remote control, running the tape back then playing it from the bit about the corner of a foreign field up to the hopes and fears of everyone present, where he hit *pause*. The picture stopped and juddered. "Well citizen, one of ours, I gather?" he said, looking at the screen.

"You didn't know?" Julian held his jacket slung over one shoulder, the loop hooked over an index finger, a prop, not to be worn.

"No. Anyone else I don't know about?"

"No other hostages, if that's what you mean. Quite a few in corners of foreign fields."

"So I see. We'll come to that in a moment. About this Peter Neville, the hostage. We still paying him?"

"I imagine so. He's not in breach of contract. Technically he's still on the story. I know accounts are a bit pissed off because he's still got a float to clear. They've had to carry it over from last financial year." Julian smiled. "I think they're worried he might come back and try to claim overnights for all the time he's been away."

Boyle didn't react. It wasn't his kind of joke. "What about trying to get him back?" he said.

"Done that; tried everything. We got a lot of airtime out of it at the beginning. Philippine Ambassador in the studio every week but these Moro Liberation people – they're freedom fighters not jihadists by the way – evidently didn't want to know, no demands, nothing. Seems the island of Mindanao is like the Wild West – settlers grabbing land from the indigenous tribes, loggers chopping down rainforests, everybody carrying guns. And these Muslim provinces are the remotest of all. By all accounts we're dealing with warlords, bandits rather than your respectable terrorist. I mean just imagine ...." and Julian paused for emphasis, "....nobody, and I do mean nobody, is on the telephone....no mobiles, nothing." He let a silence hang for a moment while Boyle appreciated the awfulness of such a thing.

"What about his family?"

"Wife, estranged, no children. We asked her to appear on the programme. How do you feel, Mrs. Neville? Told us not to bother. As far as she was concerned this was the nearest she'd come in a lifetime to knowing where he was and what he was up to."

"Popular bloke," said Boyle. "Somebody must have loved him."

"Oh, millions loved him." Julian looked serious now. He unslung the jacket from his shoulder and wedged it under one arm, plunging his hands into his trouser pockets. "The Great British Public loved him. They loved his outrage at the injustices of the world. Peter loved to make films about how outraged he was. He was outraged in Chechnya, outraged in Rwanda, outraged in Kosovo. He wept at the world's injustices. On camera of course. Public adored him. He gave them that vicarious thrill of righteous indignation."

Boyle frowned. Vicarious. What kind of a word was that? He changed the subject. "What was he doing in the Philippines?"

"Nothing really, I suppose it was a sort of 'whither' film."

"Whither?"

"You know, 'Whither Zimbabwe?', 'Whither Azerbaidjan?', 'Whither the European Union?'. When there's no real story around you do a 'whither?'"

"The shit you do," said Boyle.

"Anyway Peter had this thing about the Philippines. He'd been out there when he was just a novice reporter. He'd gone for the funeral of Benigno Aquino and then stayed on for the revolution; you remember – people power and all that?

Boyle frowned, recollecting. "When Marcos was president, you mean? The one whose wife had two thousand pairs of shoes – now *there* was a story."

"...anyway Peter made several Here-I-am-outraged-in-Manila films. In the spotlight for several weeks, till Marcos did a bunk. Adopted the revolution as his own. It's what first made him well-known. Probably why he liked to go back for progress reports. Reliving past glories. Hence 'Whither the Philippines?'"

"There was no story, no angle, no human interest?"

"There didn't have to be." Julian smiled shyly. "You'll still hear it at the forward-planning meetings, Doug. The ones without ideas will say: 'I think we ought to be thinking about doing something about..... you know....Africa'."

"Thinking about doing something about....?" Boyle repeated incredulously.

Julian shrugged apologetically. "You have to understand it's all a question of how you say it." He felt an odd elation as he spoke, a masochistic thrill of self-betrayal, high on renunciation. No-one had been able to deliver that line like Julian Jenkin. You only had to see him at those forward-planning meetings, rocking back in his chair, hands in pockets, a biro between his teeth, waiting for an invitation to contribute – *Julian any thoughts?* – and he would rock his chair forward and take the pen from his mouth, dropping it just a few centimetres onto the table. "I think," he would say, staring at the pen as if in actual thought, "that we should be thinking..." and here he would look up and flick his gaze from face to face as if to say 'and so should you, can't you see I'm way ahead of you all?'... "about doing something about..." and then with immaculate timing he'd look down at the table again, pick up the pen and tap it two or three times, thoughtfully yet decisively "....Africa!" and there would be pursed lips and nods of agreement and Julian would wait until someone said 'you mean Sudan?' or 'you mean Nigeria?' or 'you mean Chad?' and between them they would begin to invent a 'whither?' story none of them had realised existed. In this way Julian had gained a reputation for depth and sagacity, for a critical prescience and a wide perspective on events.

But now the trick was exposed and it would not be used again, or at least it would be tried only one more time. And, if Julian predicted correctly, its user would die in the attempt.

"These reporters," said Boyle, "don't they usually work with a producer, a director?"

"Well, yes...."

"So was there a producer on the Philippine hostage shoot?"

"Jonathan Dowell," Julian said uneasily, "do you want to see him?"

"Is he here then?"

"Outside I should think. He works in the studio now. He didn't much take to being on the road after the Philippine experience, couldn't handle it. Anyway he's happier doing analysis pieces. Very good on Westminster. Rather serious." Julian contrived to say 'serious' in such a guarded tone as to make seriousness sound like a secret vice.

"Tell him I want a report − on the whole business. Names, contacts. How they came across this terrorist bunch. We're going to start all over again, Julian. That's what we're going to do, start all over again." Boyle slipped off the edge of the desk, put down the remote control and rubbed his hands together enthusiastically. "We've lost an asset Julian, you know that? You lot may have thought this Peter Neville just a dickhead who wears his heart on his sleeve. But the public loved him. And this company's paying the bastard so that means I love him. There's mileage in this citizen. Think of Stanley and Livingstone. D'you think Stanley went looking for Livingstone out of the goodness of his heart? No, mate. He went looking for Livingstone for a newspaper. For a story. And that's what we're going to do. Except we're not just going to find Livingstone, we're going to bring him back," and Boyle snapped his fingers as if the achievement of this goal were no more difficult than the illusion of a simple conjuring trick.

"Who's going to play Stanley?" said Julian cautiously. "It's going to have to be someone pretty desperate to keep his contract."

"I only *want* staff who are desperate to keep their contracts. Anyway that's something I have to decide. In the meantime I'd like to know exactly who I *have* got. I've only just discovered I've got Neville. Who else is out there? I want to meet them all. Fix something up."

"A meeting? But they're all over the place." Julian frowned. "Gerry Harris is in Moscow for a start; he's interviewing the president. Damien Street's on his way back from The Gambia I think...."

"I don't care, I want them back, here, soon, from whither Russia, from whither the Gambia, from whither bloody wherever."

As Julian reached the door he heard a snap of the fingers and turned to see Boyle pointing in his direction. "Peturr Neville ah presoom," Boyle said sonorously in a mock American accent. Julian smiled as he was expected to and went out.

Outside the door he paused while he located Jonathan across the room and then began to walk diagonally away from him. When he was sure he was one hundred and eighty degrees behind Jonathan's line of sight he turned and began to thread his way quietly between the desks towards his back. He was no more than six feet away when Jonathan's sixth sense alerted him to danger causing him to press a button on his keyboard which sent the word-processor text scrolling rapidly out of sight. But Julian had already glimpsed all the evidence he needed. He didn't need to be able to read the definitions. The one word was enough... Jenkinisms.

"Jonathan," he said, grabbing a chair and pulling it alongside. "Just remind me. The Peter Neville thing. You did a report on it didn't you?"

"That's right," said Jonathan, "why?"

"Just that Doug's interested in the background. Where would I get hold of it?"

"I've got a copy if you want. I'll dig it out for you."

"Thanks. You can bring it to the forward-planning meeting. How's it going anyway? What are you working on?"

Jonathan took off his wire-frame glasses, closed his eyes and pinched the bridge of his nose. "The Cabinet reshuffle," he said curtly, putting his glasses back on.

"Anything in particular?"

Jonathan removed the glasses a second time, breathed on them and began to polish. "In particular," he continued, "cabinet members' secretaries."

"That's interesting."

"Perhaps it is to you. We're not talking about the Civil Service varieties, you know; we're talking about the kind that sits on your knee and takes a letter. It seems our editor considers it a matter of national concern that a significant percentage of the cabinet have divorced their wives to marry their secretaries at some point in their careers. I think we are supposed to be shocked. It is my privilege, with my acknowledged parliamentary expertise, to bring this to the attention of the nation."

Julian put an arm on Jonathan's shoulder and felt him flinch. "Jonathan....," he said after a moment's apparent reflection, "you know I can see your point of view don't you? Heaven knows I can see myself taking the same line at one time."

Jonathan stared at the computer screen. His face reddened.

"But we have to adapt to change," Julian went on. "You know you're very highly regarded; it's just a question of finding one's niche, where one fits, that's all. And you never know, I may be able to help."

Jonathan shrugged.

"It's just that there are one or two things coming up which might be more up your street and if you play your cards right...."

"For instance?" said Jonathan, turning to look at Julian for the first time.

"For instance," Julian lowered his voice, "I happen to know that Doug's particularly keen on doing something on Africa."

Jonathan frowned. "What about Africa?"

"Nothing too specific at the moment. It's just that Doug feels that Africa is going to become *the* focus of attention. He wants us to be in there first."

Jonathan looked puzzled. "And?"

"And I'm only trying to help, Jonathan. Just a tip, that's all. Why not be the one to bring it up at the forward-planning meeting. Then you'd be the one to handle it."

"What am I supposed to be proposing?"

"I told you. Nothing too specific. Just say that you think we should be thinking, you know, about doing something about.... well, Africa...."

Julian liked to remark that the BBC had clubs, which is to say bars, the way other companies had tea trolleys. It had become his habit, since his promotion, to spend an hour in the club at the end of each day, using it as an officer might use his mess; a place where he, a senior now, could meet his juniors off-duty; where they, grouped around him, could converse as pretended equals, listen for advice and praise, accept his opinions, laugh at his jokes. Here too he played public relations man for Doug Boyle, proselytising for the new order. Here too he kept his ear to the ground.

When Damien Street walked in, Julian had just accepted a drink from one of the acolytes and was telling a story which absolutely everyone found funny. From the corner of his eye he spotted Damien across the room. Damien was unshaven and wore a suntan so deep and eradicable that, had it been a disease, you'd have called it chronic. Somehow he always seemed to be en route from the airport to the edit suite with never enough time to shave but always enough time to appear like this, unshaven in the club. In his hand was a grip, its handle tangled with torn luggage labels. With the fingers of the other hand he pushed back a thatch of sun-bleached hair.

"Good trip Mr. Street?" the commissionaire asked ingratiatingly. Damien gave a tired, handsome, condescending smile and handed him the grip for safe-keeping. The commissionaire looked grateful. For a moment Damien stood in the doorway seeing and being seen. When his eye caught Julian's he flashed the weary smile and sauntered over, interrupting the story-telling as of right. "Julian, how's things?" he said, as if they were old friends.

"Okay," said Julian, breaking off, flattered, in spite of himself, by the attention. "How was the trip?"

"Well, you know West Africa...."

Julian nodded. He didn't know West Africa. "Story going well....?"

Damien tapped the side of his nose secretively then nodded to the barman who poured a double whisky unasked. "So," he said, "what's it all about? I gather congratulations are in order." He raised his glass. "To our new number two. How does it feel to be treading the corridors of power then?"

Julian affected indifference. "Of course you were away when it happened...." He gave a dismissive smile, at the same time inwardly exulting in the inversion of the relationship. Hitherto Damien would scarcely have given Julian the time of day. Damien befriended only those who were useful to him or, as Julian thought now with satisfaction, those whom he feared.

"So how's the new bloke, the Aussie wonder?" Damien said. He had turned his back on the others in the group, pinning Julian confidentially against the bar. "Is everything they say true?"

"I'm sure that depends on who's doing the saying." said Julian.

"What about me?" As a reporter Damien had learnt not to waste time on irrelevancies.

"What *about* you?"

"Well, what do you think he thinks of me?"

"He doesn't," said Julian.

Damien frowned. "What do you mean he doesn't?"

"He doesn't think about you. He doesn't know who you are."

Damien's suntanned features distorted momentarily with a mingled expression of panic and disbelief. "You can't be serious," he said almost in a whisper.

Julian nodded. "No idea. That's why you've been called back. All of you. He wants to find out who's who."

"So it's not just me; you mean he doesn't know about any of us? Like he doesn't know who Harris is either?"

"Oh he knows who Gerry is."

"He does?" Damien's eyes narrowed. "How come he knows who Harris is but he doesn't know who I am. What about my book? Doesn't he know about my book?"

"Shouldn't think so," said Julian. "He only knows who Gerry Harris is because I had to tell him he was in Moscow. He has an interview with the president tomorrow and won't be back till after that."

"Oh," said Damien, for the moment pacified.

"Actually," Julian went on, "I'm forgetting something. He does know a bit about you."

"What bit?"

"Well he asked me to do him a paragraph on each of you."

There was a silence. "A paragraph?" Damien repeated, almost under his breath, "A paragraph? Julian you're talking about a career, a reputation. How can someone like you....?" he checked himself, remembering to whom he was now speaking, "....I mean how can you put that into a paragraph?"

"Well you know the old expression 'you're only as good as your last story'...."

Damien drained his glass and deposited it slowly on the bar as if not to make a sound. "I see. So what you're saying is you told him about my last film?"

"Not exactly. Doug just wanted to know what people had done during this run."

Damien stared at the empty glass. "I see. You know, of course that I haven't actually....that's to say nothing of mine has been.... well.... transmitted this year. You see I've been working on this story since.... well...."

Julian finished the sentence for him. "...last August. It's been eight months."

"All right, all right Julian. For Christ sake we're talking about a world exclusive here not some bloody motorcycling parrot story. It's sensitive material and, if I may say so, not a little dangerous. I have to treat my contacts carefully. Besides it happens to be going really well; it's just that I'm not at liberty to talk about it. Look, you see if I can just establish this West African link....we already know the stuff's been arriving in the Gambia, we just need to establish the Moldova connection and then...." he broke off, "....so what exactly did you say to Boyle?"

"That you hadn't transmitted anything yet this year."

Damien ran his fingers through the blond, tangled hair. "You said that? Is that all?"

"No, I think I told him you were working on a cocaine trafficking film."

"Well that's something. And?"

"And so he asked what your previous film had been about. So I told him that was about cocaine-trafficking too. In fact I think I explained you'd made several films about cocaine-trafficking."

"So what did he say?"

27

"Why."

"Why?"

"He asked *why* you'd made several films about the same subject."

Damien looked appalled. "It's my field, Julian. You know that. I've cornered it. It's my niche. I've written a book....Anyway you must have explained to him that the films were all different."

"Not exactly," said Julian, "I explained how they were shot in different parts of the world, *The Bahamian Connection, The Seychelles Connection,* what was the other one?"

Damien looked uncomfortable. "Bali," he said.

"That's it, *The Bali connection.*"

"And what did he say?"

Julian took a swig from his glass, holding the drink in his mouth for a moment before swallowing it, as if trying to recollect. "I think he said that they all shared a beautiful climate...." He smiled amiably and put his glass down next to Damien's "....oh and he wanted to know how many of these cocaine smugglers you'd actually managed to get to talk."

"Talk?" Damien was incredulous. "You don't mean on camera?"

"I think it's what Doug meant."

"Julian you can't be serious. I mean *he* can't be serious! Doesn't he realise we're talking major masters of crime here? The Medellin Cartel. The Mafia. Do you want to get them all killed? Do you want to get *me* killed?"

Julian smiled. "As I said, Damien, he doesn't really know you at all. So why don't *you* explain it all to him. I'm sure you'll find he's a very good listener."

A phone rang in a corner. A moment later the tannoy crackled. "Telephone call for Julian Jenkin, please, telephone call for Julian Jenkin." Julian made his excuses to Damien and crossed the room to the booth, followed by several pairs of nervous eyes. Through the glass they watched Julian's expression change from surprise to gloom. (Bad news had been known to arrive this way before. People had been fired.) Julian listened but said little, sometimes nodding his head, sometimes shaking it. By the time he returned to the group each member was mentally prepared for his or her coming dismissal.

"Bad news, I'm afraid," Julian said and they clenched their

stomach muscles in readiness. "It's about old Felix. You see they've just had an e-mail from Moscow. I'm sorry to have to tell you all but it seems.....well, it seems he's dead." The ensuing silence was broken only by exhalations of relief. After a moment someone felt compelled to say, "Oh dear, but that's terrible," and then suddenly everyone agreed how terrible it was and while they were agreeing how terrible it was and being perhaps a little too voluble about it, someone else said that they really ought to drink to Felix's memory. And so rounds were bought and an unofficial wake begun in which Felix Porter would be celebrated in death as never before in life. Only Damien declined to join in the fun. He sat at the bar, one hand clutching a whisky, the other cupping his chin, persuading anyone who would listen that Felix's problems were nothing compared to his own. But even for Damien there was one consoling thought in all this. With Felix out of the way, that Olivia girl would be free wouldn't she? He'd always fancied his chances there. Of course there'd have to be the 'decent interval' but a week should probably do it. After all, it wasn't as if they were married or anything. Just bonking.

Olivia blamed herself, which did not suit her. She knew that self-recrimination, the insufferable frustration of having to recognise in one's own actions the cause of one's own misfortunes, has only one recourse – find someone else to blame. Anyone else. She could blame Gerry for a start. It was his own stupidity which had brought him to this. And thinking of stupidity she could blame the police, not just for keeping her half the night in their dingy station, but for refusing to release him in time for the interview. And as for the two Daves and their meal breaks....But then she blamed herself again. If she hadn't succumbed to Felix's advances at that ridiculous time in the afternoon she'd have been down at dinner with the others, she'd have intervened and translated when the police arrived, Gerry wouldn't have been arrested and Felix wouldn't have had his heart attack, not then at least. Not that Felix was entirely blameless either. It was his stupid idea to go to bed – and in her room too. Why couldn't they have gone to his room? But when she thought about this, she blamed herself all over again because that was horrid to Felix who was, after all, dead and it was just, well... well frankly it was all Gerry Harris's fault wasn't it...?

They were face to face in the departure lounge. Olivia had had time to change. Gerry hadn't. It qualified their relationship, she prim and tragic in black, he unshaven, his tie, recently returned to him, hanging crumpled round an open collar. Two policemen accompanied him.

"You look awful," she said, meaning it.

Gerry slung the jacket he was carrying over one shoulder, an index finger through the loop. "It all depends on whether you can see me as Frank Sinatra," he said, sounding a little drunk though in fact no more than overtired. "If I'm Frank Sinatra then the whole *déshabille* becomes positively seductive. Whoever heard of *My Way* being sung with a knotted tie?" and he began to sing tunelessly.

Olivia looked away, unamused. Across the hall the two Daves approached. Beside them an official in uniform trundled a long plywood box on wheels. "Olivia you've got to help," said a Dave anxiously as they came near, "we've got this problem you see... oh, hello," he acknowledged Gerry then continued, "...it's about Felix. *They're* saying he's excess baggage but *I'm* saying he's got a ticket and it's paid for and he doesn't weigh any more going back than he did coming, excepting the box of course. But *they* said he was going in the hold so he must be baggage and they wanted another five hundred dollars US.

Gerry turned to look at the box. "Felix....?"

"They didn't tell you?" said Olivia. For a brief moment she felt as if she wasn't going to cope. "I'm really sorry... he did it his way... heart attack" She bit her lip and looked away, regaining her composure. Then she turned to the Daves. "We'll get a refund back in London. Trouble is I only have roubles left. Did they say if they'd accept a credit card?"

They went off in the direction of a cashier's window. Gerry slumped into a chair, his mind assaulted by the preposterous images of a plywood coffin and a credit card. (*That'll do nicely sir...*). Despair engulfed him. Felix's death was so much more than its own unexpected shock, it was the un-asked-for confirmation of what he had yet failed to face up to, that in the space of a night he had brought his whole world to an end. NOTHING WOULD EVER BE THE SAME AGAIN. He tried to concentrate his thoughts on Felix. Felix after all was dead. That was worse wasn't it? Wasn't it? He would summon up recollections of shared exploits, the good old days, but when he tried he found he could think of none (though later, whenever Felix's name would be mentioned, he would say, 'I remember when he and I were in Colombia....' or 'Felix and I made this film in Angola once...' and he would regale the company with some anecdote about Angola or Colombia in which he, Gerry, would play a part at best heroic, at the very least amusing, but in which Felix hardly featured). So instead he re-examined his self-inflicted wounds. He shared Olivia's anguish of self-recrimination but lacked her ability to transfer the blame to others. Felix had lost his life but he, Gerry, had lost the big interview. He, Gerry, had almost certainly lost his job. He, Gerry, worst of all had lost face. Those who do not appear on television fail to understand the deep insecurity felt by those who do. Television personalities are the only famous people who are not famous for what they do. Gerry knew that he was not famous for being a reporter (there were a thousand or more journalists of equal ability), he was famous for being on television, i.e. for being famous. And for all that reporters will tell you that the fame is unimportant to them, that they are just doing a job, it is those little flatteries, glances in the street, autographs, invitations to open supermarkets which become indispensable to their self-image, boosting ego, stifling insecurity. The fear of losing fame is like the fear of a bereavement.

"Excuse me but I know you don't I?"

Gerry looked up. A woman held out a book to him. "It is you isn't it? My husband said it wasn't but I said it was. It's that Whatsisname from the *Worldweek* programme I said and he said you weren't but I said I've got his book. I bought it at Heathrow.....," and she poked a hardback volume towards Gerry. Gerry took the book while the woman found a pen in her bag. He looked at the cover. He knew it only too well. He'd even read it. He opened it and took the pen the woman offered him. "What's your name?" he asked, trying to sound friendly.

"Iris."

To Iris he began to write on the inside cover opposite the flyleaf where Damien Street's photograph looked out at him beneath the scarlet, embossed lettering of THE COCAINE CONNECTION,

Best Wishes
You Silly Cow
Yrs. Damien Street

31

Gerry snapped the book shut and handed it back. "Thanks," he said, "Always nice to meet a discerning viewer."

Damien snapped on the light. "This do?"

The other one stopped, put down the large boxes and glanced around. The garage was bare, lit by a single bulb.

"It's a lock-up," said Damien as if an explanation were needed, "cash.... one week. It can't be traced. Thought we might do him up against a wall".

The other stared through two hundred and seventy degrees of bare brick. "Not that much choice," he said, "unless we use the up and over."

"Up and over?"

"Door. Mind you bit of a risk that. Might not have such things in.... where's it supposed to be?"

"Moldova."

".... in Moldova. No, probably not. Not your average Moldovan background I'd imagine. Where is he then?"

Damien swung the door down with a crash. "Be here in a minute," he said. "I thought we'd get set up first."

The other looked uneasy. "You know I'm not sure about this Damien."

"What do you mean?"

"I mean it's not, well, it's not exactly.... legit is it? And anyway you know I don't like doing my own sound."

"Dave, I thought we'd been over this. The fewer people know the safer it is. Anyway you don't need a sound recordist. You can record straight off the camera mike. It doesn't have to be good quality; it's supposed to be, you know, surreptitious."

"But he's not real, is he?"

"Who?"

"This bloke you're going to interview. I mean he's not a real cocaine smuggler is he?"

"Well, in a way he is."

"What way?"

"Well the things he's going to say to me *were* said to me by a real cocaine smuggler. It's just that the *real* cocaine smuggler wouldn't say them to me on camera. So....well it's like a reconstruction isn't it?"

"No. Cause you're not telling anyone it's a reconstruction. So it's not the truth."

Damien looked at him with the special kind of intense sincerity he usually reserved for the camera. "There's such a thing as poetic truth you know, Dave. We're all trying to do truth justice."

Dave thought about this. "Don't you mean that without this interview you haven't got a story and without the story this new bloke Boyle's going to call your bluff? Then what? Bye bye world travel, Mr. Street, hello again motorcycling parrot?"

"Something like that."

Dave shrugged then got up and began to pull a tripod from a long cardboard tube. "Ok which brick wall?" he asked, "any preferences?"

They were ready and lit by the time the visitor arrived. The up and over door swung suddenly open, spilling two and a half kilowatts of tungsten light into the quiet street. Damien shrieked. "For Christ sake shut that thing. Do you want the whole of bloody Eastern Europe to know?"

"Sorry, not late am I? Bit of a hold up on the Circle Line." The door crashed down leaving two figures shielding their eyes against the light.

"Who the hell's that with you?" snapped Damien. "I told you Howard, no-one else is supposed to know."

"Sorry Damien, this is Bernard. He's going to be my dresser. Thought you wouldn't mind. He doesn't want paying or anything. He's on a work experience programme. It's just he's never done any telly..."

Damien exploded. "Howard this is not fucking drama. This is current affairs. This is documentary. This is *real*. Real people don't have dressers. In any case we don't even get to see your *face*. If I'd wanted everyone to know I was using an actor I'd have gone to *Spotlight* and got myself a real one...." He broke off. "Sorry...sorry, that was offensive, I didn't mean that, I meant a well-known one. You know perfectly well the whole reason for asking you is that you're the only actor in Britain who's *never* been on the telly. You're supposed to be ANONYMOUS...."

Howard sighed and turned to Bernard. "Sorry love, not welcome I'm afraid."

"Well now he's here he might as well stay," Damien said irritably. He turned to Bernard, "but you haven't been here right? One word and you'll be hearing from my Colombian friends....." He turned back to Howard. "How were the lines?"

"No problem. Where do I stand?"

For a minute or two Dave manoeuvred his performer in front of the bare brick wall, adjusting backlight and exposure until no more than an unidentifiable silhouette stood framed in the eyepiece.

"Right Howard," Damien said, "just look at me."

"Why?" said Howard

"For the eyeline of course."

"But you said they couldn't see me, just a silhouette."

"For Christ sake I thought the whole point of actors was that they did as they were told. You're not a real person you know. Just look at me okay? No questions." Damien cleared his throat. "Turn over," he said to Dave.

"Running," said Dave.

Damien looked down at his notes then looked up again, paused and began. "Hyena.... I believe that is your codename.... can you tell me when were you first recruited to smuggle cocaine into Moldova and how you first made contact with the Medellin Cartel?"

"That's two questions," said Howard.

"So?"

"Well I've only got the first one down here." Howard pulled a script from his pocket. "That's the way I've rehearsed it."

"Damien sighed. "Okay okay, I won't argue. We'll do it your way. We still running? Good. Okay..... Hyena.... I believe that is your codename.... can you tell me when you were first recruited to smuggle cocaine into Moldova?"

"Yes I can tell you that. The first time I was sent to Moldova...."

"Cut.....! Why did you say that?"

"Say what?"

" 'Yes I can tell you that.' "

"Well it's the answer to your question. 'Can you tell me....' 'Yes I can tell you....' "

"It's not in the script."

"I was improvising."

34

"Who said you were to improvise? You're not supposed to be acting. You're supposed to be a real person. Stick to the script. Let's go again. Turn over."

"Running," said Dave.

Damien took a deep breath. "Hyena.... I believe that is your codename.... can you tell me when you were first recruited to smuggle cocaine into Moldova?"

"The first time I was sent to Moldova," the silhouette began, "I was carrying one and a half kilos. We used condoms then which we swallowed...."

"Cut....!" Damien had his eyes closed

"Yes?"

"Howard, what kind of an accent do you call that?"

"Well.... it's sort of.... Moldovan?"

"Is it?"

"Well it's Russian anyway. You can't expect me to do all the former Soviet Republics. I reckoned as long as I got the 'R's' right and those hard 'L's'...."

"Howard...."

"Yes?"

"The Hyena is a Colombian."

There was a silence. "Oh, shit," the silhouette said quietly.

"Is there a problem?" Damien asked.

"There is," Howard said apologetically, "there is a problem. I don't do South Americans."

"What do you mean you don't do South Americans? You're an actor."

"I just don't.... can't...."

"Of course you can. That's what I'm paying you for. Have a go."

There was a pause. The silhouette cleared its throat and had a go. "Thee furst taime ah wass sent...."

Damien closed his eyes and groaned. "Okay. You can stop there. You don't do South Americans." He turned away from the camera and stared furiously at the blank wall. "So what the hell do we do now?"

"I could do you a convincing German," said Howard not very hopefully.

"Excuse me," said Bernard the dresser suddenly from the shadows, "but why can't the Hyena be a Moldovan?"

"Because the real Hyena happens to be a Colombian," snapped Damien, "anyway who asked you?"

"Sorry," said Bernard, "it's just that I think it would be a lot more convincing. I mean how's this Colombian supposed to arrive in Moldova without attracting attention. He gets off the plane and the customs say, 'Oh, look, a Colombian in Moldova. How unusual. I don't suppose he could be a drug smuggler by any chance?'"

"He's got a point," said Dave.

"But it wouldn't be *true*," said Damien emphatically. "The Hyena *is* a Colombian and he *has* been to Moldova. You can't go round making up the facts."

Dave looked around him. "You can't? So what's this then? Scene: a brick wall somewhere in downtown Kisinov – that's the capital of Moldova by the way; I looked it up."

"That's not the same."

"Please yourself."

For a moment none of them spoke while Damien paced the garage rationalising with a colluding conscience. "All right," he said at last, "You can be Moldovan – only I'm not going to say you're the Hyena. I'll say we've had to change your identity to protect you. That way at least we're still telling the truth."

"Suits me," said Howard, "as long as I get the same rate as the Hyena. Shall we give it a go?"

Damage Limitation Exercise. Gerry hated the expression. Was it military in origin or was it original, genuine, first generation PR-speak? Either way it was stuck fast in his mind, Damage Limitation Exercise.

The taxi dropped him at his flat and sped away with an uncooperative Olivia. She'd refused to speak to him about what had happened. She'd just showed him copies of the e-mails she'd sent back, one last night to say that he'd been arrested, one this morning to say that the interview was cancelled and they were on their way home. "Damage limitation exercise," Gerry muttered to himself, watching the taxi disappear.

He let himself into the flat and closed the door behind him.

Friends who had seen Gerry's flat always said they felt sorry for him, not because it was a tip or because it lacked a woman's touch or any of those things. Quite the contrary, it was serviced, sheets were always clean, floors Hoovered, dishes neatly washed and stacked in the tiny kitchenette. 'But it's like a hotel room,' they would say, piteously, so showing they knew nothing of Gerry's taste at all. Gerry loved hotel rooms. He lived most of his life in them. He wanted nothing more from his accommodation than a comfortable bed, a telephone beside it and a complete absence of domestic chores. Such women as had, from time to time, stayed with him had tried, with plants and ornaments and cushions, to bring some sense of personality to the flat but invariably, upon their departure, the plants would die and the ornaments and cushions find their way into cupboards and drawers. Only the photographs of his wives were given space on the dresser. They both shared the same frame above a handwritten caption *You think this is just a hotel!* It amused his guests. "It's a warning," he'd say to them, "not to make the same mistake again." The women in his life understood exactly who the warning was for.

He turned on the computer and threw himself into the sofa while he waited for the program to load. There was a remote control on the cushion. He picked it up idly and pointed it at the television. After a second or two the screen came alive with a picture of a white stretch limo, cruising down a suburban high street. Inside the car a woman, fresh from the hairdressers, lounged into a seat made more enormous by the wide-angle lens. She wore spangled leggings and earrings, which swung with the movement of the vehicle. "I'm so nervous," she was saying to another camera, "I really, really am," in a tone of voice which suggested that she really, really was nothing of the sort. Gerry sort of recognised her, a face from the tabloids, an actress in some soap he'd never seen. Another camera now, down on the street where the limousine drew into the kerb. The chauffeur opened the door and the woman got out clutching a large blue plastic bag. The camera followed her, wobbling, defocussing and refocussing into a room where people, mostly young, some Asian, some Black, sat in a row of chairs. There were gasps of astonishment from the occupants, then squeals of recognition. "Oh my God!" a young woman said and clasped her hands to her cheeks. "Oh my God!" someone else said, "I don't believe it!" "Oh my God!" a third voice said, "It's her, it's Debbie Belcher. We're on bloody *Celebrity Launderette*."

Gerry didn't believe it either. He grabbed for the Radio Times and flicked for the right day. There it was, 6.30 Wednesday: *Celebrity Launderette – This week, 'Mayfair Apartments' star Debbie Belcher pops in on an unsuspecting clientele in Peckham, south London, to share the secrets of her laundry basket with ordinary folk.* Gerry dropped the magazine and hit the off button. He went to the kitchenette and poured himself a whisky. He took a slug from the glass which only made him feel tireder than ever. He switched the radio on. *"And for your next record,"* a voice said, a cultured voice, elegantly modulated, received pronunciation; Radio Four's *Desert Island Discs*. He listened for a moment while the unidentified interviewee, who evidently owed his celebrity to some academic achievement, explained why Bach's Saint Matthew Passion had meant so much to him in his life.

Gerry felt sick. He took another slug of the whisky. On the radio the music had begun to play. There was a time when he'd mocked *Desert Island Discs* for its antique gentility. He'd mocked its preposterous conceit that the interviewee has to imagine that he's abandoned on a desert island with a 'gramophone' and can choose only eight records to take with him. How had this come about? Had the First Mate broadcast over the sinking ship's Tannoy, instructing the passengers to pass through the ship's record library en route to the lifeboats? *PLEASE SELECT ONLY EIGHT RECORDS. I REPEAT PLEASE SELECT ONLY EIGHT RECORDS. THERE IS A GRAMOPHONE ON EACH LIFEBOAT, THERE IS A GRAMOPHONE ON EACH LIFEBOAT.* And what of the late-comers? What if the only copy of the Saint Matthew Passion had already been snapped up? Did you have to take what's left – *Abba* for instance? Had anyone on *Desert Island Discs* ever admitted to liking *Abba*? He stopped mocking and found himself suddenly in the interviewee's chair. It was a game you played involuntarily. What records would *you* choose? Time to bare your musical soul, tell the public your intimate taste. Would you own up to playing *I just called to say I love you?*, did you want the world to know that you actually liked brass bands, worse still Country and Western? Better, perhaps, to exaggerate your interest in classical music: the slow movement from that Mozart piano concerto for instance, the one in

38

the Swedish film whose name you couldn't quite remember. Don't mock, Gerry thought desperately, don't mock for Christ's sake; at least it isn't *Celebrity Launderette*. But for how much longer? For how much longer? He was suddenly aware of another side of the *Desert Island Discs* game he'd never played before. The biography. That, in a way, was the whole point of the programme. Between each record you were guided through your life in tiny, carefully researched tranches. Between records one and two the humble beginnings, the newsagent's son who dreamt of becoming a journalist. Between records three and four, professional success at the expense of personal failure (those marriages). Between records six and seven......Gerry looked at himself in the mirror above the fridge, at the unkempt hair, the stubble on the cheeks, the sleep-deprived eyes..... between records six and seven.... "So, Gerry Harris," the silky voice of the presenter was saying to him, "a turning point in your life. You decide, after nearly a decade in which your career as a reporter has reached its heights, to leave the BBC...."

Oh, shit, Gerry thought, damage limitation, quick.

He flicked off the radio and went into the bathroom to wash. There wasn't a lot of time. He shaved, rehearsing the words in his head. When he had dressed and drunk a cup of coffee he went into the room which was not the bedroom and sat down at the computer. He looked for a number in his contacts book and rang a friend on the Guardian. Did she know anyone on the media page? A name and an e-mail address. He did the same with the Independent, The Times, The Telegraph, the Mail, the Express. He decided against the red-top tabloids in case they missed the point – they were read by *Celebrity Launderette* viewers after all. When he'd completed his list he e-mailed his recipients with addresses in the *blind copies* box so that, with any luck, each might think the story exclusive to his or her newspaper. Damage limitation exercise.

Olivia threw her head back against the hard seatback of the taxi and burst into tears. "I'm a bitch," she said softly to herself, "an absolute bitch."

"Whassat love?" the driver asked, looking in the mirror.

Olivia manoeuvred her bottom to the very edge of the ridicu- lously uncomfortable seat and spoke into the narrow slit in the glass between herself and the driver's cab. "I said I'm an absolute bitch, actually, but I think you heard it the first time."

"Life's a bitch, darling."

"Oh thanks for that. Great! Wonderful! My problems are to be solved by London cabbie ethical philosophy. Kierkegaard of the South Circular are we?"

"Sorry love, you upset or something."

"Yes I bloody well am upset, what's it to you?"

"Sorry, it's just I had this girl in my cab once who was so upset she slit her wrists."

"Christ!"

"It was that bad it took me days to clear up. Used one of those *Stain Devil* things in the end – they do one specially for blood you know."

"Excuse me… am I hearing this right? … you took her to the hospital, I take it?"

"Course I did. What on earth do you take me for?

Olivia slammed the glass partition shut. "A total prick, that's what." She leant back in her seat and sobbed. Felix was dead. That was awful, wasn't it? Wasn't that just awful? There was poor old Felix, handed over to the baggage handlers to come home as luggage, and all she'd had time to think about was how the programme had been affected. What was happening to her? She pulled out a tissue and wiped her eyes. She and Felix had been an item, hadn't they, a partnership? No-one seemed to understand that. Of course everyone could see what *he* saw in *her*. 'Sure you're not just looking for a father figure?' they'd say. Bollocks, no, she had a perfectly good father of her own for a figure, thank-you very much (even if, in his own dry, academic way, he was sometimes prone to regard her more as an intellect than as a daughter). Anyway Felix was only in his forties. What none of them understood was that being with Felix had been a great experience. That's what *he'd* brought to the partnership. He opened doors. Felix wasn't just a *member* of the Groucho club, he actually *knew* people there, first names and all. He'd taken her to dinner parties in Holland Park where there'd been cabinet ministers at the table (and hadn't their wives stared at her?) He'd written a book on the decline of socialism within the Labour Party. It was seriously grown-up stuff. Compare that to the 'boys' of her own age, their estuary accents belying their Oxbridge degrees, their pretended working-class passion for 'footie', their stupid beer-drinking a perfect match for their hopeless inability to dance. She wiped a wet cheek with the back of her hand. It was the job; that's what it was, stupid bloody television. It made you pretend you were harder than you were. She wiped the other cheek and stared out of the window, subversive anti-feminist thoughts welling up with her tears. Why couldn't life be like Jane Austen? There a woman could be wise and witty without having to prove it through a competitive career. (*And* weren't the clothes gorgeous too?) And why did it have to be so bloody competitive anyway? Not just all these stressful three month contracts but the salesmanship; you didn't only have to sell your ideas you had to sell yourself. Why couldn't they just say, 'this is a good idea; perhaps Olivia could try her hand at this'? Women would do that. But oh no, you were on your own, *in* there, testosterone-deficient, having to fight like a male.

She blamed her mother, proto-feminist of the sixties and hypocrite. She'd fed her girls all the propaganda of emancipation whilst all the while bringing up her family as a 'housewife', loudly bemoaning, of course, the (entirely voluntary) abandonment of her own academic prospects. And now, on those weekends when the whole family gathered for lunch, who *was* there more fulfilled than she, dandling the latest grandchild on her knee, promising baby-sitting and holidays for Olivia's married sisters, playing, with utter and abandoned contentment, the radiant matriarch?

Which made Olivia think of babies. Which then made her cry all over again. It had only been recent, this baby thing, but she couldn't keep it out of her mind. She was twenty-six, not that old okay, but how long would it take to find a suitable father? Was there a suitable father? She couldn't think of a single man she knew who she'd want to father her child. She didn't actually *want* a child at the moment but she knew that she *would* and that there would be an inevitable time-lag between finding the appropriate partner and getting pregnant. And then of course there's the nine months before the birth itself and... well before she knew it she'd be forty and......

'Stop it,' she said to herself, 'just....stop...it!' She closed her eyes and took several deep breaths. 'You're feeling low, a little emotional, that's all. It's only to be expected. Just change the subject.' After a moment of staring out of the window she changed the subject. "Competition is not the prerogative of the male," she announced, unaware that she was speaking out loud. She sniffed and wiped both cheeks. "You have a brilliant programme idea; you owe it to yourself to sell it. Tomorrow is the forward-planning meeting. You have a treatment to write."

The driver, hearing her speak, slid back the glass. "Yes love?"

Olivia was momentarily disoriented. She blew her nose to regain her composure. Pushing the tissue into her bag, she slid to the edge of the seat and leaned forward. "I've changed my mind," she said, eyeballing the driver in the mirror, "I don't want to go to Clapham, I want to go to Shepherd's Bush, to the BBC, White City. Oh, and by the way, I've cut my throat. You don't have a clean tissue by any chance? I wouldn't want to make a mess of your upholstery."

The taxi swerved momentarily before executing a U-turn.

The Forward Planning Meeting was no longer the Forward Planning Meeting. Until now the meeting had simply been the forum where staff submitted ideas for future programmes. Now, according to a circular from Julian, it was to be replaced by a Creative Interaction Symposium in which targets would be defined, objectives and strategies correlated, programme responsibilities editorially integrated. This would allow for output to predetermine resource allocation (he said), consequent upon structured employee-management feedback. In short, it would be a forum where staff submitted ideas for future programmes.

Ideas were the stock-in-trade of the programme researchers and assistant producers; forward-planning meetings (Creative Interaction Symposia) their market place. The participants arrived clutching their product in files and on clipboards, wearing the faces of salesmen, pretending confidence in an arena of all too public competition. Those with the fewest new ideas arrived earliest in order to take the seats nearest to the editorial team. The editor called for submissions in clockwise rotation, starting with the nearest person to the left. The nearest person, therefore, had only to suggest the most obvious ideas, running stories which the programme could not ignore – last week's scandal, next week's war, all thoroughly researched from this week's papers. Then, as the suggestions progressed around the table the ideas would become weaker or more original or both. The occupant of the final chair was either over-confident or foolish or late.

That recognition had fallen to Olivia, whom the more mean-spirited amongst her competitors suspected of timing her entrance. She took the last seat, wearing black, smiling a wan smile, accepting condolences, mostly from the women. 'It must have been terrible.... Poor you....You really shouldn't have come in you know....'

"Best just to carry on," she said tossing her hair back with calculated distraction, all the time studying their eyes for signs of knowledge. Could she trust the Daves not to have said anything? Probably not. She took a file from her bag, opened it and began to read, avoiding the need for further conversation.

Next to her sat Jonathan Dowell.

Julian came in and held the door open for Boyle. Both men took their seats. "Okay," said Julian, "I know not all of you have had a chance to meet Doug personally but well.... here he is in person...." Nervous, colluding laughter rippled around the table. "Now I'm sure you've all had a chance to read this." He held up the circular. "We want this session to be really productive. What we're looking for is creative inter-activity."

"Interaction," Jonathan said without thinking..

Julian stopped. "Sorry, Jonathan, you said something?"

Jonathan took off his glasses and began to polish them defensively. "Interaction," he repeated quietly, not looking at Julian. "Sorry, 'interactivity' is a neologism specific to cyberspeak. No offence."

"Well thank you for that, Jonathan. Your *interaction* is appreciated. Remind me to put you down for our next management training course. Now, if I may continue, the purpose of these meetings is to produce ideas. So what do we mean by ideas? Well what we don't mean by ideas is what's in yesterday's newspaper." There was a shuffling of newspapers to his left. "What we mean by ideas is ideas original to this programme. Innovative ideas. Popular ideas."

"Bums and tits," someone muttered under his breath.

Boyle heard this and interrupted. "This programme has no specific objection to bums and tits, citizen, provided there's a story behind them. I hope you have no objection to a good story? Speaking of which who'd like to start?" and he turned, unaware of the protocol, to his right. "How about you?" he said to Olivia. There was a further frantic shuffling of newspapers to his left.

"Ah...." Julian stepped in quickly, "you won't have met yet, Doug. This is Olivia Denning-Smith. She's just back from Moscow.... you know...."

"Moscow? What, you mean with the bloke who screwed up on the interview?"

"Well I wasn't just meaning that." Julian lowered his voice confidentially. "The producer, you know, Felix Porter.... he died."

"Oh.... right," said Boyle. He looked at Olivia and gave an embarrassed smile. "Hard luck eh?"

Olivia nodded and smiled weakly in return to show she was coping with the tragedy.

"You got something for us anyway?" Boyle asked.

Olivia nodded. She closed the file she'd been pretending to read, clasped her hands together and looked straight at him. "Sex," she said unblinking, "or to be more precise, sexual slavery."

Boyle sat forward.

Olivia swallowed hard. There was no going back. She was improvising, a spur of the moment decision. She started to tell Boyle the Hackney Refuge story but no longer from the prepared text. The file in front of her was fine as it went. It was all there – exploitation, African and Oriental girls becoming the virtual property of their Arab employers, unable to leave for want of a work permit, forced to work for the meagrest of wages, denied the possession of their own passports. It was just that the story in the file had a sort of sociological worthiness about it, as if were the product (which it was) of a feminist sense of injustice rather than the outcome of a journalistic investigation. It was a sexy story. That was how the Harris's and Streets of this world would have seen it. Only it had no.... well it had no sex did it? ....Except that now, thanks to Olivia's inventiveness, it did. She spoke quickly and succinctly, not too much detail, just enough to sell the story.

"So you're saying," Boyle summarised, "that these oil-rich Arabs bring innocent young girls into the country as maids – as part of their household – deprive them of their passports so they can't escape, then have their wicked way with them?"

Olivia's own vocabulary did not contain the expression 'wicked way', yet she felt obliged to concur. She knew that the story was no longer her own. Now it had moved into Boyle's world where maids were 'innocent' and masters 'oil-rich'. The fact that she had no actual *evidence* of sexual exploitation was a problem she would have to address later. She had Boyle hooked and, for now, that was what counted. Anyway it was a pretty fair guess that some of those girls *had* been abused. After all we were talking about Arabs weren't we? In Olivia's otherwise politically correct world, racist attitudes towards Arabs were unofficially okay, or at least such attitudes were not acknowledged as racist. Arabs either treated women as chattels or were rich or both. On the first count therefore they were pigs anyway; on the second they clearly regarded themselves as superior and it was impossible to be racist towards someone who thought himself superior. In Olivia's mind the Arabs shared in this Western contumely with just one other race, the Japanese.

"These girls," Boyle continued, "Who sends them to Saudi Arabia or wherever it is they go? How do they come to get hired in the first place?"

Olivia read the question correctly. He wants a villain, she thought, a Mr. Big trading in human flesh, rounding up virgins for export. She gave him one. "Agencies," she said. "One in the Philippines, for instance." She opened her file for reference. "*Filipina Services*, it's called. Run by a man called Rizal. Several of the girls were hired through him."

Boyle looked thoughtful. "Philippines," he said, "now there's a coincidence. Now there *is* a coincidence." He made a few notes then turned to Julian. "We should set up a meeting on this one. I'd like to bring in a reporter."

"What about a producer/director?" said Julian.

Boyle looked at Olivia. "What about Miss Denning-Smith here? It's her story."

"No experience I'm afraid." Julian smiled apologetically at Olivia.

"Well, she can get some doing this, can't she?" It was more of a statement than a question.

She can get some doing this! Beneath her strength-through-tragedy composure Olivia suppressed an urge to squeal.

"Well that's not a bad start is it?" Boyle continued brightly. "Sex in the very first item." It was a self-parody but not everyone was sure. Jonathan, awaiting his turn next, was sure it was nothing of the sort. How did you follow white slaving with 'something about Africa' for Christ's sake? He felt a rising sense of panic. He looked up. Boyle's eyes were already on him. "Okay citizen, looks like you're next. Why don't you shoot?"

Jonathan took his glasses off then put them on again. He cleared his throat. He shuffled his papers. He took a deep breath then exhaled again.

"We're waiting Jonathan," said Julian supportively, "you do have something for us don't you?"

"Well," Jonathan said, "I was thinking you see.... perhaps we should be thinking about...." he paused, staring at the table, confidence evaporating. From the corner of his eye he could see Julian encouraging him with barely perceptible nods: *Go on, go on*. He started again. "I think we should be thinking about.... doing something about...." But this time it was Boyle's expression he caught, the head slightly to one side, the eyes narrowing with what looked like a glimmer of recognition, or was it suspicion? He looked back at Julian for encouragement.

"Go on, Jonathan, go on. What exactly is it that we should be thinking about doing something about...?"

But that wasn't a tone of encouragement was it? That was a tone of irony. That was the tone the schoolteacher uses as he prepares to humiliate you before the class. That was the voice – and he knew he had realised this far too late – that was the voice of betrayal.

And even in the moment he knew he was betrayed, Jonathan's last words were already on his lips and so he spoke them anyway, pronouncing his own sentence, condemning himself from his own mouth, faltering in his rehearsed delivery like the forced confessor at a show trial...... "well, something about.... you know.... Africa..."

Jonathan wasn't summoned to Boyle's office until late in the afternoon. His colleagues watched him enter in a respectful silence, though

Jonathan would have preferred it had they banged their desks with their coffee cups, as prisoners were said to rattle their bars in the moments before an execution. Julian excused himself from the meeting. It was to be a brief encounter.

"I'm sorry, citizen," Boyle said, offering him a seat, "but I'm going to have to let you go."

Jonathan declined the chair. He looked at Boyle. "No you're not," he said.

"You mean I'm not sorry?"

"I mean you're not letting me go. You only let go of something which is trying to get away in the first place. You're giving me the sack, firing me. Why don't you just say so?"

Boyle looked thoughtful. "Okay," he said, "you're fired."

On the way out Jonathan passed Damien Street coming in. Damien pretended not to notice Jonathan for fear of contamination. He had put on a suit and brushed his bleached hair. In his hand he carried a VHS. Damien was seizing the initiative. How great it was to meet Boyle at last, he'd heard so much about him and how pleased he was with the timing because he'd just pulled off this amazing interview with this Moldovan trafficker and it really needed to be transmitted as soon as possible and if Boyle wanted he could have the whole film cut and ready within the week (you know there was nothing he liked better than a fast turnaround – hated sitting on a story) but the pivot of the story was this interview and anyway this was just an unedited copy of course but if he'd like to look at it.....

And then the phone rang.

"You'd better bring it in," Boyle said into the receiver and hung up.

Moments later Julian arrived with a sheet of fax paper. "They wanted your comments. We've had three of them on already, Guardian, Times and Independent. I said I didn't know what they were talking about so I got one of them to fax us this." He handed the sheet to Boyle.

Boyle took the paper and frowned. *Press Release*, he read out loud, *Top TV correspondent quits over standards.* He looked up at Julian suspiciously, then continued. *Gerry Harris, senior journalist with the BBC's current affairs programme 'Worldweek', resigned his post today in what he describes as 'disgust at the deliberate cheapening of quality programming in this country'. Harris, 38, who has reported for 'Worldweek' for the last eight years, was known to be deeply concerned by the appointment of Australian Douglas Boyle to the post of editor. 'We need someone in that job with a profound commitment to our culture, to proper journalistic standards and to public service broadcasting at the very highest level,' Harris said today. 'I felt that my continuing to contribute to the programme under the new ethos was inconsistent with some rather fundamental principles.' Harris hopes to be able to devote more time to his writing.*

Boyle screwed up the paper and threw it across the room. "Let me get this right," he said with a simulated calmness. "This bloke with the rather fundamental principles, is he or is he not the one who, according to our researcher, spent last night in a Moscow police cell for causing a breach of the peace and assaulting a police officer?"

Julian nodded.

"And is this 'Top TV Correspondent' not also the one who, in so misbehaving, caused this programme's interview with the President of Russia to be withdrawn?"

Julian nodded again.

"Then what the fuck's going on?"

"Damage limitation," said Julian.

"What?"

"It's called damage limitation. He's trying to protect his reputation. He was out of a job anyway. This way he gets his version out first. When we tell the real story it's going to sound like we're trying to smear him. Dirty tricks. By the time we can find an independent witness to what went on in that hotel it'll already be yesterday's news. Probably make *Private Eye* in a week or two but that never did anyone any harm."

"So what do we do?"

"Well, we'll have to tell them something. They want a comment."

"Okay," said Boyle, "tell them this. Tell them I've never even *heard* of the bastard." He leant back in his chair and hooked his thumbs beneath his braces. "And make sure," he added through clenched teeth, "they print the word *bastard*."

It had been Damien's programme. He stood in the middle of the hospitality room, drink in hand, receiving homage, taking plaudits in turn from his circulating colleagues. Great story, Damien. Cracking interview. How the hell did you persuade him to do it? And Damien in his turn smiled and shrugged with a disingenuous self-deprecation, though the smile was a little less handsome than a week earlier and the tan paler, the face lined by lack of sleep. But it had been his programme.

That was not literally true. There had been other items in the broadcast as well as *The Moldovan Connection*. In one corner a talkative M.P., who had once been a cabinet minister and who had divorced his wife to marry his secretary, drank large whiskies and entertained a young researcher with salacious, though anonymous, stories of Westminster cavortings (to which the young researcher, who was not at all entertained, was paying attention solely in the hope that the former minister would let slip a name or two). In another, two female trades unionists who had contributed to a studio discussion on sex and the shop floor (which they had anticipated, wrongly, to have been about 'gender' and the shop floor) stood unattended as they waited for their taxi, consoling one another with sarcastic observations about the room's other occupants, the poor consolation of prejudices merely confirmed. But in the end it had been Damien's programme.

"Good show," Boyle said to him, clapping him on the shoulder, "kinda stuff we need. Shame we couldn't see the bloke's face though. Sure he wasn't just an actor?" and Boyle laughed at his own joke while Damien forced an uncomfortable smile. "Julian tells me you work alone," Boyle went on, "without a producer. How come?"

"Just the kind of work I do," Damien said. "I need access. I deal with suspicious people. The fewer of us there are, the easier it is to operate. Take that interview for instance. Local Moldovan cameraman. That way no-one else needed to know."

Boyle nodded. "But you wouldn't object to working with someone else?"

Damien frowned "Someone in mind?"

Boyle indicated across the room with his eyes. Damien turned and saw Olivia standing by the drinks table talking animatedly to Julian. She wore a loose T-shirt with Russian lettering and a black, very short skirt. From time to time she would stop and listen to Julian, seemingly with great attentiveness, combing back her long hair as she did so with the fingers of her free hand. "Not very experienced," Boyle said, "but she's got a good story."

"I wouldn't be too sure about the experienced bit," Damien said, "what do you have in mind?"

If Boyle recognised the innuendo he failed to show it. "Come and talk it over tomorrow, citizen. My office noon. She'll be there," and he slapped Damien once more on the shoulder, shook hands with the drunken M.P. and the irate trades unionists and departed abruptly. Julian, drawn involuntarily into his wake, took his leave of Olivia and followed.

"Well," Damien said, sidling up to Olivia, "How's things with you?"

"Great film," she said, as she was expected to.

Damien shrugged.

"Pity he wouldn't show his face though, your Moldovan. I sometimes think these silhouettes might just as well be actors."

Damien laughed and waited for her to comb back that flop of hair with her fingers. But she didn't. The gesture and the animation and the attentiveness had been for Julian's benefit alone. Julian had influence to trade. "I hear we have an appointment you and I?"

"We do?"

"Tomorrow, with Boyle, twelve o'clock."

"Oh." Olivia looked surprised. "So it's you then. They didn't tell me who they had in mind. I thought you only worked alone."

"Not any more. I think they feel I should be put into the hands of an experienced producer," and he emphasised the word 'experienced' with just the slightest raising of the eyebrows. "If it's your hands they're talking about then who am I to disagree?"

"I'm sure we'll sort out a satisfactory working relationship," Olivia said coolly.

"Do you think we'll get a drink?" Gerry said.

"Carrot juice if you're lucky," Jonathan said. "You're at Channel 4 now you know. You won't find any cocktail cabinets a la BBC. It's all free aerobics, creches, bicycle allowances, that sort of thing here."

"Sod it."

"Best to put a face on it. I'm sorry you lost your job. I lost mine too."

"I didn't. I resigned. And now I'm unemployed."

"No you're not. You've got projects on the go."

"What projects?"

"You're freelance now aren't you, independent? Actors 'rest', independents always have 'projects-on-the-go'. No-one is ever unemployed. It's the first lesson in this business." Jonathan caught the eye of someone across the lobby and gave a little wave of greeting.

"Who's that?"

"Felicity Burge, Hand to Mouth."

"Hand to Mouth?"

"Hand to Mouth Productions." Jonathan cast his eyes around then leant across confidentially. "The guy next but one is Valdemar Billington."

Gerry sensed he was supposed to be impressed.

"Valdemar Billington. Front Room Films. Nearly went under till he got the Gay Cookery series. Should bankroll him now for nine months. The bloke he's talking to is Conrad Blade from Last Chance."

"Are they all here for the same reason as us?"

"Bound to be. Either on the way to see a commissioning editor or on the way back. You can't tell from their expressions. They're always confident, you see, rule of the game."

They were interrupted suddenly by a performance of the *Ride of the Valkyries* played on an electronic piccolo. After some rummaging in his briefcase, Valdemar Billington of Gay Cookery produced a mobile phone and answered it with an optimistic smile. "Hi, yeah, I'm at Channel Four. Yeah, great, yeah..."

Gerry felt like an alien. He glanced up at the great glass wall of the lobby then down at the waiting producers, supplicants in this cathedral, rehearsing their pleas, praying for dispensation "You seem very familiar with all this," he said to Jonathan, "I thought you were new to this game yourself."

"Well, I'm not exactly new to it. All the time I was with the Beeb I was moonlighting, trying to sell ideas against a rainy day."

"And the rainy day came. So does that mean you're a production company now too?"

"Yup."

"Don't tell me. 'Shoestring Productions'."

"No, that's already been done. 'One Man Band' actually," and Jonathan traced an imaginary caption in the air between thumb and middle finger: "A One Man Band Production ...new line... For Channel 4."

Gerry sighed. "Jonathan is there really any future in this? I mean this meeting we're going to, is it the first for this particular project?"

Jonathan smiled and shook his head "Third," he said proudly.

"Third."

"I've never got beyond two before. They're really keen on the idea, honestly. And you're my big selling point. You see at the last meeting they said they didn't really think I had the experience to take on this kind of responsibility, meaning they weren't going to risk their money on an unknown quantity like me, and that what the project really needed was an investigative reporter. So I said I'd got you."

"You hadn't got me. You hadn't even asked."

"It's life or death Gerry."

"And what am I supposed to say?"

"That you're really keen to do the film, that as you knew Peter Neville personally this is something of a mission for you, that you're working on various leads as to where he might be being held...."

"I'm not."

"Yes I know but...."

"You want me to lie?"

Jonathan nodded.

"I thought you were the ethical one."

"I thought you didn't have a job."

There was a silence. After a moment Gerry said, "tell me about this commissioning editor. Have I heard of him?"

"Northrop Pryce....? Information Entertainment....? Used to be quite big in Wales....?"

One glimpse of Northrop Pryce and Gerry had him pigeonholed: Middle-aged Media Juvenile. It wasn't just the clothes, though they would certainly have better suited a twenty-six year old than a forty-six year old (a tee-shirt with a picture on it worn beneath a suit jacket worn over jeans) it was a whole expression of personality, a manner of movement, a slow gyration of the shoulders while talking, as if to an unheard beat, studiedly unkempt hair, and all around the symbols (he would have called them icons) of a preoccupation with popular culture, style magazines, pictures of musicians and, on a monitor high on the wall, a recording of last week's Reading Festival concert playing with the sound turned down.

"Hi, nice to see you," said Northrop Pryce, extending a fleshy hand to Gerry, while nodding his head sympathetically at the same time, "do come in guys." They took their seats and Pryce closed the door.

"This is Gerry Harris, Northrop. I told you he was on board."

Pryce perched on the edge of his desk holding his hands aloft, palms upward like a Jewish comedian. "Ger-ry Har-ris," he said, "what a pleasure to meet with you at last." (Meet *with*. Gerry winced) "Always been a great fan of your show. Heard about your misunderstanding with the new masters. I'm sure you made a wise move. Absolutely."

Show, Gerry said to himself. He called *Worldweek* a *show*. "I gather you don't come from the current affairs side of television then?"

"There are only two sides to television, Gerry, just like there are only two kinds of music, good and bad."

"Actually I've always thought that's a silly argument." Gerry said. He nodded towards the rock concert playing on the monitor. "*That* is inferior to Mozart. I know it, you know it. Q.E.D."

Jonathan shot Gerry a pained glance. "Gerry's really keen on the project, Northrop, been doing a lot of background haven't you Gerry?" But Gerry didn't answer. His eyes had fallen on Pryce's feet. Pryce had no socks on. Black lace up brogues with no socks. What kind of affectation was that? How was he supposed to sell himself to a man who wore no socks and who thought there were only two kinds of television, good and bad? His sense of alienation heightened. A telephone rang and the crossed, sockless feet unwound themselves in front of him and disappeared round the corner of the desk. Jonathan leant over and whispered in his ear. "Do you think you might try and give the impression you respect his point of view. He respects you, you know."

"But what does he know about film making? What's he ever made?"

"You don't *have* to have made your own films to be a good editor. It's like you don't have to have been an athlete to be a good coach."

"I've always thought that's another stupid argument." Gerry said.

Pryce put the phone down and turned back to Gerry. "As I was saying, Gerry, there are really only two kinds of television, good and bad. We don't believe there has to be a separation between factual programmes and entertainment. After all, art and life are inseparable aren't they?"

Gerry caught Jonathan's eye and suppressed the urge to say no they are not, that in his case he had not the slightest difficulty in separating art from life and that what the hell did he mean by 'aren't they?', presuming on his automatic consent to his tendentious proposition. He reminded him of those awful propagandists who ended every sentence with 'right?' We live in a racist society, right? This is a male-oriented culture, right? It's down to globalisation, right? He bit his lip, first metaphorically, then literally.

"In any case," Pryce went on, "this is Information Entertainment. It isn't mainstream current affairs, you know. We offer our viewers more than just information. We offer them excitement, fun. Funfomation I like to call it. Do you think people watch exposés because they're concerned about injustice? People like investigations because they *are* entertainment. Yours should be entertainment. It's a detective story, a thriller. Intrepid Gerry Harris disappears into the remote jungle braving hunger, disease and the wrath of wild mountain tribesmen, in order to bring out alive – or dead – his old colleague and friend, Peter Neville. It's like Stanley and Livingtone. Do you think Stanley went looking for Livingstone out of the goodness of his heart? No boyo, he went looking for a newspaper, for a story." Pryce had become rather excitable whilst he said this and, Gerry thought, rather unnecessarily Welsh.

"About the hunger and disease," Gerry said, "wouldn't there be an expense account then?"

Pryce looked serious for a moment then laughed expansively "Ger-ry...."

Jonathan looked relieved. "Perhaps we could talk about the project?" he asked.

"Certainly. Well what it comes down to, gentlemen, is this. What, realistically, are the chances you can find our man?"

Jonathan stepped in quickly: "That's why Gerry's on board,

Northrop," he said, casting Gerry a pleading glance.

Gerry caught the meaning. He'd got the message now about confidence. He was there to give the project credibility; he didn't have to believe in his ability to deliver, only pretend that he did. No matter that in investigative journalism you don't know what you're going to find till you look. Pryce wouldn't want to know that. Pryce would be used to hype, to the Conrad Blades and Felicity Burges who'd walk in smiling, guaranteeing to deliver, whether they could or whether they couldn't. Pryce just wanted someone he could trust. "I'm working on my contacts," Gerry said, with a slight conspiratorial raising of an eyebrow, "can't say too much at the moment but yes, absolutely."

Jonathan gave an audible sigh of relief.

"Well if you're saying absolutely," Pryce said, "then I think I could be persuaded....."

"You mean we can go ahead?" Jonathan said.

"Well I'd have to see a budget first."

Damien gazed out of the passenger window, reading the signs. "DAL-STON LANE," he intoned in a sonorous mid-Atlantic accent, "gateway to HACK-NEY, lost world of THE SOCIAL WORKER...."

Olivia didn't respond.

"Do you know that in Hackney even the social workers have social workers? What's more all of them, social workers, their social workers and probably *their* social workers have all at some time been on television – to a man.....person. The most televised professional group after city analysts. Social Work is to Hackney what money is to the Square Mile."

Olivia accelerated as the light ahead turned amber. "You're changing the subject," she said.

"What were we talking about?"

"You know perfectly well – the fact that you've hi-jacked my story."

"Not at all. We're just giving it a Filipino slant."

"So you can use it as a cover for your Peter Neville investigation. Boyle made it pretty obvious."

"It's not a cover, Olivia, don't get so uptight."

"Damien *never* tell an uptight person they're uptight."

"Okay you're not uptight."

Olivia braked abruptly as the bus in front pulled in. "Yes I am. I'm uptight because you've hi-jacked my sodding programme."

"No we haven't, we're just making it cost effective. Doug's not about to risk all that money on a film about Peter Neville which we may never get. Yours at least is a cert."

Olivia felt sick. "Oh, Christ," she said. She opened the window for air. "Look, Damien, there's something I need to explain. It's about this refuge we're going to. You see....I may have....well, I may have hyped it a little."

"Hyped?"

She parked the car and sat, hands on the wheel, staring ahead. "The sex bit. I mean these girls *have* been seriously abused – treated like slaves really – passports taken away and all that kind of thing. So we can probably assume they've been *sexually* abused as well but you see they won't actually, you know.... say so...."

Damien looked at Olivia. Sympathetic emotions towards this pretty, vulnerable girl welled within him in equal proportions: paternalism, condescension, lust. "Don't worry," he said patronisingly, "we'll see. Let me be the judge."

Olivia said nothing. She was relying on Damien to save her. Here, after all, was the man who'd brought you the Moldovan Hyena. If anyone could stand the story up it would be Damien. Being patronised by the egotistical prick was a price she'd just have to pay. She got out of the car, slammed the door and led the way into the refuge.

The refuge occupied an upper floor of a complex of knocked together Victorian houses. Staircases within led to corridors which led to other staircases, the floors covered uniformly in the same ill-fitting donated carpet, the walls disfigured with notices and posters and the sellotape tracks of their precursors. Here were gathered the champions of the disadvantaged and the dispossessed. Damien paused by a sign which read: *Black Women for Wages for Housework. Meet here Thursdays.*

"Who are all these people?" he said.

"Oh, different organisations. Law centres. Advice centres. NGOs."

"You mean, as in non-governmental organisations. I've often wondered, what is it, do you suppose, that non-governmental organisations actually *do?* – do they just not govern? And if so does that mean that Quangos do their not governing quasi autonomously?"

"Very funny. I take it you're not greatly in sympathy with this kind of work?"

"On the contrary," Damien said quickly, anxious to appear a kindred spirit. (If liberal sympathies were required then liberal sympathies he would have. Damien could be all things to all women. Seduction is a branch of politics.) They climbed another staircase and stopped at a door. Olivia knocked. A careworn woman of about forty opened it and smiled at Olivia.

"This is Joan Little," Olivia said, "Damien Street." Joan Little took Damien's hand politely but didn't smile. Damien was used to this. Those who devote themselves to charitable work frequently temper their public regard for the press with a private contempt. Polite reserve expresses or conceals both positions satisfactorily. In Joan Little's eyes Damien was a useful publicity machine who could not be expected to understand the commitment of herself and those like her. Damien knew this and didn't care. Damien didn't pretend compassion. Compassion was for viewers.

She led the way into a room crammed with furniture like a refugee hospital. Young women, mostly African or Oriental, sat on beds and mattresses pushed together at angles. They fell silent as Damien and Olivia entered and looked up with nervous eyes. "I hear you're only interested in the Filipina girls now," Ms. Little said, the tone ever so slightly accusatory (you've got your own agenda you're not really interested in their welfare but then I wouldn't have expected any more), "we've only got the two. This is Angelica and this is Marianne. I'll leave you to it."

They sat down on a low makeshift bed opposite the two girls. The girls were small and pretty with the same long, straight, black hair.

"We met before," Olivia said, "you remember?" The girls nodded. "You two know each other don't you?"

"We are from the same village," Angelica said.

"Tell Mr. Street how you came here, Angelica."

Damien affected a look of professional concern while he undressed the girls with his eyes.

"We go to *Filipina Services* agency at home," Angelica said nervously, pulling her overlarge sweater down over her small breasts.

"Mr. Rizal, he is very nice. He tell us good work abroad, find husbands, settle down."

"And what work did he find you?" Olivia asked.

"Housemaid. Mr. Khalifa's family. I go to Dubai at first but he bring them all to London, St. John's Wood. I am Mrs. Khalifa's maid but I wash and clean and get no money and never go out and they are very, very cruel."

"Cruel?" Damien seemed interested now. "What did they do to you?"

Angelica thought for a moment. "Please?"

"You said they were cruel. What sort of cruel things?"

Angelica glanced at Marianne for support. "Things," she said.

"Like what?"

"Like," she shrugged her shoulders, "I don't know....like I may not watch *Neighbours*. Mrs. Khalifa forbids it."

Olivia jumped in quickly, "It's just a language thing, Damien. "Don't take any notice."

Damien disguised a smile. "What about *Mr.* Khalifa, Angelica? What did Mr. Khalifa do to you?"

"Mr. Khalifa?" Angelica shook her head, the long black hair falling in her eyes. "I do not see Mr. Khalifa much. He go out a lot, gambling."

"Tell me, did Mr. Khalifa ever, you know.... touch you?"

"No."

"You know you can speak freely with us, Angelica, we can help you."

Angelica looked puzzled and frowned at Olivia. "Why does he ask me this? I tell you all this last time you come. Why you always talk about sex? First *you* talk about sex. Now *he* talk about sex. Everyone from television talk about sex. There is no sex with Mr. Khalifa. Nobody fuck me. Why you want to make film about fucking?"

Damien paused and turned to Olivia, "Why do we want to make a film about fucking, Olivia?"

Olivia looked panicked. "Look it's probably just that she doesn't understand the story. You've got to realise she's hardly seen any television. She doesn't know her role, what's expected of her. It's a cultural thing."

There was a silence then suddenly and without warning

Marianne got up and left the room.

"Oh for God's sake what now.....?" Olivia sighed, "Where's she going?"

Angelica shrugged. Damien got up to follow. He stopped Joan Little in the corridor. "Have you seen Marianne?"

. "She's gone out."

"But we were talking to her."

"We don't keep them prisoner here, you know Mr. Street. She has rights. People don't *have* to appear on television you know."

Course they do, thought Damien, silly woman. He went back into the dormitory where Olivia sat with a sisterly arm around Angelica. He sat down again. For a long time none of them spoke. Then he broke the silence.

"Angelica, if nobody ever had sex with you, how come you're pregnant?"

Olivia looked astonished.

"Who tell you?" Angelica said, quietly.

"No-one."

"Then how did you know?"

"I didn't. Maybe it was the jumper. Anyway I do now. So shall we talk about Mr. Khalifa?"

Olivia quelled a sudden, rising, irrational, fury. Damn the man – not only had he successfully solicited a sensational piece of information, he'd actually arrived at it through some kind of intuition (how dare he! – whoever heard of *male* intuition?). She made a huge, conscious effort to be unimpressed.

Angelica was in tears now. "No no you are wrong," she was saying, "it's not Mr. Khalifa's baby, not Mr. Khalifa, Filipino boy back home."

"A Filipino boy? So you left knowing you were pregnant?"

Angelica looked at the floor and shook her head again. "I only find out when I get here. I am frightened to tell Mrs. Khalifa so I run away."

For a while Damien was silent again. "I see," he said at last. He got up and took Olivia by the arm, steering her away from the bed. He stopped at the window and stared out. "Tell me if I've got this right, Olivia. Angelica here ran away to the refuge because she found out she was pregnant and was frightened to tell her employer because her employer, whose husband didn't rape her, was depriving her of the basic human right to watch *Neighbours*. Have I missed anything? That is our story isn't it?"

"Don't try and humiliate me, Damien. I told you I'd hyped it a bit but that doesn't mean it isn't true. You don't know what these girls might have been through."

"Sorry but I think we might as well be going."

"You can't go yet. What about Marianne?"

"Look Olivia, you have to believe me. You don't have a story."

"Only because you've hi-jacked it." Olivia's voice was becoming strident. "What about all the other nationalities? It's not my fault we're stuck with the Filipinas. I bet loads of the others have been raped."

"Want me to ask?" Damien turned back to face the room. "Excuse me everybody, but has anyone here been raped and missed *Neighbours*?"

Around the room solemn faces stared back, uncomprehending.

Damien returned to Angelica's bed and sat down next to her. "What will you do now?"

"They have an agency here, downstairs."

"What agency?"

"Catholic agency, *Innocents Abroad*. Father Ambrose. He look after girls in trouble, au pairs, girls like me. He will help find home for me and my baby."

"I see." Damien nodded. "Just one thing, if I did want to contact Mr. Rizal where would I find him? Where is *Filipina Services*?"

"It is in the capital."

"Manila?"

"No the capital of our island, Davao. Davao is the capital city of Mindanao."

"Oh," said Damien. "Is it now?"

On the way downstairs Olivia caught his arm. "Why did you bother to ask her where to find *Filipina Services* if you didn't think there was a story?" Her eyes were moist and furious.

"I didn't say there *isn't* a story. Just that you didn't have one."

On the floor below they stopped at the door of *Innocents Abroad*. Damien knocked. The door was opened by a prematurely greying man

60

in a polo-necked sweater. "I'm sorry," he said, a trace of Irish in the voice, "but I'm tied up just now. If you'd like to make an appointment for the morning I'll be free from nine."

Damien nodded, "that'll be fine, we'll come back." The man pushed the door to, but in the fraction of a moment before it closed Damien caught a glimpse of someone else in the room, silhouetted against a window, a girl with long straight hair. "You know what," he said to Olivia when they got outside, "I'd lay a bet I know where Marianne is."

It was three a.m. when Olivia awoke with a start. "What the hell do you think you're doing?" she shrieked at Damien, peeling one of his hands from her knee and the other from her right shoulder. She grabbed the steering wheel and smouldered.

"Just play-acting. Patrol car crawled by while you were asleep. What d'you think they're going to make of two people sitting in a car outside a St. John's Wood mansion at three in the morning? So we were lovers. They looked through the window and drove on. Worked a treat."

"All right then, *lover,* why don't you tell me just what we *are* doing in St. John's Wood at 3 o'clock in the morning?. First you tell me we haven't a story, then all of a sudden you decide we're going to doorstep this Khalifa. I mean other people would telephone wouldn't they, write a letter. Doorstepping doesn't get you anywhere, it's just showing off."

"It's all part of the investigative process," Damien said softly, sliding his right arm slowly once more round the back of her seat.

Olivia removed the arm for a second time. "Look Damien, I've seen this in the movies. You get male and female partners doing a stake-out. What do they do? They eat burgers and get cold. They do not snog. The audience is titillated by the possibilities of a relationship which never materialises. Our relationship is *professional,* nothing more. I do not fancy you, right?"

"Right. I just thought we might get to know one another."

"And what kind of euphemism is that supposed to be? Is that the real reason why you've dragged me out here for half the night, to get to know me?"

"And don't you want to get to know *me*?"

"God! The vanity of it. The trouble with men like you is you can't even believe you're being turned down. It's quite simple Damien. When a woman says *no* she does not mean *yes*. Can you understand that?"

At that moment a black limousine passed in the opposite direction, slowed outside the Khalifa mansion then passed through wrought iron gates which opened and closed at its command.

"Damn," said Olivia, hitting the steering wheel with the heel of her hand, "damn damn damn! Now look what you've done. You've gone and bloody missed him. So much for investigative journalism. Ha!" She jerked her seatbelt across and fastened it. "That's it, Damien, enough of this *French Connection* crap. We're off. And if you think I'm taking you home, you're very much mistaken. There's a taxi rank at Marylebone." She started the engine and swung the car out of its parking space. "Truth is there never was any bloody story was there? Isn't that what you said at the outset? You never believed in it for a moment. You've just been playing me along the whole night. Silly, naïve little Olivia. Well I hope you enjoyed your night out with her."

Damien pulled on his seatbelt slowly. "Okay," he said, "I suppose I haven't played this one very cleverly but actually you're wrong....about the story that is. There's something you don't know; well...to be more precise, something I haven't told you."

"Oh, yes?"

"You see I went back to Hackney this afternoon."

"You did what? Without me?"

"I wasn't being devious, honest. I'd lost my mobile and thought I might have left it there. And then on the way up the stairs I passed the offices of that charity – the *Innocents Abroad* one we were going to see in the morning. Only, you see, they weren't there anymore."

Olivia slowed the car and turned to look at Damien. "Weren't there?"

"Well the room was still there but nothing else. No sign, no furniture, nothing. So I went to ask Joan Little what was going on but she'd hardly speak to me, said it was all my fault. You see it wasn't just Father Ambrose who'd disappeared. The girls had gone too."

"Damien are you serious?"

"Yes, really. The girls had gone too. You'll never guess this — it turns out that it wasn't Ms. Little who recommended Angelica to Father Ambrose at all. It was the other way round. He sent girls to her — quite a few as it happens, all Filipinas. His was the address they all had, not hers."

Olivia looked incredulous. "And you didn't tell me this? For God's sake Damien, this is *my* story. Why?"

"I was waiting for the right moment."

Olivia slammed on the brakes, squealing the tyres. "And what, I may ask is *the right moment*? Was this to be a reward for my favours or a bribe for them?

Damien shrugged. "Bit academic now. *No* means *no*, remember?"

Olivia didn't respond.

"Anyway," Damien went on, "it seems we may have a story, you and I."

"You mean a reason to go to Mindanao, don't you?" Olivia stared straight ahead.

"That too if you like."

"And what is the story?"

"It's a bit early to say but I'd lay odds we were into an international sex ring, procuring girls. These Filipinas are highly prized; very submissive, do anything."

Olivia swung round to face him. "Oh really? Do I take it that's something you've researched Damien?"

Damien ignored the question. "Look, suppose it happens like this: this Rizal, the *Filipina Services* man, places these girls with employers he knows are coming to London. He gives the girls Father Ambrose's address and telephone number — in case they have any problems. He knows they're likely to get a raw deal from the Arabs even if they're not actually abused. So, when they're feeling miserable, who is it they are going to turn to? Why, Father Ambrose, of course, kindly Catholic priest and celibate. Come into my parlour says the spider to the fly. The employer doesn't have to be part of the plot at all."

"That would be 'employer' as in our Mr. Khalifa, I suppose?"

"Well....yes....but that only occurred to me just now, really it did. If you think about it there'd be nothing in it for him to bring just one girl into the country, whatever the going rate."

Olivia begrudged him the plausibility of his theory. "You don't have much to go on," she said, "just that this Father Ambrose referred the girls to the refuge and that they've disappeared. I suppose you're suggesting Joan Little is some sort of white slaver?"

"Course not. He just uses her as a half-way house. She says she's had a dozen or so Philippine girls from him. They only stay a few weeks at most while the good father 'finds them somewhere'. She doesn't know where they go. She says she trusted him."

"And do you think she'd appear in a film and say so? If everyone's disappeared, what is there to shoot?"

"That's what we'll have to see, starting with the offices of *Filipina Services*. Now by all means drop me off at Marylebone, but I think you need to go home and pack."

"Pack?"

"I've booked us a flight, leaves at noon, Gatwick. Cathay Pacific to Manila."

"Don't be ridiculous Damien, we can't go off just like that. We'll have to discuss it with Boyle. He may not agree."

Damien gave a conceited smile. "He already has, Olivia, he already has."

"Here we are," Jonathan said at the end of the fifth flight of stairs, slightly breathless, "*One Man Band Productions* Beak Street, Soho, London, England." He pushed open the door and went in. Gerry was astonished. The room held at least half a dozen desks, most of them occupied. Young men and women, fashionably dressed in a way that Gerry wasn't, sat busily at computers or smiled persuasively into telephones. "This all you?" he said.

"Heavens no, that's me over there." Jonathan pointed to an empty desk with a lone telephone. "It's all shared. That's Carol by the window; she answers the phone. Suppose you ring in wanting me. She answers and says 'six o double six', which is the switchboard number here. You say, 'is that One Man Band?' and she says 'just a minute I'll put you through'. That way you think I'm a proper company with secretaries and things, unless of course you already know me. Or you could say 'Is that Front Room Films' in which case she'd put you through to Valdemar over there."

"That would be Valdemar as in Gay Cookery."

Jonathan nodded. "There are four of us working out of here. Or is it five?"

"And are they all gainfully employed?"

Jonathan shrugged. "Depends what you mean. Most of them are trying to come up with the next big format. Hit the right idea and you can sell it worldwide; come up with a *Celebrity Launderette* and you can afford to retire." He steered a path across the floor and sat down on the edge of his desk, moving scattered papers.

"I've got one for you." Gerry said.

"One what?"

"Idea. Could be the next big format."

"Really?" Jonathan seemed genuinely interested. "You going to tell me?"

Gerry leaned forward conspiratorially and whispered, "Gladiators".

Jonathan shook his head. "Sorry, been done."

"You don't understand, I mean the real thing, as in: 'If you want Dennis to kill Darren ring *this* number. If you want Darren to be spared....'"

Jonathan pushed a chair towards Gerry with his foot.. "Don't take the piss, Gerry, this is for real."

Gerry pulled back the chair and sat down. "Bit of a Damascene conversion for you this isn't it, Jonathan? Didn't you used to be Mr. Serious?"

"I'm surviving."

"Surviving on your new project, *our* new project I should say. What are we going to call it by the way, *Suicide Mission*? How does it go again?.... 'In which our intrepid reporter braves hunger and disease and the wrath of wild mountain tribesmen loyal only to their weapons....'"

"Read this," Jonathan interrupted, throwing a file into Gerry's lap, "I copied it before I left the Beeb. Not much I'm afraid, just what I found in Peter's hotel room really, diary, odd notes, receipts, not a lot to go on. The person we dealt with was this chap called Francisco. You'll find him in there somewhere. He publishes a sort of broadsheet, newsletter thing, you know left-wing, Catholic church. He's well connected with the hill tribes in South Cotabato – that's the district of Mindanao where it all happened. He was our go-between with the guerillas. He lives in a town called Koronadal, nearest thing there to civilisation. Hotels of sorts if you don't want sheets. Crew nearly mutinied. There's a phone in the post office. Just the one. Connects to Manila."

Gerry leafed through the photocopies. "Is this it Jonathan?" the tone one of weary incredulity, "this is the research? This all there is? I'm to go to the other side of the world to a one-phone town and ask for a guy called Francisco? Does Northrop Pryce know this is all we've got to go on?"

"Course not. You never tell a commissioning editor the truth. You'd never get any work. It's all a question of salesmanship."

"And when are you suggesting I start?"

"Sooner you start the sooner we all get paid. We'll fix you a local crew when you get out there. Better on the budget that way, saves a fantastic amount on air fares. Speaking of which you don't mind flying Mongolian Airways do you? You see they've got this great deal on – Manila via Kiev and Ulan Batur. Have you ever *been* to Ulan Batur?"

It was 3pm in Manila and the toilet had no seat. The two facts were not materially connected except in the coincidence of Gerry's thoughts, which were now ponderous and vague. Gerry called this condition *jetlag,* a state of the human body brought about by continuous travel through time zones, in this case for twenty-three hours, and in no way at all connected to the number of miniature bottles emptied into that body during the same interval. Gerry looked like a man who had seen Ulan Batur and lived.

His brain gave up trying to calculate the *real* time back home from the time on his watch and concentrated all its remaining energies on the toilet seat issue. Frequent travel over many years had nurtured what had begun merely as a curious observation into a full-blown obsession. And here it was again, a multi-million pound airport humming with technology, with computer screens and public address systems and duty free shops selling Mitsouko and Chanel and Paloma Picasso – and no toilet seats. It was the same in Africa, the same in India. For those indifferent to the question, Gerry would seek to open their eyes to its sublime mystery. There could only be one of two explanations: either the seats were broken or they were stolen. But toilet seats didn't break unless you took a hammer to them. (Did they do that?) No toilet seat in his experience had ever broken in England, or in France or in America. And if toilet seats didn't break then what was the point of stealing them, because the only point in stealing them was to replace broken ones. He looked at himself in the mirror. 'Welcome to the Philippines, Mr. Harris,' he said solemnly and flushed the topless cistern.

Outside, he argued in the tropical humidity with a taxi driver who wanted 300 pesos to take him to the International Press Centre.

"It cost half that three years ago."

"Inflation," said the driver.

"Eight percent, I checked."

"Air conditioning then. Last time you don't have air-conditioning."

"How do you know that?"

The driver shrugged. "Take it or leave it."

Gerry got in to the old Mercedes, wondering why he ever bothered to argue for the sake of a few quid of someone else's money. He slumped in the seat and closed his eyes in the cooling air. Halfway down the highway to Manila the car swerved violently and came to a stop. The driver got out and kicked at a wheel.

"What is it?," Gerry asked.

"Puncture."

Gerry got out and watched as the driver replaced one completely bald tyre with another so worn that the canvas showed through. "And I'm paying for that?" he said.

"No," the driver said, "the air conditioning."

The press centre had toilets with seats and hot water and towels. Gerry washed and changed his shirt and presented himself with his passport photographs for accreditation. The accreditation office shared a floor with the news agencies and US Networks. In the corridor a voice hailed him through an open door: "Gerry Harris, how in the hell are you? What brings *you* here. Come on in. Welcome to US News Network."

Gerry stopped and went in. The room was small and cluttered and alive with noiseless machinery. To one side, shelves of printers spewed silent copy like toilet paper; to the other, trapped in a stack of muted monitors, rival broadcasters with solemn faces mouthed the world's news with counterfeit urgency. And between them sat the source of the voice, a huge figure draped in a shapeless tropical garment which was somehow neither exactly a shirt nor exactly a jacket. He got up and extended a hand. Gerry took the hand abstractedly while his mind raced frantically for a name. "East Timor?" he said, trying to give himself time.

"Cambodia," the other said, "the landmine story," and then, reading Gerry's expression correctly and to save them both any further embarrassment added, "Barney Hedges, used to be with CBS."

"Sure," Gerry said, "Barney, know you anywhere. Great to see you."

"Great. You look whacked. Long journey?"

Gerry nodded. "Ulan Batur."

"Mongolian Airways huh? Guess everyone's into economies these days, even the BBC."

"I'm not with the BBC any more. Freelance. Channel 4."

"Really?" Barney's expression changed to one of knowingness. "Well that would explain it then."

"Explain what?"

"Well when I saw you just now I'm thinking: what the hell's the BBC doing sending two guys from the same outfit? This must be some big story. Barney, I ask myself, are you missing out on something here...?"

"Two guys?"

"Sure, the guy with the *Omen* name, Damien, Damien Street. Here yesterday for accreditation just like you. Girl with him." Barney mimed an hourglass, "boy, something else, line producer I guess, Olivia something."

The news hurt Gerry though he didn't know why. "Did they say what they were doing?"

"Sure but I didn't believe him. The marriage trade, he said. You know, British guys who can't get it back home come over here and buy themselves a nice little docile wifey. You guys were doing that story years ago. No way. Anyway so what's yours?"

"I was going to say the marriage trade. You know, British guys

68

who can't get it back home....."

Barney laughed. "Tell you what. You can tell me later. Why don't you go check in at your hotel. Get some sleep. Then I'll call by around nine and pick you up. We'll do the fleshpots. You'll talk. You see if you don't."

They dined at a restaurant where all the waiters were dwarfs.

"I come here for the small talk," Barney said, not for the first time.

"I'm looking for Peter Neville," said Gerry.

"What makes you think he's alive?"

"I'm paid to think that."

"Gerry this country's been at war with itself for a generation. Do you see any prisoners of war?"

"They took him hostage."

"Sure, they took him away in a helicopter. Then what? Cut off his head with a bolo?"

"A what?"

"It's a kind of long curved knife." Barney measured a bolo with his hands. "They do that there. Mindanao especially." He paused to taste the wine poured by a dwarf who stood on a small stepladder. "It's been likened to the wild west. It's settler country. Everyone's fighting everyone else: first you've got the communists who are fighting the government. Then you've got the Moros – when they're not fighting the Christians they're fighting one another. Then you've got the lunatic fringe, the real Muslim separatists who fight everybody. And of course you've got the pirates..."

"Pirates?"

"Uh huh, pirates." Barney didn't seem to feel any need to elaborate. When they had finished their meal, they left the restaurant where all the waiters were dwarfs for a bar where all the waitresses were boys, or so Barney said.

"Tell me about the Moros," Gerry said, sounding a little drunk and trying to keep awake. It wouldn't be for the first time if he awoke in the morning to find he had no recollection of an 'exclusive' of the night before.

"The Moros are the indigenous tribes in the south, Muslims,

came from Malaya about 600 years ago. They fought a guerrilla war for years. Thought they were being swamped by Christian settlers. Back in '95 the government bought them off with a local autonomy deal. But the extremists were having none of it. Bit like your IRA and Real IRA. So you still have your separatists, the MILF and the freaky Abu Sayyaf. They're both big into kidnappings, which I suppose was where your Peter Neville came in."

A girl who was not a girl took Gerry's empty glass and replaced it with a full one.

"As far as we know," Barney went on, "he was taken by the Moro Islamic Liberation Front who are an offshoot of the Moro National Liberation Front – they're the ones who did the autonomy deal with the government. By the way both groups deny it categorically. So don't try any direct approach. You'll be very unwelcome."

"Is that another way of saying dead?"

"Finish your drink," said Barney.

From the bar where the cocktail waitresses were boys they went to a night club where all the girls in the floorshow were naked and all the men erect. With his back three quarters to the stage, Gerry found conversation difficult. It was hard to keep Barney's attention. He wondered if Barney went to such places on his own or just when he had the excuse of a guest from abroad. "How do you cover stories when you're out on the town like this, Barney? You're the bureau chief."

"Some-one in the office calls me," he said, his eyes not leaving the stage. Doesn't happen often. Philippines only makes the news back home when there's a coup attempt."

"How often's that?"

"Often enough."

The stage act reached its climax and the performers went off to perfunctory applause. Barney switched his gaze back to Gerry. "You going tomorrow, Mindanao?"

Gerry nodded.

"There are warlords," he said. "You need to find out who's in control before you go anywhere. It really isn't very safe."

"Thanks."

"You got a gun?"

Gerry shook his head.

"You'll be the only one." A phone rang in Barney's pocket. He answered it. "Malacañang, the palace," he said, "I'll be there."

"Attempted coup?" asked Gerry.

Barney nodded. "You stick around here though, finish your drink."

Barney left and Gerry stuck around but the drink was never finished. By the end of *oral extravaganza,* which opened the second half of the performance, he was asleep. The management, believing this bad for business, put him in a taxi and sent him to his hotel. Gerry thought this kind. The next morning his wallet was empty.

He woke three times: the first time, as the dawn light broke through the picture window, to rise and close the curtains, drink a pint of water and take three paracetamol. The second, an hour later, to pee the first pint of water, take another two paracetamol and drink a second pint of water. The third to pee the second pint of water, draw the curtains and REMEMBER THE NIGHT BEFORE. He stood, swaying, staring out of the window, trying to recollect where he was supposed to be. He closed his eyes in pain. "Oh shit," he said at last, very slowly, eyes still shut. A memory, slurred and indistinct, of a smiling bouncer in a DJ taking the money from his wallet to give the taxi driver. "Oh, not that...." He searched the floor for his trousers, rummaged in the pockets and retrieved the empty wallet. Nothing. No money, no credit cards, nothing. He fell back on the bed, arms crucified, and surrendered to paranoia.

He lay motionless. For once in his professional career he had lost all sense of urgency. Since the Moscow débacle, (which was only how long ago – just days wasn't it?), his life seemed to have veered entirely out of his control, a mere croquet ball to be knocked off course by some malicious, unseen opponent. Fate, was that it? Had Fate robbed him of his job and status? Was Fate systematically stripping him of his identity? Did Fate, masquerading as a Filipino bouncer, steal his credit cards? A travelling man without credit cards does not exist. *I have credit, therefore I am.* Paranoia. He opened his eyes again and stared at the stippled ceiling. What the hell was he doing here? What *was* he doing here on this preposterous assignment? If Barney had been right about his guerrillas and his warlords and his pirates, this story wasn't just impossible it was ludicrously dangerous. Okay if you were Damien Street but this was Gerry Harris. Gerry Harris didn't *do* danger. Got that? But then Gerry Harris didn't have another job did he? Question answered. Paranoia.

He manoeuvred himself off the bed and over to the dressing table. There was a number in his briefcase, twenty-four hours, international. He called it and cancelled his credit cards. Then he called the local American Express office, ordered a new card and some cash. 'The cash you can have right away, sir,' the have-a-nice-day voice told him, 'the credit card tomorrow.' Tomorrow. Another whole day in Manila. Oh God. Gerry sprawled again on the bed and reached, in desperation, for the hotel's welcome magazine. He leafed through the reams of glossy advertisements, advertisements for retailers of Swiss watches, French couture, Bond Street jewellery – aimed perversely at a Western readership almost certainly in search of authentic rattan. He found the cover story he was looking for, an article on Manila for the international visitor. *'Manila by day and by night.'* He'd done Manila by night, thankyou very much. Manila by day didn't seem much better either. Here apparently was the one capital city in the world with not a single sight to see. Once, he read, there had been a 16th century Spanish city here of great beauty. Then had come the liberation from the Japanese in 1945. General MacArthur, it seemed, had managed to liberate Manila to smithereens (though the writer, in the Utopian tradition of these pieces, was able to see even this event as an occasion for optimism, the demolition of the old allowing for something called the auspicious birth of the new and the modern). Gerry closed the magazine, rose and went to the window. Outside, the new and the modern stretched to the horizon with unmitigated ugliness. He turned on the television, the business traveller's displacement activity, and watched a CNN commercial for other hotels with CNN. And then the phone rang.

"Don't get paranoid," the voice told him, "but you've got company." It was Jonathan.

"If you mean Damien, I know. I'm already paranoid."

"But have you heard where they're going?"

"Nope."

"Mindanao."

A silence then: "Shit. You know why?"

"My spies tell me something to do with white slaving."

"You believe it?"

"Dunno, but there's something I never told you. Before I left the Beeb I remember Julian asking for my Peter Neville file. I never told you that did I?"

"No you didn't Jonathan. I suppose I can guess why not?"

"I suppose you can. Anyway it's probably nothing. Just thought you ought to know. Good luck."

The next day's flight to Mindanao lasted little over an hour but during that time Gerry watched as the seven thousand islands of the Philippine archipelago slipped silently beneath, deep green and golden in a sea of ultramarine. He felt uneasy. It was partly that the plane was something called a BAC one-eleven which had, aeons since, gone out of service back home, partly that the area was notorious for disasters on a grand scale. But mostly it was the presence of Damien and Olivia *in his location*. It was a coincidence, of course it was. But what *were* they doing in Mindanao? However small a world it might be, Mindanao was surely the very end of it.

Davao City was shabby and overpopulated, the streets congested with motor tricycles and decorated jeepneys. (The jeepney, Gerry had read in the hotel magazine, was another legacy of General MacArthur, from whose abandoned jeeps, it claimed, the colourful Filipino bus had first metamorphosed.) They moved slowly through the traffic. The Intercontinental lay on the far side of town in what passed for a better-class suburb. The taxi swung off the main road into the hotel gardens. At the door obsequious flunkeys in white coats deferred to Gerry, whisking his luggage away and escorting him to the desk. How did that slogan go? *Outside it's Africa, inside it's Sheraton.* How despicable Gerry had always found that sentiment. Yet at the same time how appealing.

And at the desk was Olivia...

Olivia was looking vulnerable, which was something she was good at. Across the desk the under-manager, who had already succumbed to vulnerability's charm, was being solicitous beyond even the call of his profession. He gazed up into her face and she down into his (he being the smaller of the two), his expression one of profound sympathy and concern. "I am very sorry miss," he was saying.

"But are you absolutely sure?" Olivia kept repeating, her tone agitated.

Gerry held back, observing. Her appearance was quite different now. She wore long, khaki shorts with turn-ups and a co-ordinated military-style shirt knotted at the midriff. There was no make-up and the long black hair was scraped back and tied with that studied carelessness of a woman who knows exactly how attractive she is, yet wishes it to be known, for professional reasons, that she is quite unconcerned with her appearance. A broad leather belt and matching shoulder bag completed the ensemble. Tropical chic.

"Yes I *am* sure, miss. Mr. Street has not telephoned. Yes his things are still in his room. Perhaps I can get miss something, some tea perhaps?"

She flicked a stray strand of hair away from her face. It caught in the draught from the ceiling fan and blew back again. "He's been gone two days, you see. He never said he was going anywhere."

"Probably met a cocaine trafficker, you know, the *Mindanao connection*......" No sooner had Gerry spoken the words than he began to regret them. At the sound of his voice Olivia spun round. There was a moment's mute astonishment then she flung her arms round his neck, laughing and crying all at the same time. Gerry stood embarrassed, his arms sticking out like a doll's, feeling her thin body pressed against his, unsure if he was qualified to return the embrace. He hadn't seen her since she'd dropped him at his flat on their return from Moscow. Then she was hardly speaking to him. Now she wanted to kiss him. Women.

"God, Gerry you don't know how pleased I am to see you. You're the one person on earth I would have wanted to walk through that door right now. This is wonderful. What on earth brings you here of all places, to Mindanao, it's the end of the bloody world, it's...." She stopped suddenly, her voice trailing away. She took a step back, releasing Gerry from the embrace and stared at him. "Gerry what the hell *are* you doing here?"

Gerry dried. He was wordless. His mind raced down empty corridors in search of an answer. What the hell was he doing here? What the hell *was* he doing here? He had no alibi. He should have thought. It was obvious he was going to bump into her here – they were both journalists and this was the best hotel. But he'd prepared no alibi. He stared at her mutely.

"Gerry?"

"Er... jetlag."

"Sorry?" she said.

"Jetlag... forgot the question. What was it again?"

"I asked you what you were doing here. In fact I asked what the hell you were doing here. It's not exactly like bumping into someone in Sainsbury's you know."

"Er...story."

"Story? What story? You can't be doing a story. I'm doing a story, I mean we're doing a story, Damien and me. You can't be...."

"Look I've just got to check in..." Gerry turned away abruptly, giving himself time. He took a registration card and began to fill it out.

Olivia stood right behind him. "Gerry I need some help, honestly, but if you don't tell me what you're doing here how can I trust you? Gerry speak to me. I was pleased to see you wasn't I?"

He finished writing and turned round. "Look I just need to check into my room, make a call. Why don't you order us a drink or something?"

Olivia looked grateful. "Okay, there's a bar out by the pool. What can I get you?"

"Beer. Give me five minutes."

From the balcony of his room he watched, through palm fronds, as Olivia took a table beneath a pergola and ordered from the waiter. He didn't doubt her enthusiasm for seeing him but the intimacy of her embrace had quite taken him by surprise (and was not at all unwelcome). He turned back into the room and concentrated on the problem at hand. He'd told her five minutes. He had about three left to come up with a story. He knew nothing at all about Mindanao except that Peter Neville had disappeared here. He supposed he could try the marriage market story but Damien would never buy that one, too old hat for Channel 4. On a coffee table in a corner of the room lay a pile of tourist literature. He picked up a brochure and flicked through its pages, searching desperately for a subject, any subject. From time to time he stopped when a photograph caught his eye, a copper mine, an outrigger canoe, a pineapple picker, a thermal spring. He returned twice to one particular photograph, reading and re-reading the text before finally making up his mind. Outside, by the pool, Olivia was already looking at her watch.

Neither spoke until the waiter had poured the drinks and left.

"Aren't you going to tell me then?" Olivia said.

"You tell me yours and I'll tell you mine," Gerry said.

"And what if they're the same? Who gets the story?"

"First one to say *snap*...."

"Gerry you're not fair. Damien's disappeared and I'm really worried. You know this is the place where Peter Neville was abducted don't you?"

Gerry snorted into his drink. Jesus! Did she say that? What did he mean *snap*? Stud poker more likely. And the way she'd said it, matter-of-factly, innocently, as if she and Damien just *happened* to be in the place where Peter Neville was abducted. That was the bluff, it had to be. For a moment Gerry pondered the worst case scenario. He remembered the unconvincing cover story they'd given Barney Hedges about doing the marriage market thing and that stuff from Jonathan about Boyle wanting his Peter Neville file. Suppose they *were* here doing the same story. Suppose he'd come half way round the world to do the same bloody story as Damien. And suppose she knew it. He hid his face in his glass and drank.

"*Please* Gerry, tell me yours first."

His eyes met hers over the rim of the glass. Show us your cards or play some more poker, they signalled. "Okay," he said, putting the drink down slowly, ".....exploitation."

Olivia felt faint. *Exploitation*.... what did he mean exploitation? Missing girls? There couldn't be two exploitation stories in a place this remote. Surely. Could there? Then she remembered, with growing unease, that her own story had become public knowledge the day of that forward planning meeting. And that that was the same day Jonathan Dowell got fired, wasn't it? And that that was the same day Gerry had resigned....

"Pineapples," Gerry was saying.

"Pineapples?"

"Pineapples. That's my story.

"What about pineapples?"

"You've heard of the Calfruit Corporation?"

"Yes."

They operate here. Big Pineapple plantations. Usual thing. Subsistence wages, no health care, child labour. Most of their output goes to one supermarket chain back home. Claims to have an ethical buying policy. So 'Tonight, in *Dispatches*, we expose the guilty fruit....' you know the kind of thing, bit of righteous indignation, questions in the House, everyone at home stops buying pineapples, everyone here ends up out of work."

Olivia let out a long slow breath. "Well," she said, trying not to sound relieved, "It's still a good story. I don't think you have to be quite so cynical about it."

Wrong, Gerry thought, that's the creative touch that lends credibility. "Now you," he said.

"You won't tell?"

"I showed you mine."

Olivia took a sip from her coke. "There's an agency here, *Filipina Services*. They find work overseas for local girls, domestic work. A lot of them get placed with families in the Middle East. When their employers get posted to London they take the girls with them. That's allowed. But the girls don't have work permits, so they can't leave. They end up trapped in these employments, often treated as slave labour. Some of them run away to an address they've been given in Hackney, a priest, Father Ambrose. What happens next we don't know, except they disappear."

"Disappear?" Gerry sat up. This was a real story. You don't get that kind of detail in a fiction. So they were actually here to do a real story and a good one at that. Well that was it then. Great. End of game. She'd shown her cards. He'd didn't have to show his. He took a deep gulp from his glass to disguise his relief and choked.

"Are you all right?" she said.

"Sure." He cleared his throat. "Anyway, sorry, you were saying. Did you actually get to meet any of these girls?

"We met a couple – before they disappeared of course."

77

"And the priest, Father what was it?"

"Ambrose. Saw him once. Soon as he thought we were onto him he shut up shop, vanished."

"And what do you make of it?"

"Dunno. Damien's convinced we've stumbled across an international vice ring. You know he always thinks Big Picture. Maybe he's right. We got here two days ago. He said something about going out to have a look around and we'd meet for dinner. Haven't seen him since. I'm worried, Gerry."

"Sure he's not just doing his own thing? He's not used to having someone like you around."

"Oh I'm under no illusions there. I like to think I'm here as a director. Damien thinks I'm here so he can get his leg over."

Gerry shifted uncomfortably, recalling an earlier use of the expression. "Do you suppose he went to see this agency by himself?"

"Possibly. I was all for masquerading as man and wife, you know, on our travels, looking for a maid to take home with us, something like that. But not Damien. I suppose a wife was the last thing he wanted me for." There was a note of grievance in Olivia's voice as if not to be desired for one's wifely qualities were itself a form of abuse. She flicked a loose strand of hair abstractedly.

"You told the office?"

"That's the problem. What do I tell them? If I tell them he's disappeared they'll panic and pull me out and I'll never get a chance like this again. On the other hand, if I tell them I don't know what he's up to, I'm just going to look like a complete wimp and I'll never *ever* get a chance like this again." Her eyes were cast down as she said this. After a moment she lifted her head slowly and looked Gerry straight in the eye.

Gerry realised he'd never really looked at Olivia. Well of course he'd *looked* at her but he'd never looked *at* her. To look at her as he did now required an invitation. She was leaning forward across the table, so that their faces were close. A slight, pitiful smile played on that gorgeous mouth. He looked into her eyes as he was meant to. The brown of the iris was so dark that it merged with the pupil. Black pools. Deep. Impenetrable. Vulnerable. "Perhaps I could help," he said.

They bought a cheap wedding ring in a jewellers then took a taxi through congested streets to the waterfront. Between the lines of traffic, cyclists and strange three-wheeler motorcycle cabs wove dangerously. A garishly decorated jeepney drew alongside, its passengers spilling out of the open sides, clinging to the roof.

"Have you noticed that you never see a bus in the third world which isn't overfull?" Gerry said. "You never see an even *half* empty one. I mean how can you explain that? It defies the laws of supply and demand. If our buses always come along in threes, why don't theirs? It's like toilet seats. Have I told you about toilet seats in the third world?"

Olivia ignored him. She was holding out her left hand at arm's length, splaying the fingers, amused by the novelty of the wedding ring. "You know it would look much more realistic if I had an engagement ring as well."

At a traffic intersection the taxi driver fought off two small boys intent on washing his insect-splattered windscreen to opacity. Olivia dropped small coins into their outstretched palms.

"Protection money," Gerry said.

"Oh but it's all so colourful."

"Only to you. These people don't think they're colourful, just poor, Local colour is the rich man's description of poverty. Ever hear of anyone looking for local colour in Sweden?"

"Curmudgeon! I think it's exciting."

They drove down a waterfront street of timber yards and furniture shops, the rainforest come to town, and pulled in outside a two-storey concrete building. Mahogany-framed sofas and chairs, spilling from the neighbouring workshops, blocked the pavement. They wound their way towards the entrance and climbed a narrow, dark staircase to a door which said *Filipina Services.*

Until their eyes had adjusted, they saw only bright bands of light which streamed through louvred shutters Then the room and its occupants slowly grew clear. A silence had fallen with the entry of the foreigners and Olivia was reminded of the Hackney refuge. Here were the same timid young women, sitting now on chairs ranged around the wall, some in tribal costumes, richly woven fabrics and beads, others in T-shirts and jeans, all with the same long, straight hair. On the wall itself were occasional posters, their colours desaturated to pale blues and greens, Guardsmen at Buckingham Palace, The Eiffel Tower, Bonn. A downmarket travel agent, Olivia thought, which in a curious way, she supposed, is what it was.

At a desk an older woman sat behind a Remington typewriter. Without saying a word she rose and motioned to them to follow her. They entered a back office where a man was interviewing two girls. The girls were summarily ejected and their seats offered to the visitors. The man leant across the desk to shake hands. "Rizal," he said, "you are very welcome."

Olivia didn't like Mr. Rizal one little bit. In fact she loathed him all the way from his nasty little '50's pencil moustache to the way he wore the bracelet of his wristwatch loose on his skinny wrist, from the embroidery on the collar of his shirt to his two-tone shoes, from his pointed sideburns to his tacky aftershave. The man had pimp written all over him. If there were an opposite to sexual chemistry then this was it. Rizal, on the other hand, clearly found Olivia both charming and good business and fawned accordingly. It was rare, he said, for such beautiful ladies to visit his office in person, not many of his overseas clients came to the Philippines, contacts were made through advertisements in foreign papers, perhaps that was where she'd seen the name?

"No," Olivia said, sensing a dangerous inquisition, "nothing like that at all. My husband and I…" (it amused her to hear herself saying that) "…are travelling all round South East Asia, aren't we darling? He's such a darling that he doesn't want me to overdo things and suggested I have a maid, someone we might even take back to England with us if she were suitable. So we just made enquiries in the town. Isn't that right darling?"

Gerry thought she was definitely overdoing things. She was acting. She'd even affected one of those English starlet accents, all flattened 'A's and elocution lessons, '*beck* to England, *rind Sithe* East Asia'. "That's right darling, you're really not your usual self at the moment are you?" he said.

"So if you could do anything for us Mr. Rizal we'd be most enormously grateful, wouldn't we darling?"

"Of course Mrs.…?"

"Harris." Olivia said. Gerry grimaced.

Rizal put the tips of his fingers together and leant on the desk. "How long do you have?" he asked.

"We're not sure," Gerry put in quickly, stealing the stage from Olivia.

"Most of the girls who are willing to work abroad come from the hill villages. We have some on our books but it will take time to bring them down here."

"What about the girls we've just seen out there," Olivia said, "some of them look terribly sweet (*terribleh sweet*) don't they darling?"

"No," Rizal said, "they are not suitable... I mean they are not available. Of course it would save time if you travelled up country yourselves. You could combine it with some sightseeing. The mountains are very beautiful. There are lakes, thermal springs and of course you can bring the girl back with you."

"What a simply marvellous idea darling. Oh Mr. Rizal how frightfully clever of you."

Gerry closed his eyes. She's Vivien Leigh, he thought, she's Norma Shearer playing Elizabeth Barrett Browning, she's bloody Gertrude Lawrence. He cleared his throat noisily. If it was as obvious to him she was playacting, it must be obvious to everyone. But Rizal seemed unaware. In this remote corner of the Pacific, English people were a rarity and Rizal was the owner of a Betamax video cassette player. Rizal had seen far more screen performances of the thirties and forties than real English women. Rizal had seen Vivien Leigh. Rizal had even seen Norma Shearer (who he knew was actually American) playing Elizabeth Barrett Browning. Rizal thought Olivia the quintessential Englishwoman and was enchanted.

"You are too kind Mrs. Harris. Now if you'd like to step outside I'm sure my secretary will find you a cup of tea while I discuss terms with your husband."

"Oh," was all Olivia could say, suddenly quite out of character with surprise.

"Now do run along darling," Gerry said, "the chaps need to talk business. There's a good girl."

Forced to revert to a role of her own inventing, Olivia gave Gerry a saccharine smile, got up and left the room.

As soon as the door had closed, Rizal walked over and locked it.

"Now," he said, "perhaps you will be good enough to tell me who sent you. You see 'enquiries in the town' would not have brought you here. We deal directly with agencies overseas. We don't operate locally." The tone of Rizal's voice had changed.

Gerry had to think on his feet. "Someone in London," he said after a moment. "My wife doesn't know that, you see. She thinks I enquired locally."

"And the name?"

And the name. He only had the one name. That name represented his entire pile of chips. All or nothing. He mentally rolled the dice. "He's a priest, catholic, Father Ambrose."

Rizal walked slowly round behind his desk and sat down. He gave what Gerry thought was a distinctly unpleasant smile. "So. It's a child you want."

Gerry blinked. He knew what he'd just heard but his head swam. He was faint, hyperventilating. *So it's a child you want.* He thinks I'm a paedophile, a sex tourist. He struggled to control his breathing but his mind still made no sense of anything. Fr. Ambrose's girls were supposed to be eighteen, nineteen, not children. *So it's a child you want.*

Rizal poured a glass of water and handed it to him. "I can see you find it embarrassing Mr. Harris but you can be assured of our confidentiality. Now I take it from your coming to the Philippines in person that you intend to father the child yourself and that Mrs. Harris is agreeable to this?"

Gerry blinked again. This time his mind went into a terminal spin. *Father the child yourself... Mrs. Harris agreeable.* What....? So it's not children.... babies? Something to do with babies.... *father the child yourself...* There were connections. He needed time to make them. He knocked back the glass of water. "You'll have to excuse me. I just need one last word with my wife. We have to discuss these things you see..."

"Of course." Rizal unlocked the door and Gerry went out into the outer office. He paused for a moment, watching Olivia, cup in hand, sitting by the shuttered window. Connections. There were connections. Somewhere. Connections he had only moments to make. He looked around the room at the shy young girls. What did they all have in common? Poverty of course. And youth. Poverty and youth.

And gender – they were all girls. Poverty, youth and gender. Connections, think connections. Poverty, youth, gender and… babies? Was that it? He walked over and sat down next to Olivia. "Those girls in Hackney," he said after a moment, "were any of them pregnant by any chance?"

"How on *earth* did you know that?"

"Shh. Male intuition. Tell you later. The men have to finish their business." He went back into Rizal's office and sat down. "Yes Mr. Rizal. I'll be fathering the child."

"Well?" Olivia said as the taxi pulled away, "don't keep me in suspense."

"I'm going to be a father."

The taxi swerved violently to avoid an oncoming jeepney. There was an intimate collision on the back seat. They were eyeball to eyeball.

"What did you just say?"

Gerry took a deep breath. "We're unable to have children you and I. So I'm going to father a child by your Filipina maid. She's going to come back to England with us to give birth. Then we're going to adopt it. Then she'll go home again. What do you want, girl or boy?

Olivia straightened up and adjusted her shirt. "Gerry this is absurd. Will you please begin at the beginning?"

Gerry felt like the detective in the last scene of a country house mystery. All the pieces of the plot were about to be dropped into place and he alone had the script. He sat back again in his seat and took his time. "Okay what do you know about adoption back home?"

"Pretty impossible I gather, specially babies."

"Social services get to decide who adopts and who doesn't. They don't even like people in their thirties let alone people who, say, smoke. Which is why people have been travelling to places like Colombia. If you arrive back in the country with a foreign baby there's little they can do to stop you adopting it, whoever you are. Trouble is the governments in those countries are making it harder and harder to take a baby out. Even if you're lucky it can take months, years even. But suppose instead of taking the baby out of the country you take the pregnant mother instead….."

Olivia's eyes widened. "Angelica," she said, as if thinking aloud, "one of the Hackney girls. She told us she'd got pregnant here but hadn't known till she got to London."

"Of course she knew. And Rizal would also have known that her employer's family were bound for London. He'd have matched the two."

"So how do the adoptive parents explain the baby?"

"They say they came here themselves and brought it out of the country. They say it was unwanted. There's no way social services are going to take it away from the only people who care for it and there's no way it can be sent back. There's no-one to send it back to. So you see Damien got it all wrong. It wasn't the girls they were exporting, it was their pregnancies."

"Can we prove it?"

"Depends on my sperm count I suppose."

"Gerry that's outrageous. You wouldn't really... would you?"

They met for dinner beneath the pergola in the garden. Olivia wore an ankle length dress of Indian cotton and, judging by the prominence of her nipples through the thin cloth, very little else.

"Aren't these tropical evenings wonderful," she said. "I've never been this far south. You know we're almost on the equator here." She leant to one side to allow the waiter to pour her wine.

"We need to talk," Gerry said.

"I know."

"I can't go on being your husband."

"But we've only been married a day darling. Don't you want to consummate first?" The starlet accent again. The waiter moved round to fill Gerry's glass while Olivia giggled at his Jeevesian inscrutability.

"I'm being serious."

"Will that be all sir?"

Gerry nodded and the waiter withdrew, eager to disseminate this pearl of gossip among the kitchen staff.

"I'm being serious," Gerry repeated. "And by the way what makes you think you can act? You nearly blew it this afternoon with that accent."

"Nonsense. I got terrific reviews at Oxford. I was a star in the Barretts of Wimpole Street." She struck a photographic pose, eyes cast upward.

84

"I'm being serious Olivia."

"I know." She looked down at the table, as if repentant, "I know, you've got your pineapple pickers to worry about. Channel 4 are paying you. You can't be expected to traipse around the countryside with me, looking for tribal maidens to bonk. Am I right?"

"It wouldn't be so bad if it weren't so far away. Rizal wants us to go to South Cotabato. It's the other side of the island. We could be away for days. I've a job to do."

Two little vertical creases formed between Olivia's eyebrows. "Did you say Cotabato?"

Gerry nodded. (She even frowns prettily, he thought.)

"And you wouldn't want to go there?"

"Why should I?"

"Oh...." Olivia shrugged, "Well I suppose that's something anyway."

"What is?"

"Well I guess I owe you an apology. I doubted you. Now I can own up." She did the business with the strand of hair, curling it behind her ear. "You see, Damien and I are not here just to do this story. We're here to do a much bigger one, well Damien is anyway." She took a sip from her glass, prolonging Gerry's suspense. "Do you know what happened in South Cotabato?"

Gerry shook his head.

"It's where Peter Neville disappeared."

Gerry sat impassively, his visceral turmoil invisible to Olivia.

"We're here to try and find him."

For a moment neither spoke. Gerry drained his glass in one go, wondering how to react. "Why the apology?"

"Because I suspected you might be here for the same reason."

Gerry forced a laugh. "I see. And now you know I'm not because I'm not interested in going to South Cotabato. Tell me..." and he added this casually, "...is that where you suspect Damien's gone?"

"Ninety-nine percent certain."

Gerry smiled. Gotcha. "Just got to make a call," he said.

"Six oh double six, help you?"

"Can I speak to Jonathan please?"

"Can I have the company name sir and I'll put you through to the department you require."

"It's the desk in the corner by the window, Carol. One Man Band."

"…putting you through now."

Gerry lay on the hotel bed, the cradle of the telephone balanced on his stomach. "Jonathan, that you?"

"Gerry, you calling from Mindanao? How's things?"

"Give me a worst case scenario Jonathan."

"Damien?"

"Carry on."

"….is in Mindanao looking for Peter Neville."

"No, that's a bad case scenario, Jonathan. The worst case scenario is that Damien is in Mindanao looking for Peter Neville and is TWO FUCKING DAYS AHEAD OF ME. He's already in South Cotabato. He'll have seen your contact, whatever he's called and got whatever there is to get. It's what they call an exclusive Jonathan, and he's got it, geddit?"

"No need to shout. What do you think we should do? I'll have to call Northrop and tell him."

"You'll do no such thing. It's life or death, remember, your words."

"So what are we going to do?"

"Stay calm. We're going to do what you always do in these situations. If you can't stand your story up you tell them you've got a better one."

"And have you?"

"Maybe, I'll need you to do some research. I want you to find out all there is to know about hiring domestic servants from the Philippines, agencies, ads, that kind of thing. Any stories about maids running away or disappearing. There's an agency here sending pregnant girls to Britain so their babies can be sold for adoption. It's called *Filipina Services*. Olivia and I are going up country with them tomorrow posing as a married couple to choose a girl to have a baby for us."

There was a long silence "Can you repeat that?"

"What, the whole thing or just the bit about Olivia?"

"Are we talking about the same Olivia here, Denning-Smith?

She's supposed to be with Damien. Are you telling me she's working for you?"

"Not exactly. She thinks I'm helping her with her story. It was hers originally."

"But you're not helping her with her story."

"No, I'm stealing it."

Gerry returned to the table. "Sorry about that. Had a call booked. Producer. Seems the pressure's off for the moment. I won't be starting right away."

"Really?"

"Yeah, got to wait for some budget meeting next week before we can go into production proper. So I get a week to 'research', which is very nice because the research is pretty well done, so… cheers!" He raised his glass and encouraged Olivia to do likewise. "You bring a camcorder by the way?"

"Yes why?"

"We'd look pretty conspicuous towing a film crew around with us."

"Us?"

"Thought with my spare time I might do a little sightseeing. Do you know there's a rainforest in the West. South Cotabato province I believe."

Olivia's mouth fell open. "You'll do it?"

"One condition."

"Anything."

"Strictly no acting."

The car came for them at seven, a jeep made entirely of polished stainless steel. Gerry had seen them in Manila, someone's idea of a status symbol, the Filipino Jag. The driver wore white clothes and shoes and dark glasses. He opened the back door for them, then sat alone in the front. They took the road south, back past the airport, out along the coast.

"Isn't Mr. Rizal coming with us?" Gerry asked.

"He will meet us at Mr. Espinoza's."

"Who's Mr. Espinoza?"

"The owner."

"The owner of *Filipina Services*?"

"Mr. Espinoza is the owner of most things."

An hour down the coast the road turned inland and the surface worsened. The driver opened the glove compartment, took out a pistol and laid it on the seat beside him. "No good area," he said to them, shaking his head in the mirror.

Olivia looked out at the no good area. Across a field, a cloud of red dust, fired by the early morning sun, tracked the slow progress of an ox cart. On distant mountainsides, wisps of blue smoke escaped mysteriously from wooded slopes. A flock of green birds wheeled and swooped. The jeep climbed up into the mountains and then down, until they came, as is the way with islands, to the sea again. In the small town of General Santos they stretched their legs by the waterside. There were outrigger canoes here and bamboo houses built on stilts over the water. Half-naked children stood in groups and stared. Gerry pulled out the camcorder and began to film.

"I thought you weren't interested in local colour?" Olivia said.

"I merely said local colour was the rich man's description of poverty. I never said it wasn't picturesque." He panned the camera through one hundred and eighty degrees till it came to rest on the gleaming jeep. The driver held his hands in front of his face and turned his back.

They headed off again, northwest, inland. At the next small town of Koronadal they turned off the road onto a track and began to climb. The scenery grew in scale. Below were great valleys now, wet with rivers. Steep, mist-hung slopes towered above them. Rainforest trees began to mingle with the lesser species of the bush. Gerry recorded it all with the camera.

At the sight of the first roadblock he put the camera away. Soldiers with M16's. They looked at the passengers in the back and spoke to the driver in what Gerry took to be Tagalog. "They want to know what you are doing here," the driver said.

"Tell them we've come to hire a maid."

The driver translated, shrugging his shoulders. The officer, incredulous, repeated the question. The driver repeated the answer. Then the officer laughed and stroked the stainless steel door. Gerry heard the name Espinoza. The tone was polite. They were waved on.

The second roadblock was more of an ambush, the jeep suddenly surrounded on a hairpin bend. Faces and guns poked in through the windows. The clothes were military but not uniform, the interrogation terser, the language different this time. "We've come to hire a maid," Gerry said again, and again the leader of the troop brushed his hand over the polished metal of the bonnet and waved the jeep on, a stainless steel passport.

"Who the hell *is* this Espinoza?" Olivia asked.

Gerry shrugged. "Nervous?"

"Try scared shitless. Did you see those knives, the long curved ones?"

The driver, listening, mimed the cutting of his throat in the mirror. "Moros," he said.

"Moros? Gerry sat forward. "Was that the Moro Islamic Liberation Front then?"

The driver nodded and mimed the cutting of the throat again."

"Who is this Mr. Espinoza?" Olivia asked.

But the driver didn't reply. In the silence it began to rain.

They came to a stop beside a lake. From where they sat, the cloud and driving rain obscured all but the near shore, the huts of the village just shapes in the mist. Then the drumming on the roof of the jeep lessened and a transformation scene began to unfold of near theatrical contrivance. The lighting switched from blue to gold as visible shafts of sunlight burst through the cloud. Mist and rain cleared, figures came into focus, fishermen pushed log canoes onto the waters while women emerged at the top of bamboo steps in brightly-coloured clothes, for all as if they were about to break into chorus. And across the lake a gauze seemed to lift.

Behind the gauze was the house. It sat perched on the rim of a volcanic crater, the same crater which contained the lake, a sea on top of the world. From the house, all the way to the water's edge below, ran a wooden staircase like a Mayan temple's. Larger than all the village huts put together, the house, even with the perspective of distance, dominated its stage, the fairytale castle on the backcloth.

"Wicked Witch or Sleeping Beauty?" Gerry said.

"Bluebeard more likely."

They walked down to the water's edge between stilted houses and boarded a dinghy. From the glassy water Gerry took more pictures, a fisherman astride his canoe casting his net, a cluster of cabins, the big house. The house itself was enormous, a minor palace, built entirely it seemed, of mahogany. A deep verandah, ornamented with fretwork, circumscribed the ground floor, opening onto the steep waterfront staircase. Above the verandah, balconied windows sheltered beneath a steep, double-pitched roof.

Olivia looked from the house to the water, taking in the scene. "I've never seen anything so beautiful – such harmony, such peace."

"You've got a short memory." Gerry said and he mimed the driver's throat-cutting gesture. They pulled in to a landing stage at the bottom of the wooden staircase. Men with long knives helped them from the boat, took their bags and motioned them to climb. Half way up the steps it became apparent someone was watching them from the top. Olivia found it hard to look at the figure and hard not to – hard because if she acknowledged him too soon what would she do with her eyes until she was close enough to talk, hard not to as she recognised someone she'd already met. "I win," she whispered to Gerry, "It's Bluebeard."

Rizal smiled down at them, his upper lip stretching his pencil moustache. Touches of local colour had been added to the embroidered shirt and the two-tone shoes – a brightly-printed bandanna such as the villagers were wearing and a sash with a bolo hanging from it. Olivia thought he looked faintly ridiculous. "Who does he think he is?" she whispered again, "bloody Errol Flynn?"

"Just his weekend-cottage clothes, I expect," Gerry said, "that'll be like Barbour and green wellies to him. Oh and by the way, talking of Errol Flynn, don't forget that promise of yours. No Barretts of Wimpole Street."

Olivia affected a puzzled frown. "Somehow Gerry I don't recall Errol Flynn being in that particular film."

Julian answered the call on its ninth ring, seven of the previous eight having insinuated themselves into his dream and subverted its storyline to their own ends, the eighth having woken him. "'lo" he mumbled. An accented voice told him he had a call from the Philippines. He sat up and looked at his watch. It was three a.m. "Damien that you? D'you know what time it is?" A body in the bed beside him stirred and grumbled.

"Midday."

"Not here it's not. It's three in the morning."

"I thought it's what you guys thrived on, Julian. Red braces ethos. On the job twenty-five hours a day."

"Who's that?" the body in the bed murmured.

"Just work," Julian said. "Go back to sleep."

"Who're you talking to?" Damien said.

"No-one. What seems to be the problem?"

"Olivia's disappeared."

"You're married to that bloody job, Julian," said the shape beneath the duvet.

"Julian cupped the mouthpiece with his free hand. "Can you please stop interrupting Brian. You have to understand this could be important." He uncovered the phone again. "Sorry Damien, I didn't hear. You were saying?"

"I was saying Olivia's disappeared."

"You're kidding! Where are you?"

"I'm back in Davao. I went up country to that place Koronadal. Met Jonathan Dowell's contact, whatsisname, Francisco. Waste of time by the way. If he does know anything he's far too nervous to tell. Anyway I didn't tell Olivia I was going 'cause, frankly I didn't want her on my back. Far too conspicuous. However I get back today and guess what, no Olivia."

"She's vanished?"

"Not exactly. Are you ready for this?

"Go on."

"She's gone and got married."

"Fuck-ing hell!"

"Do you have to shout?" Brian said.

Julian dropped his voice to a stage whisper. "When?"

"Yesterday I gather. I think she thought it was all a secret but it's the gossip of the hotel. The happy couple left this morning in a stainless steel jeep with a chauffeur. But that's not the real news."

"It's not?"

"Guess who she's married."

"Damien how can I possibly guess who she's married?"

"Gerry."

"Gerry who?"

"Our Gerry, Harris. Reporter. BBC as was."

There was a silence then, very loudly, "Fuck me!"

"That's it," Brian said, grabbing a pillow and heading for the door, "It's just job, job, job isn't it? It's always the same. You come home late. You're tired. You eat, you watch television, you go to bed. And then the only time you're actually awake in bed, you're on the bloody phone."

"Who *is* that?" Damien said.

"Nobody," Julian said.

"Nobody's about right!" Brian said and slammed the door.

"You still there?" Damien said.

"Yes… They kept it bloody quiet didn't they? I thought she was bedding poor old Felix. Whatever happened to the decent interval?"

"The whole thing's fishy," said Damien, the line beginning to crackle now. "They weren't on speaking terms after Moscow, yet when he turns up here, according to the bloke behind the desk, she's all over him. By the end of the day they're wed. And there's something else too. This jeep that comes to collect them, supposedly to whisk them off on their honeymoon. Everyone here knows it. Belongs to some big shot called Espinoza. Now guess where this Espinoza happens to have estates? – South Cotabato. And what is South Cotabato famous for?"

"It's where Peter Neville disappeared…" Julian said slowly. "Jesus, Damien, what the hell's she up to?"

"Dunno. Look I'm going to have to pay this Espinoza a visit. You'd better hold the crew till you hear from me, if you hear from me."

"Don't be melodramatic Damien. Course we'll hear from you. Compared to the Moldovan Hyena, this one's an absolute pushover."

Rizal led the way into the bedroom. Both Olivia and Gerry's eyes flicked involuntarily towards the double bed and then away again. "The house belongs to my employer, Mr. Ferdinand Espinoza," he was saying. "He will be your host this evening. He hopes you will be comfortable here. Dinner will be at 6.30."

"Exactly who is this Mr Espinoza?" Olivia asked. She'd dropped her starlet voice and was relieved to see that Mr. Rizal was unaware of the change. Presumably all English accents were the same to him.

Rizal smiled and frowned all at the same time. "He is the owner, of course, Mrs. Harris."

"Oh," Olivia said, "yes of course, the owner of most things."

"Till 6.30 then."

Only moments after Rizal had left there was a knock at the door. A young girl entered, perhaps fifteen or sixteen, dressed in colourful tribal clothes, her long hair straight to the waist. She smiled at Gerry, dropped a little curtsey then made her way to the bed. Olivia froze. Surely not so soon? And not with *her* there? The girl pulled back the mosquito net and slowly turned the sheet down, smoothing it with her hand. She smiled at Gerry again, then walked round to the other side and did the same. Then she closed the mosquito net once more, curtseyed and left.

Gerry let out a long breath. "For a moment there I thought...."

"Gerry I sincerely hope you're not even thinking....."

Gerry walked across the bare teak boards to the window and looked out through its louvred shutters. Far below a boat glided across the glassy waters towards him. It was too far away to see any detail but he knew by now, from the colourful clothing, that its passengers, its cargo more likely, were all female.

"The problem is that's exactly what I'm thinking. I know what I'm here to do, they know what I'm here to do. And you, darling Mrs. Harris, are supposed to know what you're here to do as well. You're here to help choose the surrogate mother of your child, I'm here to father it. The only problem is....how do we film it?"

"Gerry, that's outrageous."

"Is it? How do we back out now and stay alive? We can't just ring for a taxi you know."

Olivia thought of the journey up, of the *laissez passer* granted by the military road block, of the Moros out there in the forest, of bluebeard Rizal the procurer. "Gerry I'm scared."

"Me too, if it's any consolation."

"None in the slightest. You're supposed to be the man."

"*New* man. I'm showing my feminine side."

"Look Gerry, these girls... you're surely not saying you'd actually go through with it? You couldn't. It would be like, well... rape."

"Not if the girl's willing, it wouldn't be. I'm sure they all get paid. And a free trip to Europe thrown in."

"If that's a joke it's in very poor taste. You are joking aren't you...? Gerry...? Gerry speak to me..."

But Gerry's attention was distracted by the scene at the lakeside below. The boat had come alongside the landing stage. Rizal had gone to meet it. Gerry had been wrong. Not all of the boat's occupants were female. One of them was a man. It was the man who stepped out first, spurning Rizal's proffered hand. The two exchanged words, Rizal pointing up at the house as he spoke.

"That'll be him, I guess, Gerry said, "this Espinoza."

Olivia joined him at the window and peered through the slats, squinting at the tropical light. It was the grey hair that caught her attention, premature for a man only in his early thirties. He turned and looked up at the window. "Oh no," she whispered, "it can't be."

"Can't be who?"

"Oh Gerry we're dead. You know who that is don't you?"

"No."

"That's the man from Hackney. The man from the agency. That's 'Father Ambrose'."

For the hour between their arrival and their appointment for dinner, Gerry and Olivia stayed in their room. In Olivia's case this meant mostly in the bathroom. She told Gerry it was something she must have eaten, food poisoning, though her private diagnosis favoured the less common condition of *scared shitless*. The bathroom had become her condemned cell where she explored the terrors of imminent extinction. She had read in her researches that retribution in these parts commonly took the form of beheading. It would be one of those bolo things no doubt, with Rizal as the executioner and, however much she tried, she couldn't prevent her imagination from showing her what the film course had called the POV, the point-of-view shot. From inside her own skull she could watch, horrified, as her head became detached from its body and spun to extinction in that last sky-whirling moment of sentience. And in the odd way that the brain, under extreme stress, makes inappropriate connections, she recalled that Dostoevsky had once begun a novel with some similar such thought.

Gerry was no less nervous. While it was quite possible that 'Father Ambrose' might *not* recognise Olivia – theirs had been a meeting of only a moment, a door ajar, a corridor, Damien doing the talking, it was equally possible that he *would* recognise Gerry. He need only have watched television in London. This was Gerry Harris after all, reporter, *Worldweek*. He was even here under his own name, thanks to 'Mrs.' Harris in her ingenue role. (Their positions were momentarily reversed. For once he could, and did, blame her.)

At six-thirty a gong sounded. Olivia emerged from the bathroom. Gerry was impressed. Though paler than he had ever seen her, she stood erect and dignified She had on the same Indian cotton dress as the night before but now wore a bra underneath, fortitude and decorum both being deemed appropriate to the circumstance. She was Anne Boleyn now, Lady Jane Grey; she would go to the scaffold with nobility. Without thinking Gerry offered her an arm.

Olivia took the arm and squeezed it, pulling him closer. "Gerry," she whispered, "if we survive this bit, just one thing…."

"Yes?"

"These girls. I'm not getting involved Okay? I won't help you choose."

"Sisterhood never forgive you?"

"I just couldn't bring myself, that's all. It's immoral. You're on your own, right?"

"Right."

"That's all then. Good luck."

Rizal was waiting for them at the foot of the stairs. They crossed a corridor into a large central room which overlooked the lake. Wooden walls, hung with tribal artefacts, reflected in a polished wooden floor. There were high chairs with carved backs and a long refectory table, laid only for two. Rizal indicated that they should sit down. "Mr. Espinoza presents his apologies Mr. and Mrs. Harris. He has been suddenly called away."

Olivia wanted to burst into tears. Apocalypse postponed. Gerry just felt oddly cheated. Was someone playing a game? He'd seen and heard Espinoza arrive. So he should have seen and heard him depart. A young girl brought plates of fried fish and rice and fruit and Rizal encouraged them to begin.

"Mr. Espinoza," Gerry asked, "tell us about him. Is he from these parts?"

"Mr. Espinoza is from Manila, an important family. He is a great benefactor.

"What does he do?"

"Mr. Espinoza is a very wealthy man."

That's not an answer, Gerry thought but he didn't say so. He supposed from this that that Espinoza's wealth supplied the infrastructure for the baby scam while Rizal presumably supplied the girls. Odd, though, that a wealthy man should bother himself with such an operation, whatever the income per infant. (They had agreed on $US 10,000 plus expenses). "These girls," he said instead, "what is their relationship to you?"

"What relationship?" Rizal said, his pencil moustache shrinking abruptly and quite unpleasantly with his smile.

As in pimp, you brute, Olivia thought.

"I suppose I mean how do you come across them?" Gerry said, "Do they come to you?"

Rizal smiled, relaxed again. "I am well known in the villages. *Filipina Services* recruits a lot in these parts. I make sure the girls are well looked after. They call me The Protector."

Sure it's not Procurer? Olivia thought.

"And the parents?" Gerry asked.

"Of the girls you mean? Are they happy with the arrangement? Of course. I told you Mr. Espinoza is a great benefactor. He is a very generous man." Then the Protector gave a little bow, bestowed on the 'beautiful Mrs. Harris' another sickly smile and left them to finish their meal. They ate on in silence, unable to make conversation as husband and wife and fearful to make conversation as themselves. When Rizal returned he brought the girls.

The girls, three in all, were of an even height, small, similarly dressed in tribal costume and pretty. They walked in single file and took up pre-rehearsed positions facing a pair of ornate, high-backed chairs with wooden arms. Rizal indicated the chairs to his guests. They rose and took their places. "Make you feel like royalty?" Gerry whispered.

"Mmm. The sultan selects his concubine."

Rizal walked over to a corner of the room. They heard a click, then the scratch of a vinyl record. He clapped his hands and suddenly and for no reason the girls were all smiling. From a loudspeaker somewhere out of view came syrupy strings then a male voice, crooning… '*the most beautiful girl in the world*…' Gerry and Olivia exchanged glances of disbelief. One of the girls stepped forward from the line, her smile fixed, her eyes sparkling and approached the guests. She showed first one profile then the other, then, speaking and smiling all at the same time, said in a small, nervous voice, "I am Susanna. I have seventeen years old. I am 32-24-33. I would like to travel and meet people. My interests are dressmaking. Thank you." Then she turned and walked back, her arms catwalk limp. Rizal applauded. The next girl came forward: "I am Maria. I am seventeen. I am 32-23-33. I hope to work with children." She paused, hunting her memory for a lost script, her eyes darting nervously, then suddenly continued, "and my interests are singing and needlework. Thank you."

Olivia, despite her latent fears, felt an uncontrollable urge to giggle. She leant across to Gerry, hiding her mouth with her hand. "It's Miss Mindanao," she whispered, "winner gets to spend her special year in bed with Gerry Harris."

Theresa came last. Theresa was also seventeen but an inch larger on the hips. Theresa wanted a job where she could work with people. She liked cooking. When she'd finished her presentation Rizal led his guests in a round of applause. "Now to business," he said. He stood in front of the girls and invited the clients to inspect the merchandise. He wished them to understand that all the girls had received some education at the Catholic Mission school, could speak some English and were free from communicable diseases. Olivia got up from her chair.

"I think I'll leave you gentlemen to it. I've seen all I need to see, Mr. Rizal. I'll take some fresh air on the verandah if you don't mind."

"Tell you what, darling," Gerry said quickly, "before you do you couldn't just fetch the camcorder for me? We really ought to have a souvenir of this." It was a moment before she grasped what he was about. He made her feel unprofessional. All she was thinking about was escape; Gerry somehow still had his mind on the story. She fetched the camera and watched with a grudging admiration how he cajoled Rizal, in slow persuasive steps, to re-enact the beauty parade. First he just took shots of the girls – a group portrait, individual close-ups. Then *how about if they did that bit with the music again?* Then, *tell you what, why don't the girls each say their bit for the camera?* Then, pushing his luck, *could they just do that again so I can get a wider shot?* And they did, Olivia recognised, because Rizal, in common with most of the human race, would abandon all reason for the prospect of being immortalised in moving pictures. And it was flattery, too, which persuaded Rizal to take the camera for himself and film one last shot of Olivia and Gerry seated on their thrones, watching the proceedings. "Thanks," Gerry said when the camera was returned to him. "That'll look great back home."

Olivia went out onto the verandah. The air was moist and oppressive. It was already dark. A soundtrack of cicadas and frogs played continuously, overlaid by occasional murmurs of human voices from across the water. From somewhere above, in the house, she heard a man's laughter. In the room behind her Gerry was trading for a womb.

Except that he wasn't. Because Gerry had a plan. Minutes earlier he had no idea things could work out so simply but the beauty parade had been so unexpected. And to have got it again on camera was downright inspirational. He had a story. All he needed now was to pick one of the girls and get her back to Davao as fast as possible in the morning before this Espinoza appeared. Then he could interview her and send her home. He'd already got the establishing shots, the journey, the lake, the house. He'd need an exterior of *Filipina Services*; he might even be able to doorstep Rizal there. Then it would be time to give Olivia the slip, off to the airport and bye-bye Mindanao. He walked up and down in front of the girls, whose smiles still remained set. "Okay," he said to Rizal, "Which one shall it be?"

"Which one?" Rizal queried. His eyes narrowed.

"Who's to be the girl to have our baby? I have to choose, yes?"

Rizal looked genuinely puzzled. "You misunderstand Mr. Harris. We have already chosen for you. These are the girls we have chosen. They are all for you."

Gerry stared at the girls. As if on some sort of cue they'd all stopped smiling. They stared back at him now blankly, unemotionally. "They're *all* for me?"

"All of them." Rizal held up some papers which had lain, untouched, on the table. "The *Filipina Services* contract guarantees delivery," he said. "With one girl there can be no guarantee. With three we will have success. These girls have been specially chosen for their menstrual cycles."

"Their menstrual cycles?"

"They are ready. You have perhaps 36, 48 hours. You should begin tonight."

Gerry looked round and saw Olivia standing in the doorway. She too was staring at him. All he could do was to shake his head helplessly.

"The terms are as follows," Rizal was saying, "if more than one girl gets pregnant by you, you will only receive and be charged for one child. *Filipina Services* will retain ownership of other babies sired by you. Arrangements will be made for the mother of your child to be transferred to England or another country of your choice prior to birth. Deposit of 10% to be payable in advance, the balance on delivery."

"Cash on delivery," Olivia said, "how very appropriate."

Noproblem was Damien's name for the wiry, persistent young man who hung around outside the hotel entrance. *Noproblem* hustled for a living. *You wan' souvenirs? No problem. You wan' rattan? No problem. You wan' see a copper mine? No problem. You wan' girl...?*

"If I wanted you to fuck off would that be a problem?" Damien asked. The man took a step back and shrugged, his palms turned forward in a gesture of incomprehension. How could such offence be taken at such willingness to please? Damien moved on down the line of waiting taxis. One by one their drivers declined his fare. It would be dark before they got to Cotabato province. The road wasn't safe. Sorry. And behind his back, as Damien well knew, *Noproblem* waited with the smug patience of a man about to be proved indispensable.

"You wan' a car? No problem," he said finally, when he judged all Damien's alternatives to be exhausted. Damien nodded wearily.

The car, when it came, turned out to be a jeepney, garishly decorated with Catholic tat, plastic Madonnas with starburst halos, paste jewellery, samplers stitched with platitudes and the recurrent icon of a near naked man being tortured to death. An inscription above the windscreen announced, in English, that God would be going with them. So too, it seemed, were three drivers. "How much?" Damien asked.

"Two thousand for the jeepney, two hundred for each driver,"

"Why do I need three drivers?"

"They are all brothers."

"So?"

"They all own the jeepney."

"Well I'm not paying for them all."

The men stared silently. "Well?" Damien said again.

Noproblem walked away and leaned on the jeepney's bonnet, a manifestation of patience. No-one spoke. It was silence as negotiating position, the silence of men who clearly have all the time in the world, trading with a man in a hurry.

"Okay," he sighed at last and pulled a wad from his trouser pocket.

"And two hundred for me," *Noproblem* said.

The jeepney rattled through the town and took the road south. Damien sat on one of the hard benches that ran down each side. Rosaries and crosses and bits of purple ribbon swayed and jangled around him. Dust blew in from the open sides. After about half an hour, for no apparent reason, the jeepney slowed to a halt. A woman appeared at the back of the vehicle, handed up three small children and a caged chicken, then climbed aboard herself. Damien tried to wave her away. "I'm sorry, this is a private bus," but the woman pushed past him, sat down next to the driver's cab and handed some coins through the window. "Look here…" Damien began. One of the drivers turned and stared at him. Silence again, but something in the silence now, a hint of menace. Damien dropped his protest and turned to defend himself against an infant determined to befriend him.

Additional unscheduled stops gradually filled the vehicle, adding to Damien's discomfort and slowing the jeepney to a bumpy crawl. He sat at the back, staring out into the darkness, boredom compounded with rage. After six of the longest hours he could remember, he finally arrived back in Koronadal.

The room he'd occupied the previous two nights, the one with the air conditioner, was unavailable. The compensation, the *pension*'s proprietor told him, was that the room he was being offered cost much less. He took the key and found his own way. The bedroom door opened into darkness. He flicked the switch. A bare bulb lit the bleak scene: a single bed, its stained sheet still damp from the wash; a ceiling fan dangling from a single wire; a dripping shower behind a plastic curtain, cockroaches clattering on the wet concrete. And worse than all these – no telephone.

He dropped his bag and pulled back the damp sheet to inspect the mattress stains. "Shit!" he said very softly, "Shit!… Shit!… Shit!… Shit!… Shit!" He bent down slowly and began to remove one shoe. "You know what? You're all going to have to pay for this" He stood up again, hobbled silently across the room and tore back the plastic shower curtain. As the light spilled into the cubicle, large orange-brown cockroaches accelerated across its slimy surfaces, stopping, starting, changing direction, their movements as random and unpredictable as lightning tracks. Some in the tray made their escape into the gaping drain hole, some simply disappeared, the ones on the walls twitched their antennae and froze in the hunter's spotlight.

It takes considerable force to squash a cockroach, but Damien was a champion. "You're dead Noproblem," he screamed and brought the heel of his shoe down with crushing speed onto his first victim. He heard the satisfying crunch of splintering shell, and took his shoe away. The corpse rattled into the tray below leaving a gelatinous trail on the wall. At the first strike the other cockroaches began a frenzy of movement. He waited for the first one to stop. "Now you bloody drivers," he screamed and slammed the shoe down again. Crunch. Clatter. Slime. "You're dead, the lot of you! Dead, you hear that?" Then he thought he'd slaughter the chicken of the woman who'd ridden on his jeepney. That'd teach her. And if he could do that, why not the stupid woman herself? The more you kill the easier it gets. So he murdered the woman, though it took a while and then, for good measure, as there were still two cockroaches left, he dispatched two of her three brats, though he felt ever so slightly guilty about that and deliberately chose the two older ones. When the deed was done he cleared the abattoir, scooping the bodies onto a sheet of paper and throwing them out of the window. (If you tried to flush them down the drain they floated up again. Only the live ones somehow could stay down there.) Then he turned on the shower and stripped. With the curtain drawn it was unpleasant inside the fungal concrete box but compared to the sweat and dust of the last six hours, the cold water and clean smelling soap were a luxury no Hilton could better. He dressed, transferred his wallet and passport to his clean shorts, and went out.

Francisco Lopino's house, which also contained his office, lay adjacent to the big Catholic church separated by a patch of grass. Damien had not quite worked out the relationship between Francisco and the church, nor had he bothered much. Francisco was of a type you found everywhere, left-wing, do-gooding, a human-rights activist who thought that Christianity was socialism and socialism Christianity. (Tell that to Karl Marx.) He'd seen Franciscos in Guatemala, he'd seen them in Lebanon, he'd seen them just about everywhere in South America, the same offices with their broadsheets and their Amnesty posters and their photographs of mutilated corpses. God they were so worthy, struggling on their pitiful resources to change a world which neither knew nor cared of their existence. Perhaps, Damien thought cynically, that's why they called it the Struggle. It was never going to be a fight. They didn't have the strength for that.

The light of Francisco's office was on and Damien set out across the spongy grass. At each step two or three, sometimes as many as five or six frogs leapt forwards and sideways out of his way. It unnerved Damien, the sudden movements in the dark and the realisation that if a frog-free path was opening before him then it was certainly closing behind him, trapping him in a sea of frogs. He was relieved to reach the building's verandah.

Francisco didn't seem particularly pleased to see him, but greeted him anyway in the manner of international solidarity, shaking hands first in the normal way then with palms clasped, as if they were arm wrestling. Damien wondered why people like him always fell for the idea that journalists were like-minded souls, radicals campaigning for justice for the oppressed, part of the greater movement. Damien didn't even believe that human rights were 'inalienable', having seen at first hand that they were alienated from more than half the world's population. Human rights, no differently from fishing rights, were things one person granted to another. Every dictator knew that. But it was true that by listening sympathetically, Damien encouraged his subjects to believe that their beliefs were shared. That way you drew them out. That way they delivered. That way, if it came to it, they could betray themselves and you them.

"I didn't expect you back," Francisco said, "I have no more information for you."

"I'm here on a different mission."

"Oh?" Francisco pointed to a chair, took a cigarette from a packet and lit it.

"How would I get to meet Mr. Espinoza?" Damien asked.

Francisco drew the smoke deep into his lungs then exhaled a slow, diffuse cloud. "Why should you want to meet Espinoza?"

"I need to trace my director. I believe she's at his house."

Francisco played with the cigarette, rolling it between the smoking fingers. "That seems unlikely, Mr. Street."

"Why?"

"How old is she?"

"I don't know, twenty-something. What's that got to do with it?"

"Mr. Espinoza has many houses, in Manila and elsewhere. The house in the mountains here is his retreat. He does not receive outsiders there."

"What's that got to do with Olivia's age?"

Francisco laughed. "Simple, Mr Damien, she's too old."

In the silence which followed, Francisco watched Damien's slow realisation translate into facial expressions: first the frowning, then the quizzical, then the wide-eyed. "You mean girls, young girls? He likes young girls? How young?"

"Thirteen, fourteen.. Fifteen's pushing it a bit."

"And everyone knows this? Isn't anything done about it?"

Francisco laughed out loud. "Mr. Damien, your western outrage does credit to you. Haven't you learnt yet? This is Mindanao. Even in the Philippines they call it the Wild West. There is no law to speak of in the mountains. Besides, amongst the tribes a girl is considered marriageable once she reaches puberty."

"He's hardly marrying them, I imagine."

Francisco drew on the cigarette. The smoke escaped slowly through his nostrils. "What makes you think your colleague is there?" he said, changing the subject.

"She was collected in his jeep from Davao. Stainless steel. Lots of people saw."

Francisco looked puzzled. "And she too is involved in your search for Peter Neville?"

"Well… yes. Why?"

Francisco shrugged and looked away, deliberating. He pulled an ashtray towards him and stubbed the half-smoked cigarette out amongst other half-smoked butts. Then he looked at Damien. "I didn't tell you this when I saw you before," he said, "but they met."

"Who met?"

"Your Peter Neville and Ferdinand Espinoza. They met. The day before Neville disappeared."

"Why didn't you tell me?"

"I suppose because I felt responsible."

"Responsible for what?"

"Responsible for you. I was already in part responsible for him; I didn't want you on my conscience too."

"How were you responsible for him?"

Francisco pulled the cigarette packet towards him again, took one out, rolled it between his fingers and reluctantly put it back. "I helped them, Neville and that boy… what was his name? Jonathan. I produce a paper here as you know, a kind of newsletter for subscribers overseas. They hired me for my contacts; you'd call it a fixer. It was me who set up the meeting for them with the Moros."

"And Espinoza?"

"Oh he already knew about Espinoza. He just wanted me to arrange a safe passage. He went up there alone, well with a driver anyway."

"He knew about Espinoza? What did he know about Espinoza?"

Francisco shrugged. "He was knowledgeable about the Philippines. If you know about the Philippines you'll know about the Espinozas. They're an old family, one of the 'illuminati' as they call them here. They're big in minerals, copper, gold, property. I think Neville was just curious to know what this particular Espinoza – he's the youngest son – was doing hiding away on the edge of a rainforest a thousand kilometres from Manila."

"Indulging his sexual preferences?"

Francisco shook his head. "He doesn't need to come this far for that. No, he likes to think he has some affinity with the tribal peoples; wears their clothes, talks about spirituality a lot, the purity of the forest, noble savage stuff. Of course it's just a rich man's indulgence. In Manila he's a playboy; out here he likes to think he's some sort of a monk. He buys the people's affections with cash – literally hands it out. They humour him by calling him *Tao Bong* – it means *Good Man* in the T'Boli language. He has it painted on the side of his helicopter."

Francisco left a silence now and waited for the word to register.

"His helicopter?"

Francisco nodded.

"Peter Neville….." Damien paused.

Francisco finished the sentence for him. "…..was abducted in a helicopter."

"You're surely not saying……I mean it was a military helicopter."

"It was painted with camouflage colours if that's what you mean."

"And you think this Espinoza…..?"

"I don't know Mr. Street, I really don't know, but I do know that some of the Moros still use poison arrows. I do not think it likely that a helicopter comes within their arsenal."

"But why would this Espinoza..?"

"I have no answers Mr. Street. I promise you I have no answers. I only know that Peter Neville paid a visit to Espinoza in the mountains and that the very next day he was abducted. This is why I am now giving you the information. You say you wish to pay the same visit yourself. That can be arranged. It is simply my duty to inform you of the risk."

"Compared to the Moldovan Hyena this one's a pushover," Damien muttered under his breath

"I didn't catch that Mr. Street."

"Nothing," Damien said, "it's nothing. Just a saying."

Olivia was locked in the bathroom once again, this time to be sick. "I'm not coming out," she screamed when Gerry knocked.

"Look nothing's happening. I've had a word with Rizal. Nothing's going to happen tonight."

A silence.

"I said nothing's going to happen tonight. You can relax."

The door unlocked and banged open. Olivia stared at him, nauseous, her hair dripping from where she'd put her head under the shower. She swayed and held on to the door. "Relax?" she said, "relax? Just because you're not going to start raping virgins until the morning,

I can relax can I? And how did you manage to persuade the Lord Protector to allow you a good night's sleep eh? You have mebbe 36, 48 hours. You should begin tonight." She mimicked Rizal's accent.

"I told him I needed to wash my hair... For God's sake Olivia what d'you want me to say? It was man to man stuff, international machismo, you know," he clapped the palm of his right hand over his left bicep and raised the forearm, fist clenched. "I told him I was too tired tonight." He lowered the arm again. "In short I wouldn't be able to get it up. Hasn't done a lot for my South Cotabato street cred. I can tell you."

Olivia smiled with mock sympathy. "Poor Gerry, poor baby," She ran the back of her fingers down his cheek. Gerry grabbed the hand and held it. "Look, Olivia, you've got to believe me. I never had the slightest intention of ravishing maidens. I honestly thought I was going to choose one and we were going to take her back to Davao. That way you'd have been able to interview her for your film and send her home again. You'd have had a terrific story then, even if the London end didn't come up with anything. You've got all the stuff I shot on the way up here. And the beauty parade, for heaven's sake...."

Olivia looked at him and bit her lip. "Gerry I'm sorry. You are sweet. You're doing all this for me and I'm being ungrateful, aren't I?" She looked up at him, raised herself slightly on her bare toes and kissed him on the lips – not for so long a time as to imply mutually discovered passion, but quite long enough to begin to restore Gerry's South Cotabato street cred. She pulled away "Gerry what are we going to do?"

"I know what you're doing. You're going sightseeing."

"SIGHTSEEING?"

"While the men get down to business the wives are taken sight-seeing. It's quite usual. You know like the PM's wife. They've arranged for you to visit the village across the lake in the morning. You'll enjoy the weaving apparently."

"While you attend the fucking summit?" Her voice rose.

"In a manner of speaking only."

"Gerry you're avoiding the question. WHAT-ARE-YOU-GOING-TO-DO?"

Gerry turned and walked to the window. There was moonlight

now on the water. On the verandah below, Rizal, a small cigar clamped between his teeth, leant on the rail, smoking hands free. "I honestly don't know, Olivia. And you know what the worst of it is? I know you think it's all highly immoral. Well I think it's probably illegal as well, that is if there *is* any law around here."

"Well of course it's illegal. You can't just go around hiring out wombs for profit."

"I'm not talking about that, I'm talking about the sex bit."

"The sex bit?"

"How old do you think those girls were?"

Olivia frowned. "They said they were seventeen."

"Yeah, all three of them. That was a bit of a coincidence. Did you see the second one, Maria wasn't it, the one who forgot her words?"

"Gerry what are you saying?"

"I'm saying, Olivia, that I doubt she was a day over fifteen."

Olivia grabbed hold of the doorknob. "No Gerry."

Gerry nodded.

"Isn't it just that they're small?"

Gerry shook his head. "It's more than that. They're not virgins either. Look at the way they behaved. When they switched those smiles off they looked totally indifferent. These weren't girls about to face losing their virginity to a total stranger. Those were the expressions you see around King's Cross, the faces of girls who've become accustomed to their situation, girls who've become complicit in their own abuse."

"Gerry, no!"

"How else do you explain it? You can't just go round the villages buying girls to have babies, whatever the culture. These girls have been groomed."

"Espinoza? Having his 'wicked way' with them as Boyle would say?"

"Possibly. Or Rizal."

"Oh Gerry what a mess." Olivia slumped on the bed and began kneading her hands in her lap. "I got you into all this, I'm sorry."

"It's okay."

Neither spoke for a while. It was Gerry who broke the silence. "Perhaps I could get sick?"

Olivia shook her head. "Anything like that's going to look suspicious. Rizal probably thinks it's suspicious you're not already hard at it, if you'll pardon the expression."

"Look, do you mind if I go for a wander round? I can't think in someone else's presence."

"No, wait a minute." Olivia got up from the bed and came over to him. "Don't go. I may have an idea. Listen, how much cash have you got?"

"Dunno, a few thousand."

"Me too."

"Why?"

"Well this may be a way out. You know you mentioned Kings Cross just now. Well, if you think about it, that's what it's all about isn't it, money. Prostitutes trade sex for money."

"And?"

"Well why not the other way round?"

"What, trade money for sex?"

"No stupid, you trade money for abstinence. You pay the girls not to have sex with you."

Gerry frowned.

"You don't get it do you?" Olivia said. "Look, for us to get out of here Rizal needs to believe that you have inseminated his three girls. But he only needs to believe it. You don't actually have to do it."

"Oh," Gerry said, "I see...I think."

"The girls come in one by one. They stay for, say, ten minutes — you'd just be after a quickie after all, need to ration the testosterone and all that. Maybe you bounce up and down on the bed in case Rizal's listening at the door — I wouldn't put it past him — and the girl leaves."

"What if they tell?"

"That's part of the deal. You pay them money not to have sex with you and not to tell, not even each other. Believe me, no girl who's ever been coerced into sex is likely to turn down an offer like that."

Gerry looked thoughtful. "Hey, you know what? I could do all three in thirty minutes. Now that'd mean real street cred around here."

"You'll do no such thing. You're supposed to be an English wimp. Spread them out, breakfast, lunch, tea. Even that would be going some for some of my partners. We'll just have to take our time and keep our nerve." Olivia waited for a response. "Well? What do you think?"

Gerry looked at her. A strand of damp hair stuck to her cheek. He lifted it carefully and curled it behind her ear. "I think you're brilliant. I think I'd like to kiss you." He leaned towards her but she turned her head so as to take the kiss on the cheek. Her lips had been hers to bestow only. A reward for services rendered.

"Sorry ," she said by way of explanation, "but as we're going to have to share that bed tonight I really don't want to send out any wrong signals. I take it you like the idea then?"

Gerry nodded. "I don't think we have another one. Better start turning out your purse."

They came for Damien at midnight. A knock on the door and the proprietor's voice: "You have visitors Mr. Street." He lay on the bed, fully dressed on top of the stained sheet on top of the indescribable mattress. A fresh batch of cockroaches clattered somewhere in the corner. He sat up in silence. There was no point in replying. Friends don't come calling at midnight. After a moment he heard the master key in the lock and the door burst open. Someone flicked on the light. Through squinting eyes he saw the proprietor back away to admit two men. "Police," one said, "you come with us."

They marched him to the police station, gripping him by the upper arms like the bobbies in the old black and white comedies, *Now come along quietly sir.* At the station there were no formalities, no paperwork, just a search. They took his passport and watch and opened his wallet, counting the cash with their eyes. Then they took his shoes and belt and put him in a cell. The cell must have been a legacy of the American colonisation, three of its four walls being entirely of bars, a cage. That apart, it wasn't so different from the room he'd just left – concrete floor, stained mattress, cockroaches. He sat on the bed and looked at the bars. What was it with the Americans and their penal attitudes, these cages, those shackles and their hideous electric chairs? Medieval. Something to do with puritanism no doubt. He lay back on the bed and allowed his mind to follow its own train of thought from puritanism through Catholicism to Francisco.

Francisco was the only person who knew who he was and why he was here. He must have told someone. But why should wanting to see Ferdinand Espinoza be an arrestable offence? An hour passed, maybe more, he had no watch. He drifted into a shallow sleep. In the dream from which he would finally awake, the face of a man he knew to be Espinoza stared down at him. Other faces crowded in at the periphery to get a look, the faces of young girls. "Go on," Espinoza was saying, "you have one. It's perfectly okay round here. Everyone does it you know. Go on, choose one" and Damien was struggling to see beyond the faces to the camera lens. Where was the camera? This was a story he would expose to the world but there was no camera. This is Damien Street for '*Worldweek*', Mindanao, the Philippines. But there's no camera. Where's the camera for Christ's sake... where's the fu... and as the dream reached the point of the irreconcilable storyline he awoke. A face was indeed staring down at him. "Good evening," it said. "I am Ferdinand Espinoza. I believe you wished to see me."

There was something faintly absurd about Espinoza. It was the dress, of course. He wore the casual clothes of a certain kind of wealthy man – a silk shirt, monogrammed, 'slacks' with sharp creases, slip-on buckskin shoes with basketwork uppers, but all this overlaid with the incongruous ornamentation of the local tribes, a plaid shawl, strings of beads and a piece of cloth wound into a rather ridiculous turban. He took a chair from the guard and sat down. "You wanted to see me Mr. Street. Well, here I am."

"I wanted to see you. I didn't ask you to have me arrested," Damien said, still lying down.

"One can never be too careful. There are many subversives in this area, guerilla activity, pirates... journalists...."

Damien sat up slowly. "And who are you to order arrests?"

"I am a... a sort of magistrate."

"What sort? Appointed, elected?"

"Appointed."

"Who appointed you?"

"I did. Now I think it better for you if you allow me to ask the questions. I'm quite unused to answering them. Why did you want to see me?"

"I believe you have guests at your house. One of them is my colleague. I need to talk to her."

"Her name?"

"Olivia Denn... no sorry, Olivia Harris. She just got married. To a former colleague of my mine. He's with her I understand."

Espinoza looked confused. "I think you'd better begin at the beginning, Mr. Street. In what enterprise is it that you are all colleagues together, were all colleagues together?"

"The BBC."

Damien was quite surprised at the effect his answer had on Espinoza, though he'd seen the reaction often enough on camera. It's where the subject's eyeline keeps moving anywhere but in the direction of the interviewer (the astute cameraman zooms in for the big close-up here). It's the reaction of a man caught off guard by a question, finding himself unexpectedly in a trap, a man suddenly struggling to think on his feet.

"There was a BBC journalist here just over a year ago. Another colleague of yours?"

"He was abducted," Damien said.

"I know, the Moros. Very sad."

"Did you meet him?"

"You're asking the questions again Mr. Street. Why are you here?"

"I told you, I need to see Olivia."

"I mean why are you here in the first place? Why are you in Mindanao? What journalistic enterprise are you and Mrs. Harris undertaking?"

"I think that's confidential."

"I really don't think so, Mr. Street." Espinoza got up and slammed the bars of the cell door shut, so that the sound of the lock echoed along the corridor. The policeman outside stood unmoved. "How long do you think I can keep you here?"

"You can't keep me here. You've nothing to charge me with."

Espinoza turned and called the guard over. From one of his trouser pockets he pulled a wad of notes, peeled a couple from the top and handed them through the bars. The guard nodded his thanks and took them. Espinoza turned back to face Damien. "How long?"

Damien's nerve gave. With the slamming of the door, he'd convinced himself that violence was about to occur and had begun the necessary psychological preparations. But the sudden reprieve, replaced as it was by Espinoza's apparent power to keep him imprisoned for as long as he chose (the wad of notes would never run out) undermined his will to fight. In any case, it was now evident that finding Peter Neville would almost certainly require his gaoler's co-operation. He took some deep breaths to compose himself. "Okay. We're trying to find out what happened to Peter Neville, the one who disappeared."

"We?"

"Olivia and I"

"So what is Mr. Harris doing?"

"I honestly don't know. At a guess he's probably doing the same thing. For another channel or a newspaper. I can't see there's any other story in these parts that would interest an audience back home."

"And *Filipina Services?*"

It was Damien's turn to be wrong-footed. How the hell did Espinoza know about *Filipina Services*? His eyes began darting in all directions. He saw the camera lens zoom in for the big close-up. *I'll just ask you that question again shall I?* He felt sweat break out on his brow. "What about *Filipina Services?*"

"You tell me."

"Er….it was Olivia's story really," Damien said, betraying her in an instant. (Well, she'd betrayed him hadn't she?) I didn't really have anything to do with it. The editor just thought it might be a fallback if we couldn't get anywhere with the Neville enquiry. You don't come all this way and go home empty-handed, if you like."

"And the story?"

"Not much as far as I could see. Never thought it would stand up myself. Just some girls from the Philippines gone missing in London. No big deal. Filipina Services just came into the picture because they'd acted as employment agents. Olivia and I were going to follow up the lead when I got back from my first trip here. But when I got back to Davao she and Gerry Harris had got hitched and were whisked away by your chauffeur. It's my belief, Mr. Espinoza…"

Espinoza held his hand up for Damien to stop. He leant close into his face and spoke very softly, "You were going to follow up the lead when you got back from your trip? But in the meantime your colleague had got married, right out of the blue, to this other journalist, Harris, and was being whisked away by my car….?" He got up and walked over to the door, grabbed the bars with both hands and

112

pressed his forehead against them. "Rizal you are a fucking idiot. An absolute fucking idiot."

"Can I go now?" Damien asked.

Espinoza didn't seem to hear.

"I said can I go now?"

Espinoza rounded on him. "Course you can't. You're more of a liability than ever." He signalled to the guard to open the door. Damien got up to follow but was pushed back into the cell. He grabbed the bars.

"But I've told you everything I know. It's not fair."

Espinoza stopped, peeled a couple of notes from his wad and passed them back through the bars. "Here, this makes everything fair."

In the absence of even so much as a hard chair, in which Gerry might do the traditional, gentlemanly thing, it had been tacitly understood by both he and Olivia that they would have to share the bed. Now that Olivia had actually mentioned the subject, the embarrassment level had risen markedly. She retired to the bathroom, leaving Gerry to ponder the actual mechanics of climbing into bed with someone who was not your sexual partner, especially someone as exquisite as Olivia. Would they lie under the same sheet? Would they kiss good night? Would she smell delicious? Would they touch in their sleep? Would he.....well, get aroused?

Exactly this same last thought pre-occupied Olivia as she dried herself after her shower. She picked up the bottle of cologne nervously out of habit, then thought better of it and put it back. She climbed into a pair of cotton pants (very plain) and pulled on a T-shirt long enough almost to cover the buttocks. In the mirror she brushed her hair straight back from the forehead (maximum severity) and tied it with an elastic band. She removed her pearl stud earrings. When she felt as satisfied with the effect as she could be, she unlocked the door and went back into the bedroom.

Gerry thought the effect was stunning.

"Your bathroom," she said.

Gerry rummaged in his bag for a clean pair of underpants.

"Before you go, Gerry, the rules. When you come back I'll be asleep okay? And I mean asleep – that side of the bed if it's all right with you, facing outwards. I shall sleep under the sheet. You can sleep on top. No goodnight kiss, no touching, nothing, okay? Is that understood?"

"Understood."

Gerry took his time in the bathroom, giving her the outside chance of actually falling asleep before his return. He knew that finding her asleep was just a strategy, that if necessary she'd feign sleep the whole night to avoid contact. It was a shame she didn't feel she could trust him but she was probably right. The sexual part of a man's brain and the rational part are not connected. He'd done stories himself on public figures who had ruined themselves caught kerb-crawling or cruising, politicians humiliated by kiss-and-tell bimbos. Why risk everything for a fleeting orgasm? But they do and the reason why is simple: when it comes to sex versus sense, sex is the supreme champion. Love conquers all.

When he returned to the bedroom the light was out. Pale slats of moonlight fell on the white bedsheet, changing direction with the outline of Olivia's body. Her breathing was slow and rhythmic. (I'm asleep, Gerry, get it?) He lay down on his side of the bed in his underpants on top of the sheet and turned onto his side, careful that their bottoms shouldn't touch. He could smell her shampoo. Sense number three. He'd seen her, he'd heard her, now he smelled her. That left only two, didn't it? The forbidden senses, touch…..and taste.

He couldn't sleep, or so he thought, but when, once or twice, he looked at his watch, intervals of an hour or more had passed, which his sense of time could not account for. It was odd, like coming round from an anaesthetic. He recalled a tonsillectomy at about the age of twelve and its curious consequence of his own apostasy. He'd remembered the anaesthetist pushing the needle into his hand and the feeling of oblivion closing around him, then woken only a second later on a trolley, with a nurse calling his name and the sorest throat imaginable. The operation had taken place without any sense of time having passed, quite unlike the usual awakening from a sleep. It was incredible. They'd just switched his brain off and that was it. Nothing. Oblivion. Hence the apostasy, because for a child brought up to believe in a soul this was nothing short of a revelation. This meant that death could be like that. Just nothing. Oblivion. And from that moment, lying in the recovery room between the rails of a hospital trolley, he'd abandoned belief in the soul and the afterlife forever and vowed, when he returned to school, to give the Reverend Smithson a seriously hard time, because there's nothing men of faith liked less than a logical argument.

But the next time he checked his watch he knew for sure he'd been asleep, because he surfaced from a dream of erotic pleasure to find Olivia curled around him, her lower abdomen pressed against his buttocks, her knees tucked in behind, transmitting the warmth of her body. A slender arm lay draped across his waist, its hand barely touching his stomach with its fingertips. Gerry recognised the hand as the cause of his erotic dream. A few inches below it, his underpants bulged in a shaft of moonlight.

Olivia was clearly in a dream of her own, emitting periodic moaning, snuffling noises and shifting her position. Gerry looked down at the hand and dared himself. He just wanted to know what it would be like if she touched him there. That's all. She'd never know, she was fast asleep. So it wouldn't be taking advantage or anything would it? He reasoned with himself, sex versus sense, and waited for sex to win. Then he lifted the hand by the wrist and repositioned it on the swollen delta of his underpants. For a moment it lay there limply while he stiffened. Then suddenly the fingers clenched. Gerry gasped. Olivia's whole body shifted position. He heard her mutter something as if she were coming round. He closed his eyes and pretended to be asleep. He could feel her sitting up. She must be wide awake now, yet the hand stayed in place, motionless. Gerry lay in fear and silence. She was considering her next move and she had him, quite literally, by the balls. Then he felt the hand begin to move, slowly at first, up over his belly, feeling the musculature with its fingertips like a blind person reading a face. And then down again, this time beneath the waistband.

"Don't pretend you're asleep, Gerry," she murmured at last in a drowsy voice. "It's okay. You want it. I want it. Let's just do it shall we? But no post mortems eh?"

It was the noise which woke Olivia. It had penetrated her sleep, its slow crescendo lifting her to consciousness. For a moment her waking brain struggled with the noise's identity, like a stroke victim searching for a familiar word. It was an unmistakable sound, she knew that, but still she couldn't quite name it. It was the incongruity. It was a noise that didn't belong here, not here, in this village, on the edge of a rainforest, on top of the world, at the very end of the earth. It was….she sat up suddenly. "Gerry," she said, nudging him in the ribs, "Gerry listen to that. It's a helicopter."

Gerry opened an eye, saw a naked breast and reached out a hand. She slapped it. "Listen," she said.

Gerry listened and began to frown. The throb of the rotors fluctuated with the atmosphere like an ill-tuned radio signal, first louder, then more distant, but there was no question the helicopter was heading straight for them. He swung his legs out of the bed and tiptoed across to the window. Olivia threw a pair of underpants after him. "Must be something military," she said,

Gerry ignored the underpants and opened the shutters quietly.

"You'll be seen," Olivia hissed.

"Look. It's coming. I can see the light."

Above the near horizon a cone of light hung from the sky, tracking its follow-spot across an undulating hillside. As the pulse of the rotors grew louder, so the ring of spotlight on the ground grew smaller and brighter until finally it burst onto the water, shooting its reflection towards Gerry in a river of silver, whipped up by a Lilliputian tempest.

"I don't think so," Gerry said.

"Don't think so what?"

"I don't think it's military. Come and look. It's white. And it's got something written on the side TAO BONG. What do you suppose that is?"

Olivia padded over to join him, clutching the sheet around her. The helicopter had landed on a floating platform. They watched as a man got out and began to run, stooping beneath the rotors, a strange headdress unravelling wildly in the cyclone. Suddenly there were people there to meet him, hard to count in the darkness, people they hadn't noticed until now, but people who immediately began to cheer. Parents held up small, sleepy children. Women whooped as young girls came out from the crowd and hung on the visitor's arms. The visitor allowed himself to be kissed.

Gerry looked at his watch. "It's two fifteen in the morning," he said incredulously, "it's the middle of the bloody night."

"Gerry, d'you see what I see?"

Gerry looked where Olivia was pointing. Pushing through the crowd towards the visitor was the man with the prematurely greying hair, his hands clutching a small overnight bag. He stopped for a short, shouted conversation with the new arrival then made his way out to the helipad and boarded the aircraft.

"I thought Rizal said he'd been called away," Olivia said.

"He said Mr. Espinoza had been called away."

"Exactly. Still at least we don't get to meet him now and run the risk of being recognised. That's a piece of luck we deserve."

"On the contrary Olivia, I think you'll find we'll be making Mr. Espinoza's acquaintance a lot sooner than you imagine."

It took Olivia a moment to make the connections. She looked at Gerry. She looked at the newcomer below. She looked at Gerry again. Gerry's smile was ever so slightly condescending. Then she got it. "Oh," she said, embarrassed now, "you mean….. it's him."

Gerry nodded.

"You must think I'm awfully slow," she said.

Gerry glanced from Olivia to the unmade bed and back again. "Not in the slightest," he said.

Boyle stared out of the window at White City. He was in truculent mood. Where was this White City.? What was this White City? Two tower blocks and a motorway flyover that's what. He'd been ripped off by these Brits. He'd been invited to BBC London, not BBC White City. The view out there should be of Tower Bridge, Trafalgar Square, The Palace of Westminster. That's what you saw when the reporters filed their pieces back home. People in Paris got the Eiffel Tower; people in Moscow got the Kremlin. Everyone knew that. This was supposed to be the television headquarters of the greatest broadcaster in the world and all he got was a traffic jam. You can bet your life Rupert Murdoch never fired anyone without at the very least a national monument over his shoulder. The view only added to Boyle's ill-temper. He turned to face Julian. "Offer him his job back," he said.

"What, Gerry Harris?"

"No, stupid, this Jonathan whatsisname, the one I fired. Offer him more money?"

"How would that help?"

"We're victims of a conspiracy here, Julian. This marriage you're telling me about, Harris and the girl, it's got to be part of a bigger picture and this bloke knows what it is."

"But he's already got a job. As I understand it Channel 4 have commissioned him – Northrop Pryce, Information Entertainment."

"Commissioned to make what?"

"That's the big question; my spies couldn't say. But we do know they hired Gerry as the reporter and you don't have to be a conspiracist to work out the rest of it. Think about it: Jonathan Dowell is asked to bring in his file on Peter Neville. That very same day he gets fired. So there he is; he has no job but he has a story – a story we've unwittingly just handed him. He thinks, hey, they must be planning something on the Neville case. I could do that; I could sell this one. That would serve them right wouldn't it? Of course I'll need an experienced reporter but guess what, Gerry Harris is looking for a job too. Q.E.D."

"And the girl?"

"Not so easy. I can't work that bit out. Everyone thought she was sleeping with Felix, the one who died in Moscow. Maybe the Russian experience threw her and Gerry together, who knows."

"We need to talk to Damien Street. Get him on the phone."

"There are no telephones, Doug."

"That's an impossibility."

"'Fraid not. They're in this little town up country. Frontier land. No phones, no mobiles."

Boyle clearly didn't believe in such a place. He stared out at the crawling traffic on the Westway. "You'll have to go and see him then."

"Damien?"

"Nah, this Jonathan Dowell. Tell him the file he took belonged to the BBC and we've informed the police. Tell him we hold the intellectual rights to the property. Tell him we'll sue. Tell him we'll take him for every penny. Tell him he'll never work again. Anything you like. Just scare the shit out of him."

A plastic nameplate, one of many, directed visitors to One Man Band Productions to the fifth floor of the Beak St. house. On the top landing Julian looked for a sign but found none. He chose a door and went in. From behind a cluttered desk a young man looked up at him lopsidedly, a telephone wedged between shoulder and chin, his fingers typing automatically on a keyboard. "This One Man Band?" Julian asked. The young man, unwilling to pause either activity, swivelled his eyes towards a girl at a desk by the window. Julian went over. "I'm looking for One Man Band Productions."

"Certainly sir, who in particular do you wish to speak to?"

"Jonathan Dowell."

"I'll just see if the managing director is available. Who shall I say's here?"

"Julian Jenkin."

She picked up a phone and dialled a number. Julian turned away from the desk just in time to see Jonathan pick up the call in the corner.

For all Julian liked to think of himself as ruthless (the term, for his generation, had entirely lost its pejorative associations) he lacked the mettle for confrontation. He admired Boyle, a man who could fire ruthlessly, a man who had no need to be liked. Ruthlessness, the management bibles told him, was a necessary condition for success and ruthlessness was incompatible with a wish to be liked. But, absurd as it was in the circumstances, he wanted to be liked by Jonathan now; he wanted to be forgiven. He wanted to say it was Boyle who fired you Jonathan, not me, honest. But instead he was here on instructions to scare the shit out of him. He'd never scared the shit out of anybody. How did you do that?

Jonathan, for his part, had not the slightest wish to be liked by Julian. While Julian smiled his greeting, Jonathan's mask was as grim and concession-free as a Sinn Fein spokesman's. "What can I do for you?"

"Can I sit down?"

Jonathan shrugged and indicated a chair with his eyes.

Ruthless, Julian said to himself. Be ruthless. He cleared his throat. "You have property belonging to us, a file. The police have been informed. The contents of that file are our intellectual property. If you act on that information you will be sued. We'll take you for every penny. You will never work again."

Jonathan said nothing.

"Did you hear me, Jonathan? What do you have to say?"

Jonathan leaned back in his chair, took off his glasses and screwed up his eyes. "What I have to say Julian is bollocks. Utter bollocks." He opened his eyes again and stared at Julian. "This you or Boyle talking? I'd somehow never seen you as Mr. Ruthless; Machiavellian yes, under-mining by stealth, like you did with me, but this…. threatening me to my face…. I do believe you're shaking Julian?

"You know what I'm talking about, Jonathan."

"Do I?"

"You're trying to steal our story, don't pretend you aren't."

Given that this was as literally true as it was possible to be, Jonathan wisely said nothing. He polished his glasses and put them back on. Had they really found out? Or was Julian just guessing that Gerry wasn't really 'helping' Olivia with her adoption story.

"We sent Damien with Olivia Denning-Smith out to the Philippines," Julian went on. "You, quite *coincidentally*, sent Gerry Harris to precisely the same island, one of a mere seven thousand in the archi-pelago, may I add. Suddenly, while they're out there, Gerry and Olivia pair off and disappear. And where do they disappear to? South Cotabato. And what happened in South Cotabato? It just happens to be where Peter Neville disappeared. Enough coincidences for you? She's sold you our story, Jonathan, our story. We'll sue, I promise you. Every penny."

Jonathan let out a slow breath. "Ohhh… that story…" He reached down into a drawer, pulled out a file and dropped it onto the table. "The Peter Neville file. There you are. Take it. Please give it to Scotland Yard and tell them I've returned it so they can drop charges. But do be careful. It contains priceless hotel receipts or, as you would say, intellec-tual property."

Julian picked up the file suspiciously. It hadn't been that easy, had it? Had it actually worked, this ruthlessness thing? Had he actually pulled it off? He looked at Jonathan quizzically, "And you'll call Gerry off the story?"

"No need, Julian. You have my absolute word on oath that Gerry is not working on a story about Peter Neville."

"I do?" Julian looked astonished. "Then what's he doing in Mindanao?"

"You wouldn't expect me to give away my story, would you. After all you might steal it. That would be the ruthless thing to do wouldn't it?"

"And Olivia?"

"I'm as surprised as you are. But then she did seem to prefer older men."

"I don't mean that, I mean she's not working for you?"

"Certainly not. I've never spoken to her. Whatever her relationship is with Gerry it's certainly not professional. Can I ask you a question?"

"Sure."

"Why doesn't Damien know what's going on? According to you, he and Olivia are supposed to be working together."

"It happened while Damien was away. He'd gone up to this place Koronadal to see your friend Francisco, the one in here," he tapped the file.

Jonathan sat forward. "And what did Francisco have to tell him?" he asked innocently.

"Nothing apparently. Didn't want to get involved."

"So Damien's back to square one then?"

Julian nodded.

"Well," Jonathan said, getting up, "I suppose that wraps things up for now. Now if you'll excuse me...."

When Julian had gone he clenched his right fist, whispered "yessss...." to it and punched the air, fashionably.

"Success?" Carol said across the room.

"Yup," he called back, "Listen Carol, if Gerry calls when I'm out, give him this message. Tell him we're in the running again. Tell him he can stop bonking maidens. Tell him we're back in the kidnap business."

"I think I'd better write that down." Carol said.

Olivia rose and dressed as soon as it was light, the more easily to avoid Gerry's testosterone-primed awakening with its anticipated gropings. The sex had been enjoyable enough, quite tender in fact, but his professions of love during their intercourse bode ill. She rehearsed familiar lines. It was a one-night stand, Gerry, just sex. Women can do that, you know, just like men. Just have sex. No relationship. No commitment. Gerry would probably refuse to believe this, convinced, like most men, that coitus required a woman to surrender her body to the male, and that the female's only possible motivation for such a gift had to be love or at least affection. It was just physical, Gerry, just physical. She turned the doorknob quietly so as not to wake him and stepped out into the corridor.

The corridor led past the head of the staircase onto a balcony at the rear of the house. She followed it out into the cool early-morning air. The view from the balcony took her by surprise. Climbing up to the lake from the other side, she'd seen patches of woodland alternating with the bare clearings of the slash and burn farmers. But here, rising almost to where her feet stood on the balcony, lay the unbroken, awesome canopy of a virgin rainforest. From where the house stood on the rim of the crater, the forest fell away at first, five hundred feet or more down the slope of the volcano. Then it began to rise and fall again, in and out of the cloudbase in a series of rolling hills, a vast green ocean swell, its surface made turbulent by the uneven heights of the trees. She peered down through the branches beneath her, trying to make out the floor of the forest. There was only darkness.

"Welcome to my rainforest," a voice said.

Olivia spun round with a little shriek of surprise.

"I'm sorry if I startled you....Ferdinand Espinoza." the man held out a hand, "and you will be Mrs. Harris."

Will I? Olivia thought. Oh God do I have to be? She held out her own hand, for a moment unable to speak. Espinoza took it, lifted it to his lips rather limply and kissed it. Olivia felt a shiver go down her spine. She was face to face with Espinoza. Although he was younger than she'd guessed, in his early thirties probably, this was definitely the man from the helicopter last night. This was Espinoza. This was the baby trader, the millionaire with the child harem, the owner of most things.

"Mysterious is it not?" he said, indicating the forest.

"Awesome," Olivia said, "quite awesome."

"I am its guardian."

"Oh." Olivia turned to the forest, grateful for the excuse to break off eye contact. "Do you own it?"

"The gods own it. The spirits of the forest."

"Oh."

"Do you believe in spirits, Mrs. Harris?"

Mrs Harris didn't remotely, but thought it wise not to say so. "I'm into alternative medicines," she said, hopefully.

"The people here believe that spirits reside everywhere in nature. There are spirits in the trees, in the rivers, in the animals."

"And do you believe that?"

"I believe that the forest is an organism and that organisms have souls. Can you feel the soul of the forest out there, Mrs. Harris?"

Olivia closed her eyes and felt for the soul of the forest. "Sort of," she said.

"Later today I will take you there and you will feel it properly. While your husband is busy there is much for you to see. You will be my guest and I will be your guide."

Please don't, Olivia thought. Please. Childhood fears of fairytale forests and abandoned children surfaced from her subconscious. He was playing with her. He knew all about her. He was going to get rid of her. He was going to take her into the forest and leave her there and......

"There's breakfast laid on the verandah," he said, "please take your time. I'll come and find you when we're ready. Meanwhile you must excuse me. I need to talk to Rizal. He'll be staying behind to look after Mr. Harris."

She watched him turn and walk away down the stairs, waiting till he was out of sight before she rushed back to the room. "Wake up Gerry. Wake up!"

Gerry rolled over and opened his eyes. A slow expression of disappointment crossed his face at the realisation that Olivia was clothed. "What is it?"

"Gerry he's going to take me into the forest."

"Who?"

"Espinoza. I've met him. He was the man in the helicopter. He's going to take me into the forest Gerry."

"Why?"

"Why do you think? To get rid of me. He knows all about us Gerry, I'm sure he does. He says Rizal is going to LOOK AFTER you. And he's going to take me into the forest and lose me there."

Gerry stared at the ceiling. "Olivia, if that happens you know what to do don't you?"

"No, what?"

"Well you stay calm and look around you. What you'll see is a little cottage. Inside there'll be a tiny table with seven tiny chairs and seven unwashed plates. Go upstairs and you'll find seven unmade beds with seven... ow!"

A pillow landed on Gerry's head. "You bastard," Olivia said, "You absolute bastard," and she hit him again, sobbing with impotent fury. And then she hit him again for good measure and even once more but by now the sobs began to mingle with her own giggles, and she stopped and wiped her eyes and he put his arms around her and kissed her. "Okay, I'm over the top, Gerry but I'm really scared. He's really creepy, this Espinoza. He talks mystical, all about the spirits of the forest. He's a kind of Central Casting evil genius type. Come to think of it he sounds a bit like a film script."

"Couldn't be your fertile filmic imagination, I suppose? How long did you speak to him for?"

"Must have been at least a minute."

"Exactly."

"First impressions are usually the best."

"What makes you think he knows who we are?"

"I don't know. He just had that tone of irony, you know, knowing."

"How could he know anything about us. The only person on the whole island who knows who we really are is Damien....." Gerry broke off. Their eyes met in an eloquent silence.

"You don't suppose...." Olivia began.

"His name's Damien Street," Espinoza said, throwing the passport onto the desk.

Rizal picked it up and studied the picture. "You want me to have him removed?"

Espinoza sighed. " I am a great admirer of your problem-solving skills, Rizal, but that might not be appropriate this time. You see Mr. Street is a journalist. With the BBC."

Rizal wiped his moustache with a fingertip. "With the BBC?"

"Exactly."

Rizal flicked his eyes down to the picture then up again to meet

Espinoza's. "Neville was a journalist with the BBC."

"Exactly. And that disappearance caused us enough fuss, if you remember. People down here from Manila asking questions. Besides it's more complicated than that. A great deal more complicated than that. What did you make of Mr. & Mrs. Harris?"

"She's very beautiful."

"She's clever too. Oh and by the way she's almost certainly not Mrs. Harris. They're investigative reporters. They're colleagues of this Damien Street, rivals as well it seems. And guess what they're investigating? You and me Rizal, you and me."

"Investigate me? What am I doing wrong?"

"You sell babies."

"So? People want babies. I supply babies. It's a free market economy."

"It's illegal."

Rizal shrugged. "So they'll have to disappear."

Espinoza sighed again. "I've already explained; that's not an option. The BBC is influential. There'd be enquiries at government level. We'd just draw attention to ourselves."

"Offer them money."

"That's a possibility. But they may refuse. You've arranged for Harris to inseminate the girls today?"

Rizal nodded.

"Do you think he'll do it?"

"Do it?" Rizal said incredulously. "I present him with three beautiful girls and you think he won't do it?"

"Rizal I won't try and explain but in the world outside Cotabato there is something called morality. It is quite probable that Harris subscribes to some version of it. He was only posing as a potential father. He probably expected to take a girl away with him – to talk to her you understand. Now you've gone and lined him up with an orgy."

"If he's a real man…."

"…maybe he'll succumb to temptation, yes, I agree. In which case we have no problem. Make sure you get the evidence on tape. He can hardly expose his adoption scandal to the world if he's caught investing his own sperm in the business."

"But if he doesn't do it he must know we'll find out."

"Not if he bribes the girls not to tell. In any case it's not a solution we can rely on. We need an alternative."

"We could take them into the forest and lose them."

Espinoza laughed. "A fairytale ending for the honeymoon couple. As it happens I've been thinking about the forest but not in that way." He reached into a drawer and pulled out a photograph. For a moment he stared at it in silence. "Suppose….. suppose we use the forest as a diversion; suppose the forest has something better to offer them."

"Better?"

"A better story. A story they won't be able to resist, a world exclusive which only we can give them access to. They're journalists, they'll understand a trade-off. As long as they *need* us they simply can't afford to expose us."

Rizal frowned. "If you mean what I think you mean… do you think these are the right people for it?"

"Why shouldn't they be the right people? The BBC has come knocking at our door, Rizal, don't you think that could be fate? The British Broadcasting Corporation, the world's most famous broadcaster. *This-is-London – dum diddy dum, di dum diddy dum.*"

Rizal frowned, failing to recognise the tune.

"It's destiny, that's what it is, Rizal, destiny. And their good fortune. The forest itself has summoned them. They are the ones chosen to tell the world before it is too late. There are things to be done, Rizal. Send ahead to Father Ambrose, we'll need the helicopter. Lucky Mrs. Harris eh? Little does she know it, but she's in for the scoop of a lifetime."

Gerry watched them depart from the window, Olivia in the prow of the boat, nervous in dark glasses, Espinoza next to the helmsman, lounging proprietarily, adorned with turban and beads. Espinoza had made no attempt to meet Gerry before the departure, sending Rizal to fetch Olivia. Gerry was thankful for that. Fooling Rizal had relied in part on his unfamiliarity with their culture. If British wives accompanied their husbands on their breeding trips then that is what they did. The sophisticated, urban Espinoza would be more suspicious; indeed Olivia seemed convinced he already knew. Female intuition maybe, or paranoia?

He took out the camcorder and switched it on. From his spongebag he took a sticking plaster and stretched it over the red, glowing LED. Then he zoomed the lens out to its widest angle and placed the camera on the top of a cane tallboy from where the shot would cover most of the room. When he was happy with the arrangement he lay down on the bed and waited.

There was a sound directly above him, indistinct, something the other side of the wooden ceiling, an animal perhaps, trapped in the attic space. For a moment he took no notice. But then he became conscious of something else, something he might or might not have seen, a momentary glint of light, a reflection perhaps? There was a rose in the ceiling, a circle of wood with a defunct electrical fitting at its centre, just a brown plastic cone with no flex. The noises had ceased now and Gerry got up slowly, first on his knees, then to his full height. When he stood on the bed his face came to within an inch or two of the ceiling. The centre hole of the cone was too large for an electrical flex. He moved directly beneath it and looked up. And screamed.

The scream was short and involuntary. The sight of a human eye looking back at him had tapped into a primeval memory, the prey surprised by the predator, the hunted eyeball to eyeball with the hunter. But whose eyeball? He took several calming breaths and looked again. As he stretched up to the light fitting, the eye came closer; when he drew back, the eye receded. He blinked and the eye blinked. Carefully he unscrewed the fitting and came face to face with his own reflection in a small circle of convex glass. The writing round the edge said *Panasonic*.

"Kinky bastards," he said out loud. He examined the installation. Undisturbed dust suggested that that the camera had not just been put there for today's performance. This was Espinoza's guest bedroom, or one of them. The camera evidently came as standard, along with the hot & cold running water and lakeside view. He felt suddenly queasy at the thought of last night's lovemaking. Surely it would have been too dark... wouldn't it? He got down from the bed, took a tissue from Olivia's box and stuffed it angrily into the light fitting. Then he climbed back up and screwed the assembly together again. Somewhere in the house Rizal, watching his picture go suddenly black, spat with rage.

Susanna was first; Susanna for breakfast, he thought, cynically. He told himself that he was here to expose Espinoza's venal trade, but even so he felt dirty at leading the girl on this far, like some News of the World reporter about to make his excuses and leave. If he were truthful he wasn't really doing this to save these girls from exploitation at all; he was doing it for a story. And while the audience would bleat moral outrage, most of them would just be watching out of prurience. So how different did that make his camera from Espinoza's?

Susanna began to undress as soon as the door was closed. "No, don't do that," he said quickly, "not yet."

The girl spied the camera on the tallboy, picked it up and handed it to Gerry. "You want this. You want to film it?" she said and continued to unbutton her blouse.

"No," Gerry said, replacing the camera carefully in the same position, "it's not even on." He turned back to face Susanna who was already naked to the waist. He grabbed her blouse from the stool where she'd dropped it and handed it back to her, trying to look her only in the face. He really didn't need this; he was a journalist not a priest for God's sake. Please don't put his virtue to the test. He recalled that Hollywood cliché where the angel perches on one shoulder and the devil on the other. In the movies the angel's arguments always prevailed. But that was comedy. This was big-time melodrama and in this movie the devil's speeches were positively eloquent. "Put it back on," he said, desperately, "please. I just want to talk."

He motioned her to sit down on the bed, where she'd be facing the camera. "Why do you want to do this?" he asked.

The girl looked puzzled. "I go to England."

"You'd have someone else's baby just to go to England?"

"Here we are very poor. In England many rich husbands, like Filipina girls."

"Who tells you that?"

"Rizal, Espinoza."

"How old are you Susanna?"

"Fi...Seventeen."

"Tell me about Mr. Espinoza."

"He is great man. He give us poor people money."

"Does he give you money?"

"He give my parents money."

"For you?"

Susanna faltered for a moment, dropped her eyes and nodded.

"And were you expected to do something in return."

The eye contact had gone. Susanna looked at the wall and gave a little shrug. "We are Espinoza's companions."

"We? How many of you are there?"

"Three, four, sometimes more."

"And how old are the girls?"

She paused and swung her eyes back towards Gerry and the camera. "Younger than me now." The effect was dramatic and Gerry instinctively left a professional pause. So this was the girls' reward. Once you were too old for Espinoza's bed he set you up in the baby trade. Girls with such 'grooming' would no doubt take the sex in their stride. Gerry stood up and pulled a wad of notes from his pocket. He peeled off several and handed them to Susanna. "Take these, Susanna. They're for you. I don't want to have sex with you; I don't want your baby. When you leave here in a few minutes tell no-one about this conversation, not Mr. Rizal, not the other girls. If anyone asks, tell them we had sex and it all went satisfactorily."

Susanna looked at the money and counted it. "Why?" she said.

"Why what?"

"Why don't you want to have sex with me? I want to have sex with you. I want to have your baby and go to England."

Gerry hadn't rehearsed this bit. What had Olivia said? No girl who's ever been coerced into having sex would turn down an offer like that. A lot she knew about women. Typical.

Susanna came over to him and made to unbuckle his belt. Gerry grabbed her hands. "Look you don't understand. You've been abused. You shouldn't be having other people's babies. It's against the law in England. You'll be arrested and have a criminal record and then they'll never allow you to marry an Englishman. Anyway we don't need a baby any more, we're… getting one from somewhere else."

"Somewhere else?"

"Yes, we're…. getting one of our own. We're *having* one of our own. Yes that's it. Mrs. Harris is pregnant you see. Never thought it would happen. Just found out. Last night. But we don't want to upset

Mr. Rizal and I'm sure you don't either, so…. we're pretending we're going ahead as planned… only we're not."

Susanna counted the money again. "You don't want to upset Mr. Rizal?"

"No."

"So you don't want to upset me either."

"Of course I don't want to upset you Susanna, I'm your friend."

"Good. Pay me double," and she held up the wad of notes, "two thousand pesos."

"Two thousand?"

"Now I am getting upset. When I get upset I must tell Mr. Rizal. When The Protector hear I am upset he get very upset. Maybe he cut of your head with bolo," and she mimed the execution together with a suitable whistling sound effect. "Now *you* are very upset."

Gerry was beginning to tire of this particular piece of mime. "I don't think I want to be quite that upset, thank-you," he said, already peeling notes from the roll.

It suddenly dawned on Olivia that she was being taken shopping. By the time she'd clambered up into the fifth or sixth bamboo house containing yet another home-made loom, she was already encumbered with her purchases: a woven wrap-around skirt in brilliant colours, a strip of cloth you wound into a turban like Espinoza's, long strings of exotic beads, a chain-mail belt, hung with brass ornaments. She felt cross with herself. Espinoza had simply taken it for granted in his contemptuous, male way that shopping was what she'd enjoy (while her husband was off siring children by other women; could you believe that?) Trouble was he was absolutely right. She did. She found the objects irresistible. *And* she allowed Espinoza to pay for them.

That bit was easy. Espinoza's need for conspicuous generosity was compulsive. The roll of bank notes, once taken out, never returned to his pocket. A crowd followed him wherever he went like an insect cloud. To these he gave money. He gave money to the women who pushed through to kiss him, to the little children, to the young women whose hair he would brush with his hands and who would drop their eyes shyly. In each village they rushed out to pay him homage and in return he paid them cash. It would be easy to say he simply bought their adulation, but Olivia increasingly had to admit that their enthusiasm seemed, surprisingly, sincere. Theirs were the same expressions of foolish delight you might see in news reports back home when 'ordinary people' were seen chatting to the Queen. Once, in a documentary, she'd seen a Nigerian chieftain on a walkabout handing out money in exactly the same way. His status amongst his people had demanded a conspicuous demonstration of his wealth. Monarchists require their monarchs to be rich.

To Olivia it was mere *folie de grandeur*. Rock stars bought Hebridean islands for the same reason. It was vanity's ultimate fantasy, the fiefdom, the private kingdom. But to the tribespeople of South Cotabato (and to Espinoza himself no doubt) here was a genuinely superior being, rich and educated, a man from a great city who arrived, godlike, from the skies dispensing banknotes. He'd built a mission school and brought in travelling clinics. If he wished to anoint himself king, why should he not receive the homage due?

"What does *Tao Bong* mean?" she asked him, waving from the jeep to a crowd of well-wishers for all the world as if she were his queen.

"How do you come to know the expression?"

"Your helicopter. I watched you land last night, You didn't expect me to sleep through it?"

Espinoza smiled. "I'm sorry I woke you. It means 'good man' in T'Boli. The T'Boli are the tribe who make the fabrics you like so much. It's a name they gave me."

"Good man," Olivia repeated. "So you're *The Saint* then?" It was an open invitation to self-deprecation.

"I hadn't thought of it like that, but I suppose you're right. *The Saint*, yes, that's good."

Delusions of grandeur indeed, Olivia thought. The situation was looking serious, pathological even. "How did your interest in these people begin?"

"In my lifetime I have watched our wildernesses sacrificed, one by one, to 'development'. Our population has doubled in a generation. There is a race for land as people move into ever remoter places. They cut down the forests and destroy the cultures of tribal minorities. I have resolved to become their guardian."

Robin Hood syndrome too, Olivia thought, even though she didn't know if there was such a thing. He had an odd way of speaking, prophet-like, as if his lines were rehearsed. It went with the legend, she supposed. It was the way Mrs. Thatcher used to speak, once she'd come to believe in her own myth. All power deludes; absolute power deludes absolutely.

They were nearing the top of a hill. Another village, another welcome, another loom. Still she'd be happy to stretch her legs. These zig-zag climbs up tracks gouged by rainfall were slow and uncomfortable. The humidity, the heat, the whine of the jeep's low gears assaulted different senses simultaneously. When they came to a stop in front of a gate she was the first to dismount. A child ran up and opened the gate from the inside and Olivia walked through, the stainless steel jeep following. The compound had high, whitewashed walls. Olivia saw a church and a number of low buildings with open, louvred windows and heard the sounds, unmistakable in any language, of classroom teaching. What she didn't see was the priest in the white cassock, at least not until it was too late, not until he was already bearing down on her, hand outstretched to shake hers. "Welcome to Santa Barbara Mission," he said in a faintly Irish accent, "I'm Father Ambrose. Now don't tell me, you must be Mrs. Harris. I've heard so much about you."

While Gerry ate his lunch, taken, at the insistence of Rizal, on the verandah, Rizal crept into the bedroom to remove whatever foreign object now obscured the lens of the hidden camera. But being shorter than Gerry, he was unable to reach the light fitting without first placing the stool on the bed. The resultant platform was so predictably unstable that it toppled just as Rizal was unscrewing the cap. He fell heavily, striking his head on the iron bedpost during his descent, and passed out. When Gerry returned from his lunch he was convinced, for a moment, that he'd found a corpse.

He checked for pulse and breathing. The discovery that the patient was still alive was both a relief and somehow a disappointment. He unwound the fingers from the electrical fitment and noted the toppled stool still lying on the bed. He examined the bedpost, found a tiny smear of blood and, in an inductive argument worthy of the great Holmes himself, pieced together the correct interpretation of events.

Then he began to laugh, uncontrollably.

It was at this point that the door opened.

It was Maria; Maria who was next on the list for insemination; Maria who'd nearly forgotten her words last night, who was already nervous. It was Maria who now saw The Protector dead on the floor, slain by the mad, laughing Englishman. She gave a shriek of terror and rushed from the room. Two minutes later the door creaked open a few inches and a small female hand pushed a wad of banknotes at floor level into the room. When the door had closed again Gerry picked them up and counted them. Two thousand pesos.

Olivia didn't have time to panic. It was obvious in an instant that Fr. Ambrose had failed to recognise her, even though he claimed to have heard so much about her. (What had he heard? That she'd accompanied her husband on his paternity mission?) He was polite, solicitous, rather charmingly Irish and yet she felt desperately ill-at-ease in his company. The incongruity of the iron-grey head with the youngish face spoke to her of deception. He was an alien. Things were not as they appeared. And that was perfectly true wasn't it? This supposed Catholic priest was, in some way or another, up to his ears in Espinoza's adoption racket. It unnerved her to think that she knew all about them, while they supposedly knew nothing of her.

She smiled politely. "Delighted to meet you... Father." She found it hard to say father, an absurd form of address, as if duty, respect, filial love even were due to this total stranger. He led the way across the compound. She realised it was First Lady time again – after the shopping, the Good Works. She was taken into classrooms where cute children stood to attention and chanted GOOD MORNING MRS. HARRIS. She admired their work. In the clinic they put a darling baby into her arms; she goo-gooed as required. In the church she crossed herself, then genuflected, or did you genuflect first then cross yourself? (Jackie Kennedy would have known.) At last they sat down to lunch at an outdoor table where an extravagant view across a cloud-filled valley ended at the very edge of the rainforest.

They were served by some of the older girls; Espinoza followed them round the table with his eyes. "Is it just a primary school you have here Father?" Olivia asked.

"We'll keep them till they're thirteen if they want to stay but there are no secondary schools for them to go to around here. We teach them some English just in case – secondary teaching all takes place in English, which is why it's so widely spoken. But by the time they're that age, most of the parents want them at home to work in the family. Mr. Espinoza, though, has been most generous with scholarships. The lucky ones get to attend school in Manila and stay at his mansion there." (What do the unlucky ones get? Olivia thought.) "Tell me Mrs. Harris, are you a Catholic?"

For a moment Olivia wondered whether to add one more lie to her profile but decided against. As a committed, born-again atheist she'd almost certainly give herself away. "No Father."

"It's just that you crossed yourself in the church back there."

"Well, you know… when in Rome… Tell me, do you make all your children into Catholics?"

"We are a mission. That is God's purpose. That is why I am sent."

"I've often wondered about that." Olivia frowned a little to suggest naïveté. "I mean if it's God's purpose that we should all be Christians he's jolly inefficient isn't he?"

"Inefficient?"

"Mmmm. I mean look at poor old South Cotabato. It's taken him two thousand years to get around to South Cotabato. Was there no-one else he could send in the meantime? All those generations who could have been saved."

"God moves in mysterious ways, my dear."

"Then there must be at least a thousand million Chinese still waiting to hear the Good News. I think that's racist of God don't you? What do you think Mr. Espinoza? Mr. Espinoza believes in animism, Father, did you know that? He believes that spirits inhabit plants and rivers, that the forest has a soul. Isn't that right Mr. Espinoza?" Olivia could hear herself becoming shrill. It was just nerves.

"I think Mr. Espinoza means that figuratively, my dear. I think he means that natural phenomena are a manifestation of God."

Espinoza stroked the leg of the girl clearing the table beside him and stared out across the valley. "I think we should let Mrs. Harris decide for herself what I mean."

"And how is she to do that?"

"You can't show me your God, Ambrose. It's just guesswork as to whether he exists or not – what you insist on calling 'faith'. Now when it comes to the soul of the forest, I intend to show Mrs. Harris. It's as simple as that. Then she can decide."

"Is that why you wanted the helicopter prepared?"

Espinoza nodded.

"Well now Mrs. Harris. There's the twenty-first century for you. You're about to be taken on a spiritual journey.....by helicopter."

"Really?" said Olivia, "that sounds rather fun."

Gerry sat on the bed, waiting for the brouhaha which would inevitably erupt. But none came. Evidently the girls had told no-one, except each other. Maria must have pictured Gerry to them as Rizal's killer and so far more to be feared even than The Protector himself. But Gerry had his own fear, that Rizal, suffering nothing more than concussion, might come round at any time. He opened the door and checked that the corridor was empty. The household was silent, most probably asleep in the midday torpor. He dragged the body by its feet to the head of the staircase, then turned Rizal around and manoeuvred him, wheel-barrow-like, down the stairs until his head came to rest on the floor below, feet pointing upwards. If he came round in this position, or if anyone found him first, there'd be a ready explanation for his condi-tion. He checked no-one had seen him then returned quickly to his room.

In the security of the bathroom he removed the tape from Olivia's camcorder and placed it inside the soap dish in his sponge bag. Then he returned to the bedroom and took a new tape from the box. On its label he wrote: *Philippines Roll 1* and the previous day's date. Then he loaded the camera and returned it to its position on top of the tallboy.

Moments later there was a roar followed by the sound of footsteps converging at the foot of the stairs. He waited a few moments then opened the door to look out, just as if out of natural curiosity. Two men already held Rizal upright by the arms, while a maid swabbed congealing blood from his temple. Rizal caught sight of Gerry and began to stagger up the stairs, shaking the men off. He pushed past Gerry into the room and stood, swaying, gazing up at the light fitting above the bed, frowning with puzzlement and pain. "The girls?" he said, clasping a palm over his skull.

"The girls? Oh they're all done, thank-you. As soon as Mrs. Harris returns we'll be pushing off, if that's okay."

"All done?" Rizal closed his eyes and slumped onto the bed.

"Very efficient. I enjoyed working with them, nice bunch. By the way I've left my signed copy of the contract on the side there. The deposit money is in this envelope. I'll need a receipt of course. Mr. Rizal....? Mr. Rizal can you hear me...? But Rizal could no longer hear. Rizal could no longer see. Rizal, to Gerry's delight, had fallen back senseless onto the mattress, out of harm's way, his chest rising and falling to the rhythm of his snore.

"I demand to see the British consul," Damien shouted. "Can you hear me? I know you're out there. I want to see the British consul. El consulado Britannico. Le consul Britannique. Whatever it is in Tagalog. The British consul, you understand? You can't keep me here you know..." He turned and leaned his back against the bars in desperation, bending his knees slowly until he'd slumped all the way to the floor. They *could* keep him there though, that was the trouble, as long as this maniac Espinoza kept paying for his keep. They could keep him there forever, hidden from the outside world in this cell, this *oubliette* which prisoners only ever *entered*, where they died from starvation and madness, not necessarily in that order. He missed his watch. Badly. They'd done that to hurt him of course. Sensory deprivation they called it, a form of torture, like having no phone. How long had he been here? It must have been daylight for half a day at least. But what's half a day in twenty-five years? Twenty-five times fifty-two makes thirteen hundred. There are one thousand three hundred weeks in twenty-five years. You scratched a line on the wall didn't you to keep count? On the seventh day you scratched a diagonal line through the first six. Week one. One thousand two hundred and ninety-nine to go. Oh shit....

There were footsteps behind him and the jangling of keys. He turned round and got up. The guard was standing there, the one who'd taken the money from Espinoza. He held up a forearm for the prisoner to see; on its wrist was a watch, Damien's. He turned the face of the watch towards Damien, tapped it with a finger, then pointed the finger at himself.

136

"You want my wristwatch?" Damien said.

The guard tapped the watch face again and said something in Tagalog.

Damien shrugged his shoulders. "Okay you have my wristwatch. Look, YOU... HAVE... WRISTWATCH... OK? ... ME..." and he pointed to the keys, miming the turning of a key in a lock, "...GET... OUT... OF... HERE."

The guard shook his head. He tapped the wristwatch once again and pointed to himself. Then he took a key from the bunch and mimed its turning in the lock, at the same time rubbing together the upturned thumb and forefinger of the other hand.

"Money? You want my watch *and* you want money. I don't have any money. You've taken my wallet." Damien pulled out empty pockets and turned his palms upward in a gesture of impecuniousness.

The guard shook his head. He mimed money again then patted his breast pocket and pointed at Damien.

Damien copied the gesture and patted his own breast pocket, only to feel, unexpectedly through the fabric, the notes which Espinoza had given him. The man wasn't stupid. He reached into the pocket, took out one of the 50 peso notes and held it up.

The guard, who'd witnessed the original transaction, held up two fingers. "Two," he said, in one of his few words of English.

Damien shook his head. Impasse. It wasn't that he minded in the slightest giving both notes in exchange for his freedom but if he handed them both over *before* the guard unlocked the door.... "LOOK... I... GIVE... ONE... *BEFORE*..." he said, and he mimed the turning of the key, "AND... ONE... *AFTER*... OK?" The guard stared back in silence. Damien rolled his eyes in frustration. How did you mime *before* and *after*? No wonder he'd always hated charades. No wonder he'd always hated that Marcel Marceau creep, the one who went around feeling imaginary walls with those stupid, white-gloved hands. You bet *he* couldn't do *before* and *after*. Okay Marcel baby, watch this. He held up one note and mimed handing it to the guard. Then he turned his back and pretended to be the guard accepting the note and unlocking the door. Then he mimed swinging the door open, walking through it and closing it behind him. Then he held up the second note and pretended to offer it to the guard. The guard stared back, stupefied. Damien sighed. "Okay, have it your way," he said, passing both notes through the bars. The guard unlocked the door.

They returned his belt and shoelaces to him and a wallet with credit cards but no cash. They denied all knowledge of the passport. He didn't argue. It occurred to him that Espinoza might well have given him the money precisely for the purpose for which it was eventually used. He probably had no real power to keep him locked up for any length of time. Anyway taking his passport would have the same nuisance value in the short term.

He found Francisco at the back of the church. There was a mass being said. At the altar robed figures held books for one another, swung incense and rang bells while a small, scattered congregation, seemingly excluded from the ritual, meditated, read and gossiped.

"You got me arrested," he whispered to Francisco.

"I just did as you asked. I said you wanted to see him. I didn't know he happened to be in town."

"What do you know about *Filipina Services*?"

"Nothing. What is it?"

"It's a front organisation."

"For what?"

"I'm not exactly sure. But Olivia and Gerry are onto it. I need to get up there, Francisco. Can you arrange it?"

"To Espinoza's? You won't make it by vehicle. You'd be ambushed, Moros. It would have to be on foot."

"Is it possible?"

"It's possible. There are guides. It would take you a couple of days across country."

"I'd like you to arrange it. Listen, I need to talk to London. Jonathan once said this was a one-phone town. Is that true?"

"Yes. There's one in the post office. Connects with Manila but don't be too hopeful. You could be in for a long wait."

"Francisco?"

"Yes?"

"You couldn't lend me some money could you?"

Damien gazed over a roomful of heads, counting the numbers snaking towards the counter. There was a law, there had to be, a universal law. It would have a name, something like *the post office inverse customer ratio law* and it would dictate that the greater the number of customers being served the fewer desks would be open to serve them. And it *was* universal. This tiny outback in South East Asia was no different from any post office in Johannesburg or Berlin or Los Angeles or Adelaide. Never in the history of the world's postal services has a customer ever walked straight from the door to the counter to be served. The Koronadal post office had four desks and one clerk. Those wanting to use the telephone waited in turn behind the stamp buyers and parcel senders until they reached the counter, where they gave their number, only to be re-directed to the queue for those wanting to use the telephone. After twenty-five minutes in the first queue Damien was relieved that at least the second was seated. He sat squashed on a hard bench and stared up at the ceiling. A wobbly fan recycled the same, heavy air. An hour passed. It was 3pm when he was finally called to the booth so it would be 6am in London. Think of it as a wake-up call Julian.

He picked up the phone, a heavy old-fashioned bakelite receiver with a brown cloth-sleeved cord. There was already a voice on the end, distant and echoing. "That you Julian?" Damien asked.

"No, this is Brian."

"Damn. This isn't Julian Jenkin's number then?"

"Yes it is, I'm his partner."

"It's a business line then?" Damien heard the words *...business line* echo the thousands of miles back to him.

"No. I'm his partner in the modern sense of the word, in this case as in 'same-sex partner'."

There was a silence. Damien thought for a moment then said, "Do I really need to know that? *...know that?*"

"You most certainly do. That's Julian's problem you see. He doesn't want you all to know. He wants to keep me a secret. Well let me tell you I'm not something to be ashamed of. Julian's jolly well going to come out if it's the last thing..." There was a scuffling and the sounds of an argument at the other end of the line then, "sorry about that. This is Julian Jenkin speaking, who is it please?"

"It's Damien, Julian, listen this is a terrible line *...terrible line.* "I'm in Koronadal again. Listen it's serious *...serious.* Gerry and Olivia are onto something. It's to do with that *Filipina Services* story *...story.* Seems

139

she might have been onto something all along ...*along*."

"They can't be. Jonathan Dowell swore to me on oath that Gerry wasn't doing the same....." Julian broke off. Oh shit. Oh no he didn't. He didn't swear he wasn't doing the same story at all did he? He swore on oath he wasn't doing the *Neville* story. Oh my god..... "How do you know this Damien?"

"Espinoza brought the name up ...*up*."

"You've been to see Espinoza ?"

"He came to see me...*me*, Listen there's more. Peter Neville went to meet Espinoza the day before he disappeared... *appeared*."

"You're kidding!"

"Nope. And guess what? Espinoza has a helicopter....*copter*"

"A helicopter....?"

"Listen, I'm arranging to go up there myself and confront Olivia...*Olivia*. If she's got a story it's legally ours. She's here on a contract and at the BBC's expense...*expense*. She can't just take the story and give it to Gerry and Channel 4...*annel 4*."

"Take my advice Damien, scare the shit out of her. Tell her we hold the intellectual rights to the property. Tell her we'll sue. Tell her we'll take her for every penny. Tell her she'll never work again. Anything you like. Just scare the shit out of her."

"Doesn't sound like you Julian. You all right...*all right*?"

"Fine, just be ruthless."

"Whatever you say. Listen, can you organise a crew to get out here before I get back...*get back*. I should have something to film by then. Oh and tell them to bring me another passpor..." there was a click on the line and silence. Damien gestured to the clerk that the line was dead. "Could you get me that number again please?"

The clerk ignored him.

"Excuse me but I've lost my connection."

"Your call is finished," the clerk said, not looking at him, "Next please."

"Well I'd like to make another one if that's the case. Is that a problem?"

"That is not a problem sir. Stand in line please.. Everyone will be attended to in turn. Please join the line; it begins there by the door. Everyone is attended to in turn..."

It was only when they strapped her into the helicopter seat, that Olivia's primal fears of abandonment returned. Shopping and luncheon had been unthreatening activities, but a journey into the forest by helicopter put her again at Espinoza's mercy; if you went into the forest by helicopter then you really had to have a day return. She sat next to the pilot, who wore mirrored shades and carried a pistol in a holster on his belt. He lifted the aircraft slowly from the ground, rotated it though 360 degrees then tipped the nose forward to head out over the valley. Olivia held her breath as the ground beneath the glass floor fell away at precipitate speed, 100ft... 300ft... 500ft.... The view was awesome. Wisps of cloud drifted between wooded hills; shining ribbons of water glinted momentarily in the sunlight and vanished; further and further below, their own tiny shadow tracked them across the valley floor.

The noise of the jet turbine relieved her of the need to make further conversation. Nor did she have to look at Espinoza, who had taken the back seat. She didn't like Espinoza's riddles. She'd asked him outright what he'd meant by 'the soul of the forest' but he'd told her she must wait and see. Not for the first time she sensed she was being played with.

The landscape was changing. Fewer of the hillsides were farmed now. The wooded areas were merging and unifying, consuming the landscape, becoming forest until eventually there was nothing else, just the great, green, fabulous ocean of leaves, stretching unbroken to the horizon. The pilot took the chopper down and flew low above the canopy, surfing the swell just feet from the treetops, climbing and falling with its undulations. Olivia, exhilarated, gave herself up to the experience so that she'd quite lost track of how long they'd been flying when the pilot nudged her and pointed ahead. On top of a hillock in the distance was a clearing.

The helicopter approached the clearing, circled and came down slowly through the trees like a lift in a shaft. As they touched the ground the pilot leant across and unbuckled Olivia's straps, gesturing to her to keep her head down as she left the aircraft. She did as she was told and ran, stooping beneath the rotors, until she was far clear of their circumference. Then she turned.

She wanted to scream but couldn't. The aircraft was already off the ground and rising slowly through the funnel in the towering trees

towards a circle of sky. Don't go, she mouthed. Please don't go. Please…
It wasn't true. Surely it wasn't true? It couldn't be. You joked about it
Gerry, you and your puerile Disney jokes. But he's done it. He's
actually gone and done it. He's abandoned me….

"How did you enjoy the flight, Mrs. Harris. Quite spectacular
isn't it?"

She wheeled round…. Espinoza. She could never have imagined
she could be so pleased to see Espinoza under any circumstances. She
let out a long breath and tried to compose herself. "I didn't see you get
off," she said.

"That's because I was behind you."

"Of course. Silly of me. Why has the chopper left?"

"He needs to refuel. Carrying three people uses so much more."
There was something reassuring about the answer, knowing that her
exit was already planned. "What happens now?" she asked.

"We wait for Galan."

"Galan?"

"Galan is a hunter. He knows the forest. He will be our guide.
He'll have heard the helicopter and be on his way here. Would you like
some water? I have some in my bag."

They sat down and drank the water from a plastic bottle. It was
already warm. She looked up at the immense hardwood trees. "How
tall are they?" she asked.

"Two hundred feet, sometimes more."

"And they've been here pretty well for ever. Makes one feel small
doesn't it, insignificant?"

"There you are, Mrs. Harris, you've only been on the ground for
one minute and already you are sensing the great mystery of the
forest."

"Is that the soul you're talking about?"

"No no, that's something altogether more tangible. Be patient
Mrs. Harris, be patient."

There was a rustle in the undergrowth and a man emerged onto
the far side of the clearing. He was barefoot and raggedly dressed in
knee-length trousers and a torn shirt. On one side of his belt hung the
long, curved bolo, on the other a dead rodent of a species unknown to
Olivia; across his back, a bow and a quiver of arrows. Espinoza rose to

greet him. The man took his hand but showed no expression. Likewise when Olivia was introduced. It was clear he did not live in the company of men, nor have any particular liking for them. She wondered how Espinoza had pressed him into his service – Galan would appear to have little use for money. His face made her think of a snake, not just the eyes, those little slits, slanting upwards, hardly open, but the shape of the head, high cheekboned with flat cheeks narrowing to the mouth. It was easy to imagine a forked tongue darting in and out.

"Now we have to walk," Espinoza said. "It may take an hour or more, I'm afraid. Depends on the undergrowth."

They entered the forest in single file, with Olivia in the middle. Galan led the way, intermittently cutting a path for them with his bolo (she was told to be careful of the rattan leaves, which could be razor sharp). Once her eyes were accustomed, it wasn't as dark as she'd imagined, rather like being in a Gothic cathedral, the sombre floor-level light contrasting with the brilliance of the clerestory high above. It was quieter though than she had imagined. The bird calls, when they came, were sudden and shrill against a background of near silence. Occasionally the canopy above swayed and rustled with the leap of a monkey. Down below black butterflies danced in shafts of light.

After maybe an hour they emerged into the day again where a wide mountain river crossed their path. They sat on boulders in the middle, drank from the clean, cool water and refilled the bottle. Olivia looked up. There was space here. All around her the mountainous forest spread in folds to distant blue horizons. There was no other world but this one. She saw orchids growing on the far bank and crossed the river, wandering in amongst the trees to pick them. She'd lost interest in time, awed by the magnificence of nature. She'd never seen nature so raw, so untamed by man, so sufficient to itself. Mankind was neither needed nor wanted here.

And then she saw the child.

It would be hard to say who was in the greater state of astonishment, she or the boy. For it *was* a boy, his nakedness left that in no doubt, though his soft features and waist-length hair had first made her think it was a girl. He was six or seven maybe and in that life-defining moment (as Olivia would later describe it) without question the most beautiful thing she had ever seen. He was no more than ten feet away, standing above her on the top of a small waterfall which fed the river. He stared at her through round astonished eyes, his mouth slightly open, transfixed. His brown body quivered with tension, like a doe, she thought. The eyes began to dart sideways He gave a little squeal of fear then suddenly turned and scampered with breathtaking agility up the rocky stream and away into the forest.

Olivia felt unable to move a muscle. It was as if she'd opened a storybook and by some magic the storybook had come alive. She stared after the boy until long after he was gone. Then she slowly made her way back to the middle of the river where the others sat. "I think I know what you've brought me here to see," she said to Espinoza. "I think I've just seen the soul of the forest."

The helicopter approached from the forest side of the house. Gerry watched from the verandah, feeling the downdraft as the thunderous silhouette passed low overhead, yawing into position for its descent over the water. It was Olivia who disembarked first, running and stooping all the way to the steps. She was animated, her face flushed, hair tangled. Gerry met her half way down. "Gerry you'll never believe what I've seen. It's been the most amazing experience. You've just got to see…"

"I've done it Olivia," Gerry said quietly, "and it didn't cost me anything. We can get out of here. Right away."

"Gerry it's the story of a lifetime. I've seen the Garden of Eden, Gerry. Do you believe me? The Garden of Eden. These people, in the forest….You wouldn't believe…."

"I've *got* your story Olivia. Big time. I've got one of the girls on tape….."

"It's sensational Gerry, it's like they're wild, part of the forest, part of nature itself and yet they're human like us and they're so peaceable and they're so beautiful and they're under terrible threat, Gerry. They're cutting the rainforest down and the loggers are getting closer and closer….."

"Olivia will you listen to me! You're not making any sense. I've managed to get the evidence without having to screw the girls. Do you hear me? It's what we came for, remember? Now we have to get out as fast as we can before Espinoza finds out the truth. I'd rather not be around when Rizal wakes up."

"Espinoza....." Olivia faltered for a moment. "Look, Gerry, things have changed. We're going to have to put the baby thing on hold. We're going to need Ferdinand."

"FERDINAND?"

"That's his name, Gerry. He's a friend. And he's a real philanthropist."

"For heaven's sake, Olivia, what's happened to you?"

"He's not all bad, Gerry."

"NOT ALL BAD? He's just a child molester who trades in babies."

"He probably sees it differently. It's a cultural thing. Anyway can you keep your voice down." She indicated with her eyes that someone was behind him. Before he could turn around three teenage girls had swept past him, running excitedly down the steps. Down on the landing stage Espinoza was leaving the helicopter.

"Look I can't meet him now," Gerry said abruptly, "I really can't. You and I have got to talk." He grabbed Olivia by the arm and began hurrying her back up the steps to the house.

"Okay, okay, but things have changed Gerry, they really have."

"I thought you said Espinoza was creepy – 'central casting evil genius' wasn't it?"

"That's just an affectation. He's eccentric that's all. He's rich, so he has delusions about his own importance; it's hardly uncommon. But I honestly think he cares about these tribal minorities, I really do Gerry, especially the Sandula."

"The who?"

"I'll tell you inside; God it's so exciting."

They'd reached the verandah. Looking back Gerry could see Espinoza at the bottom of the steps, sheltering young girls with both arms, bestowing kisses. Jesus, what was Olivia thinking of? Impressionable or what?

In the bedroom they found the maid turning down the sheet. She curtseyed shyly, just like the day before, and left hurriedly. Only twenty-four hours had passed, Gerry thought. It felt as if he'd been trapped in this house for ever. "Listen, we need to get out of here Olivia."

"Not till you've seen what I've seen."

"Which is what for heaven's sake?"

"The Sandula."

"And they're a tribal minority?"

"I suppose you could call them that. More a family really. You've never seen anything like it Gerry, believe me. Here…" she handed him something from the pocket of her shorts.

He looked at it in the palm of his hand, turning it over. "It's a stone," he said.

"Look closer, describe it to me."

"Triangular …. flat….thin at the edges."

"How thin?"

Gerry ran a finger down one edge then pulled it away suddenly. "Ow sharp!"

"Exactly. One of them gave it to me Gerry. So what do you suppose it is?"

Gerry looked at the stone then up at Olivia then back at the stone. "You serious?"

Olivia nodded. "It's an axehead, a stone axehead. I saw them being used.

Gerry frowned then said very slowly, "you mean like…..in the stone-age?"

Olivia nodded, "neolithic if you want to be precise." She came close and looked him in the eyes. "You know what I did this afternoon, Gerry? I walked into a rainforest and straight into pre-history. It was like walking through one of those stargate things in the sci-fi stories, passing through a time warp into another dimension. They're a stone-age people, Gerry, cave-dwellers. They're several millennia adrift from the rest of the world. And they're absolutely bloody magnificent."

Gerry stared at the stone. " Wow," he said, "from the space-age to the stone age eh."

"From the space-age to the stone-age." Olivia repeated the phrase quietly to herself, "from the space age to the stone age. You know what, Gerry, that's quite a line. You don't mind if I use it do you?"

Rizal lay on the sofa where they'd first carried him and spoke without opening his eyes. "It was the camera," he was saying, "this Harris, he sabotaged the camera. I went to fix it. Something happened. I don't know...."

"Harris attacked you?" Espinoza said, incredulous.

"Maybe."

"And the camera? Did you record anything? Do we have any evidence?"

Rizal shook his head, sightlessly.

Espinoza rolled his eyes and turned away. "What do the girls say happened in there?"

"They don't say."

"They don't?"

"They ran away."

"What, all three of them, you're kidding?" The voice had shot up.

Rizal opened his eyes, saw the contempt on Espinoza's face and closed them again. He nodded in silence.

"Jee....zus." Espinoza threw himself into a chair and groaned.

"We're going to have to remove them," Rizal said.

"No we're not. Now that Damien Street knows they're here you can be sure London knows as well. This would be the first place they'd come looking for them." He opened his wallet and took out a photograph. For a long time he just stared at it. "I suppose that decides it then. At least 'Mrs. Harris' was properly impressed by the Sandula. I think she'll do the story justice. You know they're truly magnificent, Rizal, truly magnificent, humanity in a state of grace. She thought so too, it was obvious. She was dying to tell me who she really was, you could see that, how she could be the one to break the story." He laughed. "She suddenly remembered she has these 'friends in the media' back in London, people who could handle a story like this sensitively. Convenient eh? Oh and did you know she has a camcorder with her? She proposed taking some pictures of the tribe to send back to them."

At the word 'camcorder' Rizal's eyes shot open again. "He took pictures," he said.

"Who took pictures?"

"Harris, last night, he took pictures of the girls, with the camcorder."

"And you let him.....?"

147

Rizal sat up. "I didn't know who he was did I?" He sounded aggrieved. "I thought he was a good client. It's only today you tell me differently."

Espinoza began to pace. "So you think he's taken pictures today, is that it, interviews? Is that why the girls have run away? They've told him too much?"

Rizal shrugged. "I'll get the tape from him."

"No, not yet. That would make them suspicious. Just see if you can get a look at it. I'm relying on Mrs. Harris for the moment. Right now Mr. Harris will be hearing about the Sandula for the first time. She'll be working on him, you can be sure of that. He'll come round to her point of view. It's only a matter of time."

"How can you be sure? You tell me they're not really married. How can she tell him what to do?"

"They may not be married but they *are* lovers."

"You know this?"

"Of course, it's on the tape. Not much of a picture. Much too dark to enjoy it properly. But you can make out what's going on. Oh yes, they're lovers all right and he's mad about her. He'll do what she says."

"I'm not saying it's not a great story," Gerry said, "it's just that we've already got a story, a cracking one and you want to throw it all away for your long lost tribe."

"I didn't say throw away; I said put on hold. We can do it later." There was frustration in Olivia's voice. "We need Ferdinand.... sorry Espinoza....to get us to the Sandula. It's called access, Gerry. Have you taken a look out there?" They were standing on the balcony at the rear of the house. Beneath them the forest canopy, black now in the twilight, rolled away to infinity.

"You can't put the adoption story on hold," Gerry said. "If you do this Sandula thing then Espinoza's going to be a central character. He's going to want to be the hero, the man who discovered the last stone-age tribe. You can't set him up then turn round after the world's applauded and say, 'Oh, by the way, he's a pervert who breeds babies for adoption, I'm sorry, did we forget to mention that?'"

"You're overdoing this pervert bit, Gerry. The girls are regarded as mature here. They're marriageable."

"You're not suggesting he marries them?"

Olivia said nothing.

"We could do it the other way round," Gerry said. "Do the adoption story then come back later for the tribe. By the sound of it they won't be going anywhere."

"Don't be ridiculous Gerry, look at it out there. Give me a needle in a haystack any day; you'd never find them on your own – even from a helicopter you can't see what's on the ground you know." She turned and brushed past him. He followed her back to the bedroom.

"I could always just leave on my own," he said, closing the door behind him. "If you don't want the adoption story, I'd be very happy to find it a home. Come to think of it, I've shot everything so far myself."

Olivia stared at him, momentarily silenced. She crossed to the tallboy and picked up the camcorder. "Who does this belong to?"

"You."

She ejected the tape and held it up. "And this?" She read from the label "'Philippines Roll 1?'"

Gerry shrugged, "Don't I get moral rights?"

"How about a *camera* credit?" She put the tape in her shirt pocket, replacing it in the camera with a new one from the box. "It's my story, Gerry, I decide."

"Then I leave without it."

"You're not leaving without me?"

"Why not?"

"Gerry you wouldn't, you couldn't."

"Why not?"

"Well…well….." Olivia pulled back a strand of loose hair and wound it behind her ear, searching for words. She looked up at him, her expression suddenly vulnerable, the eyes, dark and pretty, exploring his face, questioning his betrayal, "…..after last night I thought….." She left the sentence unfinished, her lips slightly apart.

Gerry, exactly as he was meant to do, bent forward slowly and kissed them. Wow. Had she really said that? Did she really feel that way about him? And to think he thought she was all sex and no commitment? "You know this is blackmail," he said.

She smiled sweetly and put her arms round his waist, nestling her head beneath his chin. "I know, but you could learn to love it. Think of it as a kind of bondage."

"So where do we go to from here, Mistress?"

"Well now. I think there's someone you need to meet don't you? I know he's been dying to meet you. I'm sure you'll get on frightfully well. By the way he asked me what you did for a living."

"And what did you say?"

"I told him you were an accountant."

"An ACCOUNTANT....!"

Gerry came to realise the good sense of Olivia's fiction – no further elaboration would be needed on his part. No-one could possibly make dinner-party conversation out of an accountant's career, so he was at least spared the need to invent a history. They sat around the large refectory table eating the same frugal meal as the night before. Espinoza made no mention of how Gerry's day in the bedroom had gone, perhaps out of delicacy towards Olivia's feelings; Olivia herself was more relaxed than at any time since their arrival. She called Espinoza *Ferdinand* and ran the table talk as she might a studio discussion, steering the subject matter in the direction of her choosing. Before long the conversation was of the Sandula.

"Tell Gerry how you first found them, Ferdinand," she said enthusiastically.

Espinoza put down his knife and fork and pushed his plate away. He looked first at Olivia, then at Gerry and then straight ahead, his eyes focussing on infinity. Going into prophet mode, Olivia thought.

"It was Galan who first found them, not I," he said, "and he only found them because the forest is shrinking. Ten years ago their home would have been too deep into the jungle for a hunter to have travelled so far, but with the logging it's now only a few days' walk from the forest's edge. It's only a matter of time now."

"Olivia says they use stone tools," Gerry said, "that's pretty exceptional. Surely if the government got to know about them they could just put a stop to the logging."

"This is the Philippines, Gerry – I may call you that? – this is Mindanao. We are not one of your rich Western democracies. Even if the government wanted to protect the tribe – and they've shown little enough interest in tribal minorities in the past — they'd still capitulate to the logging companies. Where do you think the votes are? I can't imagine the Sandula are on the electoral register."

"You must tell Gerry what they're like, Ferdinand," Olivia said, "tell him what you told me."

Espinoza looked at Gerry directly, pausing before he spoke. "Imagine, Gerry, a society which has no word for war....."

Gerry was silent for a moment. "Is that why Olivia called it the Garden of Eden?"

"Look for yourself." Espinoza took the photograph from his wallet and handed it to Gerry.

Gerry stared at the picture in silence. It was an odd experience, not like looking at a photograph at all. The composition more closely resembled a painting or a book illustration. It drew him in, exotic, mystical, strangely compelling. He saw a pool in a forest glade, fed by a waterfall some ten feet high. On top of the waterfall a naked child with long black hair stared wide-eyed at the camera. In the sparkling water below, other children, stopped in their play, turned their faces towards him, smiles transfixed in a column of light. And, all around the banks, naked men and women, brown-skinned with black hair tumbling round their shoulders, sat and lay and squatted in shafts of sunlight, their benign faces illuminated, *chiaroscuro*, against the dark of the forest.

"The Garden of Eden, Mr. Harris; you're looking at mankind before the Fall. The Sandula have no weapons and no knowledge of conflict. They have no guilt, no shame. They eat, they play, they procreate, they die."

"Gerry stared again at the photograph. "Extraordinary. How many are they?"

"About thirty we think. It's just about the minimum sustainable number. Of course there may be others in the forest with whom they interbreed. We don't know yet. Our communication is limited. Galan has mastered only the basics of the language, concrete nouns, a few verbs. They may not even deal in abstractions."

"What do they make of you?"

"Difficult to say. They seem to associate us with aeroplanes — they point at the sky and make jet noises. Aeroplanes have hitherto been the only intrusion from our world into theirs so it makes sense for them to assume that's where we've come from. They may even think of us as gods, though I rather hope not."

Gerry doubted the sincerity of the hope. "So what's going to happen to them?"

"Until today I wasn't sure but your wife has given me an idea. She suggested publicity – not here in the Philippines but around the world. A campaign in your country, in Europe, in America might put suffi-cient pressure on our government to act. Olivia has already kindly offered to use her contacts in the BBC. I don't suppose you have any media contacts yourself Gerry? Being an accountant presumably not." There was a sufficient hint of irony in Espinoza's voice to cause just a frisson of alarm in Gerry. Once again came the faintest suspicion that he was being played with.

Olivia seemed unaware. "We're going again tomorrow, Gerry, you too. We'll take the camcorder. I thought we might show it to Douglas Boyle; you remember him, we met at that dinner party. He edits the *Worldweek* programme."

Gerry was taken by surprise. He was continually impressed by Olivia's ability to leaven her lies like that with just enough truth to sound convincing, even to him. He followed her lead, one lie one truth. "Of course I remember the occasion," he said, "though person-ally I couldn't stand the man...."

They parted company after dinner. Espinoza had business, he'd be back in the morning for their expedition. They took coffee on the verandah and watched the helicopter take off. When they returned to their room Rizal was already coming out. At the sight of them he clenched his right hand as if to conceal some small object. His eyes darted. "Er....."

"Er...?" Olivia enquired.

"Er....change light bulb," Rizal said without conviction.

Gerry leaned over and whispered into Olivia's ear, "how many pimps does it take.....?"

Olivia stifled a giggle. Rizal made a quick bow and disappeared towards the rear balcony. "What do you think he was after?" Olivia said once they were inside the room.

"Wanted to check the camera, at a guess."

Olivia walked over to the tallboy and picked up the camcorder. "He's taken the tape out. Why would he do that? Good job I'd changed it for a new one. You'd have thought he'd have had the sense to replace it with one from the box, wouldn't you? Then we'd never have noticed unless we counted the remain…." She broke off, holding up the tape box and peering inside. "Gerry, there were ten tapes in this box. There's one in my pocket, Rizal's taken one, there should be eight left. There's only seven. Gerry have you…..?"

"I didn't mean that camera," Gerry said quickly, distracting her, "I meant this one." He climbed onto the bed and unscrewed the ceiling fitting. A tissue fell onto the sheet. Olivia peered up and saw the shiny reflection of the lens. She put her hand in her mouth and bit her knuckle. "Oh Gerry that's disgusting. How could they…..you don't think they…..I mean did they….I mean us….?"

"It would have been too dark," Gerry said, not entirely sure himself.

"Oh Gerry it's revolting…."

Gerry picked up the tissue, replaced it in the cup and screwed the fitting back together again. He climbed down from the bed and made to put his arms around Olivia. She drew back. "Not here," she said, "we can't now, not with that thing there."

"It can't see," Gerry said, "I've blocked the lens."

"I don't care. How do I know there aren't others? How do I know I'm not being watched. I can't do it Gerry. I'm not doing it again."

"You're not doing it again? I thought I was only staying because…."

Olivia stared at him. "What did you say….?"

Gerry said nothing.

"You were only staying because what, Gerry? Tell me. What were you only staying for? Is it because I'm a good lay is that it? Is that the only reason you were prepared to help me with my story? Where are the protestations of love now eh?"

"Olivia….."

"Sod off, what do you take me for?"

Gerry glanced across at the camcorder. The tape box lay open beside it, quite forgotten now. Out of the bloody frying pan, he thought. "Look I'm sorry. I only meant you didn't want me to leave you after last night. It's what you said. Of course you mean a lot to me."

"Oh yeah? Even without the sex bit?"

"Well.... yes....of course."

"Good, 'cause that's how it's got to be from now on Gerry. I'm just not doing it in this room."

Gerry lay back on the bed, closed his eyes and groaned quietly.

He couldn't get to sleep that night. Olivia lay beside him, she under the sheet, he on top. He listened to her slow, regular breathing and smelled her soap, her hair, her body. Forbidden fruit. That was the moral wasn't it? That was the point of the Garden of Eden story. The fruit is tempting not because it's an apple but because it's forbidden to you. And now that Olivia was forbidden to him he desired her more than ever. He got up, wrapped a towel round him and walked out into the corridor. Moonlight spilled along the passageway from where it opened onto the rear balcony. He walked silently, feeling the warmth of the teak boards beneath his feet. As he neared the balcony the noise of cicadas and frogs multiplied, the unceasing chorus of a tropical night. But then something else.

It wasn't speech but it was human. There were doors off the balcony and the sounds seemed to come from the far end, mumbles, grunts, sometimes rhythmic mostly male with the occasional female 'oh' or was it 'ow'? After a moment the sounds stopped and Gerry heard the cadences of speech, though too quiet for him to pick out words or recognise a voice. Then a door opened and a girl came out, clasping a sheet around her, spilling light across the boards. She stopped for a moment and stared out at the forest, swaying, drawing in deep breaths. A voice called out from the room. The girl didn't move. The voice called again, more persistently. She lifted a hand and ran a knuckle across each cheekbone. Then she caught sight of Gerry. For a moment she just stared. Then she gathered the sheet about her, turned and went back in.

Boyle sat at his desk, leaning back in the big swivel chair, his feet on the table, shoes removed. He'd heard it was what television executives did. "Say it again for me Julian, I like the sound of it."

Julian forced himself to repeat the words, "there's a bigger picture emerging, Doug."

Boyle gave a smirk. "There's always a big picture when you look for it Julian." He sat with his back to the White City panorama, a tower block rising from each shoulder. "Okay, shoot!"

Julian stuck thumbs into braces, turned the first page of a mental flip-chart and began firing bullet points. It was the way Boyle liked it. "Okay, we now know the following: *One* – Peter Neville met this Espinoza the day before he was abducted. *Two* – Espinoza is in some way connected with *Filipina Services*, whatever it is they're up to. And *Three*," Julian paused here, "*Three* – Espinoza is the owner of a helicopter." He leaned forward, resting his knuckles on the edge of the desk. "Which all points to what, do you think?"

"You tell me."

"It points to the possibility, probability even, that Espinoza could be the one who abducted Neville."

Boyle's eyes narrowed with anticipation. "Theory?"

"As in *conspiracy*? How about this? Espinoza has a place up country in South Cotabato. South Cotabato is largely controlled by the rebels. So, Espinoza must have some understanding with the Moros, probably financial, which allows him to come and go unmolested. Now let's suppose Neville stumbles across this *Filipina Services* story, white slaving or whatever it is they're up to. What does he do? He visits Espinoza and confronts him with it….." Julian paused, allowing his audience to consider the supposition and come up with a consequence (management training).

Boyle obliged. "Espinoza wants rid of him….?"

"Right," (flatter your audience) "Espinoza wants rid of him. But does he want anyone to know that?"

Boyle shook his head.

"No. So what better way to rid himself of this troublesome reporter than to get his friends the Moros to do it for him. Let them be seen to take him hostage and carry him off in a helicopter so he's never seen again." Julian paused, timing another page turn. "Just one problem."

"Problem…?"

"They don't have a helicopter. You saw those rebels. Their infantry were still in the archery phase."

155

"But the helicopter was military. We saw the pictures."

"It was painted in military colours, that's all. When the RAF exercises in the desert they change the camouflage with emulsion paint. It washes off afterwards. The helicopter we all saw was a Hughes 500. There are lots of civil versions. It could have been privately owned."

Boyle leant forward and put his elbows on the desk, locking the fingers of both hands together. "That's quite a story. You get all this from young master Dowell?"

Julian was about to say no but had a better idea. He pushed his hands into his trouser pockets, perched himself on the edge of Boyle's desk and leaned confidentially towards him. "Once I'd scared the shit out of him he told me everything he knew. Swore he wouldn't be doing the story. Oh, and he returned the file." The truth of the last two statements mitigated in Julian's own mind the lie of the first. His ability to collude successfully with his own conscience had grown noticeably with the job.

"Good man. And Damien, where's he at?"

"Wants a crew."

"What's he going to shoot?"

"I don't know to be honest. But that's the way Damien works. He investigates as he films. Seems to pay off."

"Oh I've every confidence in Mr. Street," Boyle said rising from the desk, "we won't be forgetting the Moldovan Hyena in a hurry. I just hope he realises the risk he's running. To lose one reporter is bad enough."

"But to lose two would seem like carelessness........." Julian began to laugh then saw the expression on Boyle's face, "....sorry, just a joke, Oscar Wilde....but then you wouldn't........no....no I don't suppose you would...."

Northrop Pryce didn't look up when Jonathan entered the office. His eyes were fixed on a monitor; his ears, plugged with earphones, leaked a tinny rhythm. Jonathan moved round and caught his attention. Pryce unplugged himself and jabbed a finger in the direction of the monitor. "That, boyo, is the only true art form of the twenty-first century – music video."

Jonathan glanced at the screen. A bald, female singer was mouthing silent passion, first in a supermarket, now on a construction site, now in a coffin, the random locations somehow made all the more absurd by the absence of sound. He was glad Gerry wasn't around to argue the point. "More of a factuals man myself," he said, "never done any arts."

"Arts, factual, entertainment, what's the difference? There's only two kinds of television my friend. Know what they are…?"

"Good and bad?" Jonathan said, trying not to sound wearied.

"Right on. Now then, what's your Gerry Harris been getting up to eh? We've been hearing stories, naughty rumours."

"He's gone to South Cotabato where Neville disappeared. I won't hear from him till he gets back to Davao. No phones."

"And what about this Olivia-something-double-barrelled? BBC I gather….rumour has it they're married."

"Rumour has it wrong. It's a cover. He's just helping her with her story. Well, that's what she thinks. Actually he's trying to steal it, except that he doesn't need to any more because Damien didn't get anywhere with his initial enquiries with Francisco, which means he's not ahead of us as we thought, so we're back on track with the original Neville story and don't need the pregnancies for adoption one. So as soon as Gerry gets back to me……."

"Just stop there Jonathan," Pryce interrupted, "what did you say?"

"I said the rumour's got it wrong."

"No, not that, the last bit, pregnancies for what did you say?"

"For adoption. It's their other story, Damien and Olivia's, sort of back up if they couldn't get anywhere with the Neville one"

"Pregnancies for adoption?"

"Mm. There's this agency which sends domestic servants to England. And they're pregnant. And when they get here they sell the babies for adoption. Clever idea really."

"Clever idea? Bloody fantastic story I should say."

"Oh?"

"Well don't you think it's a great story? I presume these girls are *forced* to have sex in order to get pregnant?"

"Well, I don't know really….."

"I mean that would be fantastic wouldn't it, if they were *forced* to have sex. I mean in order to satisfy the emotional demands of white middle-class Englishwomen there are young girls in the third world being *raped*."

Jonathan took off his glasses and began polishing them. "Well... we really don't know how it happens."

"I want it Jonathan."

"Want it?"

"This story. I want it. And One Man Band Productions will get it for me, won't you boyo?"

"But what about Neville?"

"He'll keep. What do you think the public's going to be more interested in: the disappearance of a middle-aged reporter, who's not even a celebrity any more or pretty young Asian women being *forced* to have sex to supply a product to childless couples?"

"We don't know they're forced into it," Jonathan said.

"Oh yes they are, Jonathan, Oh yes they are. You'll see that they are. I mean there wouldn't be a story otherwise would there?" Pryce's smile said it all. You're the seller in a buyer's market Jonathan. In a buyer's market you supply what the buyer wants. This buyer wants sex with violence. So supply.

They breakfasted on the verandah, Olivia and Gerry alone. Heavy rain had fallen towards morning but already the sun was over the rim of the crater, steaming the land. "Smell that!" Olivia said, "the dampness, isn't it delicious? That's the smell of the earth, Gerry, the smell of unadulterated nature."

"Don't look now but what I'm picking up is a distinct whiff of the odour of sanctity." Gerry was looking over Olivia's shoulder. She turned to see Father Ambrose approach. In an instant she was in character again. "Darling this is Father Ambrose, you know I told you all about him, his wonderful mission, those sweet children. I didn't know you were here Father. When did you arrive?"

"Last night."

"We didn't hear you arrive, did we darling?"

"No, but then it's a big house."

"When it's late I use the back staircase," Father Ambrose said, "to avoid disturbing anyone."

Gerry frowned. "The back staircase? You have a bedroom here then?"

"When I need to do business with Mr. Espinoza it's more convenient. The round trip is a little too strenuous for one day. So a room is kept for me at the back of the house; it's quieter for my meditation there. Now, may I join you?" The priest took a chair and signalled to the maid to bring another cup. Gerry watched him puzzled.

"I'm sorry Father, I haven't introduced you," Olivia said, "this is my husband Gerry."

"Pleased to meet you Mr. Harris. You have a delightful wife, you know, though I'll admit I'm a trifle concerned about her soul." Father Ambrose winked at Olivia as he said this. Gerry wondered if he wasn't a trifle concerned about her body too.

"And what brings you here Father," Olivia continued, "business with Mr. Espinoza?"

"Nothing special, just the accounts, you understand. Mr. Espinoza is the mission's principal benefactor."

"You're not coming with us then?"

"With you?"

"To see the Sandula, the soul of the forest, remember? I'm taking Gerry to see them"

Father Ambrose smiled. "I'd love to but Mr. Espinoza would never permit it."

"Not permit it? Why ever not?"

"Because I'm a missionary. He thinks I would proselytise, convert them to Christ. He describes them as mankind before the Fall. I think he likens me to the tree of knowledge." Father Ambrose laughed, "or maybe I'm the serpent."

Serpent's about right, Gerry thought.

"You know they're naked," Olivia said.

"I've seen the photographs." .

"So you think they're sinful."

"We are all born with sin."

"Even you Father?" Gerry said. Olivia shot him a silencing glance.

The maid put down a cup for the priest and filled it with coffee. Father Ambrose lifted it to his nose and inhaled. "Mmmm... well there's *gluttony* for you for a start." He sipped from the cup.

"Tell me Father," Olivia said, "the Garden of Eden – what's the point of the story? I mean God creates Adam and Eve naked. They aren't ashamed of being naked until they eat the fruit of the tree of knowledge. Then they are ashamed. So, according to God, there's nothing to be ashamed of until you *know* you're supposed to be ashamed of it. Isn't that a paradox?"

"My dear Mrs. Harris I'm afraid I'm no theologian. God's ways are indeed mysterious."

"What I'm driving at, Father, is that the Sandula are just like Adam and Eve; they have no concept of nakedness either – or sloth for that matter, even though they do hardly anything all day. So, like Adam and Eve, as long as they don't know these things are supposed to be sinful, they remain innocent. Mr. Espinoza is right. You would be the bearer of the fruit of the tree of knowledge. You'd take their innocence and swap it for good old Catholic guilt."

"Surely the moral of the Garden of Eden," Gerry said, "is that sex is the root of all evil and that women are to blame, which is why men such as yourself remain celibate, am I not right Father?" A tone of hostility had crept into Gerry's voice.

"Dear dear me, this is getting far too deep for breakfast time. And to think I thought all you English people talked about was the weather. Now, if you'll excuse me, I'm going to take this coffee and get back to my books." Father Ambrose pushed his chair back and got up. "The helicopter won't be long now I believe. In any case I think I need to mug up on my Genesis before I see you again, Mrs. Harris."

Olivia held her smile only until the priest was safely inside the house. "Being a bit heavy on the irony there were we Gerry? Something you know I don't?"

Gerry looked over his shoulder then leant across the table, his face close to hers. "Last night I couldn't sleep. I'll leave it to you to guess why. Anyway I went out onto the balcony at the back and there were these sounds coming from a room at the end."

"What sort of sounds?"

"Those sort of sounds. The sounds it takes two people to make. Then this girl came out. Not one of the ones we saw at the beauty parade but the same sort of age. Seemed a bit upset. I just took it for granted it was Rizal you see."

"What was?"

"You're being slow, Olivia. I'm talking sexual intercourse here, or more likely rape."

"Ssh! Keep your voice down!"

Gerry dropped his voice to a whisper, "With Espinoza gone I'd assumed it was Rizal in the room; he was the only other male in the house. Except that he wasn't was he? Because Father Ambrose just happened to be occupying a room *at the back of the house.*"

"Christ!"

"A fitting expletive if ever I heard one."

Olivia let out a long breath. "Well, I did read somewhere that only fifty percent of catholic priests are actually celibate. In South America they say it's nought percent."

"Olivia that's hardly the point. You seem to forget that he's up to his neck in this baby scam. That's the story we came here to do and here's yet *another* reason why we should be doing it."

"You said you wouldn't bring that up again."

"Why won't you trust me? Look I'm a journalist."

"Don't you think that's an oxymoron?"

"What?"

"Trust me I'm a journalist."

Gerry gave an audible sigh. "What's happened to you Olivia? It's like you've undergone some kind of conversion. What is it with this lost tribe? Did they hypnotise you or something?"

Olivia looked away out across the lake. "In a manner of speaking, maybe they did. Have you ever had a religious experience Gerry?"

"Categorically not."

"Well then don't judge me till you've seen them for yourself."

Gerry poured himself another coffee. For a moment they sat in silence, then Gerry said, "Speaking of religion, if Espinoza doesn't want the good father to convert the Sandula, then what's he doing supporting a Christian Mission?"

Olivia shrugged. "Hegemony, philanthropy, who knows? Bit of both probably. The mission was already there doing good works. He buys into it. That way he gets the credit. He doesn't have to believe."

"How do you think he seduced Father Ambrose into joining the business?"

Olivia turned and looked at him. "How do you seduce a man?"

Gerry smiled. "Silly me. Pretty obvious when you put it that way." He leant across the table and kissed her forehead. "You know what, you look really beautiful when you're cynical. You won't go all spiritual on me now will you?"

Rizal joined them for the journey, taking the front seat next to the pilot. He wore his bandana and laid his bolo across his knees as if riding shotgun. In the back seat Olivia sat between Gerry and Espinoza. Even with her knees together, she couldn't escape the contact of Espinoza's warm thigh, an intimacy as unwanted as it was disconcerting (if she could feel his thigh he was feeling hers). Espinoza handed out headsets with microphones so they could talk above the engine noise.

"Don't you think it's curious the Sandula aren't frightened of us?" Olivia said

"Frightened? Why should they be. Remember there are no predators in the forest. The Sandula have no enemies so they don't know what fear is, except perhaps the fear of death."

"No fear, no shame, no guilt, no word for war," Gerry said, "in short no stress. Ergo, paradise is the absence of stress. Should go down well back home." He lowered the camcorder, ejected the tape and inserted a new one. This one was for Olivia. The first tape would be his. He'd got shots on it that morning of the helicopter landing, with Tao Bong himself getting out. Luckier still, he'd got a shot of Father Ambrose, who'd come out to say goodbye (bit on the brief side but once he'd frozen the frame and crash zoomed in, the man would look guilty as hell). Except for Rizal he now had all the leading *dramatis personae* on tape. It was looking good. He pointed the camera out of the window again and began to record for Olivia the spectacular panorama below.

When they saw the clearing Olivia became excited and began a running commentary for Gerry, establishing her prior experience and vastly superior knowledge of the subject. "This is the clearing I told you about; they made it for the helicopter to land.....this is Galan I told you about....he's a hunter....he found the Sandula first.....this is the path I told you about.... watch out for the rattan leaves, they're sharp....it'll take about an hour.....there's a big river just up ahead...."

Despite his natural cynicism Gerry found the enthusiasm infectious and his sense of anticipation grew. The forest was mysterious, awe-inspiring even. But he felt like a trespasser. Men didn't belong here in this wilderness. Wildernesses belonged to the beasts of the earth and the air or something biblical like that. When they came at last to the river they paused to refresh themselves while Galan went ahead to forewarn the tribe. "We've never brought so many visitors before," Espinoza explained, "we don't want to surprise them."

"Do they like being visited?" Gerry asked.

"You'll see for yourself." Espinoza said.

It began to rain and they scrambled up the riverbank beneath the shelter of the trees. "Listen to that," Olivia said, looking up at the canopy, "it's like a drumroll isn't it? Curtain up." They stood in silence, listening as the drumroll gradually quietened to a patter then became extinct. Then, perversely, came the rain, as accumulations of droplets began to slide from the canopy leaves to land heavily on their heads and down their necks. Galan returned and they followed him, climbing in single file up the stream where Olivia had first seen what she called her fairy child ("He was standing right there...") until they came at last to the glade.

The photograph had not prepared Gerry for the reality, even though the picture before him scarcely differed from it – there was even a child standing in the same position on top of the waterfall. But the experience was unnerving. It was as Olivia had described it to him, the sensation of stepping into a storybook, finding oneself actually on the page, turning a corner in a woodland to come upon a centaur or a unicorn in a shaft of sunlight. Every movement of the Sandula was momentarily frozen, every face turned towards him, men propped on their elbows, mothers suckling babies, adolescents caressing one another, long black hair tumbling to the shoulders of male and female alike. And on all their faces that same expression, tranquil, benign, beatific.

It was a child who broke the silence and he did it with a laugh, a low suppressed giggle, shared with another in the pool. Suddenly he splashed water in the direction of the visitors and now everyone laughed and the laughter was infectious and the visitors joined in and with that, as quickly as they had come across it, the tableau unfroze. Men got to their feet, children clustered round, giggling and touching the arrivals' clothes. The women pointed and laughed. It was only now that Gerry realised he had forgotten to capture the moment on camera.

"Isn't it wonderful the way they laugh," Olivia said to Gerry. "They're happy you see. Isn't that fantastic? They have no possessions, no careers, no ambition and they're blissfully happy. Just think of that. Hadn't you better start filming by the way?"

"Do you think they'll mind?"

"They won't have the slightest idea what's going on."

Gerry began filming, watched by bemused adults and children alike. Soon the children began to mimic him, holding their fists up to their eyes and wandering about bumping into trees then collapsing into fits of laughter.

"Aren't they enchanting?" Olivia said.

"Enchanted I'd say. Have you noticed the light, Olivia? It's like magic." Patterns of light, reflections from the pool, danced across naked bodies igniting droplets of water on velvet skins. From above, a single shaft of sunlight burst down through the forest with the impossible romance of a Victorian painting.

They climbed up beside the waterfall to a rocky ledge where caves opened into the limestone. "This is where they live," Olivia whispered, "in there."

"So they really are cave men?"

Olivia nodded. "Just watch this." Three of the men were squatting now around a ring of stones. One of them held a stick between his palms, its point engaged in a hole in a piece of wood in the middle of the stones. He began to roll the stick rapidly between his palms. As his hands slid slowly to the bottom a second man took over at the top while a third pushed dried moss around the point of the stick and blew gently. In less than a minute there was smoke and then a tiny flame and soon a fire. A woman appeared with a root of some description which she cut into slivers with a stone tool then dropped into a hollow green bamboo. Then she held the bamboo over the fire, turning it occasionally.

"Pretty fantastic eh?" Olivia said.

Gerry nodded, "incredible.".

"And do you know what? They're not even hunter gatherers."

"No? What are they then?"

"Just gatherers I suppose. Everything they need is here you see, within walking distance of their home, roots, nuts, fruit, fungus. There are fish in the river and frogs and tree crabs. It's a cornucopia. They have no need to hunt, to kill animals. See what I mean about the Garden of Eden?"

"Are you telling me they're veggies, Olivia?"

"I hadn't thought of it that way but yes, I suppose so."

"Were Adam and Eve vegetarian then?"

"Don't be facetious Gerry. I can see you're impressed."

"Impressed and seriously worried."

"Worried?"

"They're hardly in safe hands. Espinoza's a serpent in paradise if ever I saw one."

"I know but they're not safe anyway. You haven't seen how close the loggers are getting – you'll get to film it on the way back. There isn't much time left for them. We might be talking only months."

"I can't help feeling he intends to exploit them in some way."

"That's what we can stop Gerry. Oh Gerry look, oh how sweet…" A small girl had pushed her hand into Olivia's and was looking up at her wide-eyed. Olivia crouched down and put her arm around the child's waist. The girl smiled and looked away shyly. "Gerry run the camera. I want to say something. Quickly, while no-one's looking."

Gerry crouched down to the same level and switched on.

Olivia cleared her throat and looked straight at camera "You running?….okay." She cleared her throat a second time and began:

"This morning it took me just one hour to walk from the space age directly and unbelievably into the stone age. These are the Sandula, a society entirely unpolluted by modern man, a society at peace with nature and at peace with itself, a society which takes only what it needs from the earth, a society uncorrupted by vanity or ambition, a society which has no weapons and no word for war. Yet these beautiful people are about to be sacrificed to the selfish interests of transnational agribusiness, their paradise destroyed for profit. Unless international pressure can be brought to bear to stop the loggers very soon, we will all

have to bear responsibility for the destruction, not only of a way of life, but of the veritable Garden Of Eden itself. Olivia Denning-Smith for Worldweek on the Philippine island of Mindanao......

How was I?"

"One take, impressive. Hit all the right buttons – 'space age/stone age', 'no word for war', 'Garden of Eden' and a pretty child to boot. Knock em in the aisles."

"Gerry you don't have to be so cynical."

"Sorry, no you have a great story. You do really."

"It's not just a story, Gerry, I really care. Now we need to film them gathering food and we'd better do an interview with Espinoza, if only to keep him happy. Oh, and Gerry, I did sound okay didn't I?"

".... the veritable garden of Eden itself. Olivia Denning-Smith for Worldweek on the Philippine island of Mindanao." The editor pressed the stop button and Olivia's picture froze on the monitor. Julian waited for Boyle to speak.

"When did this arrive?" he said at last.

"Today. It was air-freighted from Davao yesterday. There was a note from Olivia saying she had a story for us but she didn't say what it was."

"Bloody amazing, that's what it is. She's only gone and found the bleeding Garden of Eden."

"Metaphorically speaking," Julian said.

Boyle looked at him. "I'm not stupid Julian. Metaphorically speaking, yeah, but what a metaphor, a metaphor for our age, a metaphor for the new millennium. It's got everything: destruction of the planet; greedy multinational versus noble savage; a race of men that doesn't make war; people who have no possessions, people who respect the environment, people Julian, and let's not forget this, who are in every respect *naked*."

"Could have a bit of a problem with that actually," Julian said. "Tits are all right pre-watershed but male genitals are always a difficulty."

"Mosaic them out. I don't particularly like seeing dangly bits myself."

"What about the sound quality? It's only coming off the little camera mike. The engineers won't like it."

"Bugger the engineers. Make a virtue of it. Say how she managed to get in there alone with only her amateur camera. She's quite a girl, our Olivia. Got a way with words. I liked that 'from the stone age to the space age' stuff and what was the other one 'they have no word for war.' Poetry."

"I'd like to know how they know that?"

"Know what?"

Julian frowned. "How do they know they have no word for war? You can't ask them if they have a word for war unless they know your word for war."

"Details, Julian, details. Schedule it for tonight…and I want it trailed – *Have we found the garden of Eden?* that kind of thing. Has Damien Street's crew got there yet?"

"Should be just about arriving."

"Get them into that forest as fast as you can. We need a proper shoot. Tell her to make it more personal this time. We want to know who these people are. What are their names, relationships. I want the public to fall in love with this tribe. I want them to know them like they're their own friends, like they're characters in a soap opera. This one's going to run, Julian."

"I'd like to speak to the managing director of One Man Band please," Gerry said. He'd decided it was easier to humour Carol.

"That you Gerry? You sound miles away. He's not in at the moment but I've got some messages for you. Can you hang on a bit they're here somewhere." Gerry heard a rumbling in his ear as the handset was put down then a moment later picked up again. "Right here we are. First one says you can stop bonking maidens, we're back in the abduction business." Carol frowned. "Does that make sense to you Gerry? Oh no that's an old one. Here's the latest one. It says here I'm to tell you that Northrop Pryce says forget the abduction story for now, he's more interested in smuggling pregnancies as long as there's an element of coercion." Carol screwed up her nose. "Is that good news or bad news?"

"Good news tempered with bad I guess. Tell Jonathan yes, I do have material on bonking maidens but the coercion could be hard to prove. I still need to tie up the *Filipina Services* end."

"How do you spell that?"

"*Filipina*?"

"No, *coercion*."

"Just write *force* Carol."

"Is that it then?"

"No. Tell him I'm back at the Intercontinental in Davao. He's not to ring me here because I'm sharing the bridal suite with Olivia and I don't want her overhearing my conversations."

Carol gave a little shriek, "congratulations, that's fantastic Gerry."

"I said I was sharing the bridal suite, Carol, not that I was married. Don't try and understand. It's just that everyone here thinks we're married and it's easier to play along. Just write the message down."

"Ah, you had me all excited there. That's not the Olivia that was on television last night is it?"

"What was on television last night?"

"Well it's where you are, Mindanao. That's what made me pay attention. She had this amazing story about this tribe who live in the Garden of Eden and they're nude and they're chopping down the rainforest. Anyway she was called Olivia something. Is it the same one?"

"Yes it's the same one. So they've shown the film then?"

"Yeah. They said they'd be bringing us more reports. They're starting a campaign to save them or something. You should see it; it was really good, although they wouldn't let us see the men's thingies. It was daft really, these little blobs of mosaic following them round the screen as if you didn't know what was underneath. But amazing really, from the space age to the stone age."

"That's a good line."

"Do you think so? Thanks."

"My pleasure. Listen Carol, tell Jonathan I'll call again later."

"Okay, will do. Is that it then?

"That's it."

"Okay byeee."

"Bye for now." Gerry replaced the receiver. Through the glass door of the booth he could see Olivia at the hotel reception being handed a piece of paper by the clerk.

"Gerry I've just had a fax," she said excitedly when she saw him, "from Julian Jenkin. It's a herogram. Just listen! *Congratulations on fantastic story. Doug delighted. Transmitted last night. Switchboard jammed, newspapers all over us. Crew en route to Damien (where is he by the way?) We want follow up story fast, at least 15 mins. This time more up close and personal, characters, relationships. Tie up exclusive access at all cost. Call so we can talk. JJ* Isn't that fantastic?" She read the piece over again to herself. Suddenly her face fell. "Oh no, you don't suppose they want Damien to do the follow up?"

"Probably."

"Gerry that's not fair."

"It's what he's paid for. Where do you suppose he is, by the way."

"God knows. The hotel told me he came back while we were away. Maybe he's got a lead in the Neville story. I'd better phone. Are they nine hours behind or ten?"

"Nine."

"You coming back to the room?"

"No, thought I'd take a stroll now the sun's down."

"See you later then." Olivia made to go then suddenly turned back, flinging her arms round Gerry's neck. "I'm so happy Gerry," she said, hugging him tightly, "thanks for sticking by me. I could never have done it without you, you know that." She released him, allowed him to kiss her momentarily on the lips then turned and ran teasingly away. "Don't be too long," she called back, "I think you deserve a reward for this."

Gerry stared after her. For a moment he actually felt ill. *The coward does it with a kiss.* No Olivia, he thought, Judas deserves no rewards. He returned to the booth, removed the camcorder bag from beneath the telephone, walked out of the hotel and hailed a cab.

It was that precise time of day in the tropics when day turns to night with none of the protraction of sunset and twilight. By the time the taxi had reached the waterfront it was quite dark, though Gerry was relieved to see there was street lighting outside the *Filipina Services* building. He asked the driver to stop across the road so that he could take a picture through the car window. It was his intention to return in the morning before his departure to try and doorstep Rizal. But to take film in an area like this carried a high risk, not just of violence but of forfeiting the camera and tape. Tonight's pictures were just an insurance against tomorrow's failure.

He took a shot of the upstairs window where the office was situated, then asked the driver to cross the road and park directly outside the building. From there he got out of the car and slipped unseen into the entrance. He felt for a light switch and clicked. A fluorescent tube flickered at the top of the staircase and came on. He ran quickly up the stairs to the glazed door and stopped. Where on earth was it? It was all he'd come to get and it wasn't there. The sign, the sign painted on the glass, the sign that said *Filipina Services*. It was the wrong entrance, it must be. No it was the right entrance but the wrong door. No it was the only door so it was the right door. He crouched down and examined the glass. Tiny flecks of gold paint dusted its surface. At the touch of his fingers the door swung slowly open. He got up and walked into the room, his own footsteps the only sound. On the walls only the torn corners of the blue-faded posters remained. The chairs beneath had vanished. So too had the filing cabinets, the desk, the Remington typewriter. Through the door beyond he could see the bare floor of Rizal's empty office.

It was the second time Gerry had stood in this same room, his mind racing for an explanation. They'd left, done a flit. Why would they do a flit? Because they didn't want to be found? Because they wanted to disappear? Fr. Ambrose had done that in Hackney. He'd left because a couple of journalists were snooping around, just closed up and vanished. Gerry felt his hands go clammy. Journalists snooping around. He and Olivia were journalists snooping around. Which meant…. they couldn't know could they…..? The back of his neck went cold. No that wasn't it, it was Damien. Damien had been snooping around in South Cotabato. Fr. Ambrose had got to hear and thrown a wobbly, imagining Damien had pursued him all the way from London. He'd temporarily closed down the operation until Damien gave up and went home. Yes that would be it. That would make sense. Gerry exhaled with relief.

The revelation didn't hit him till he reached the top of the stairs. *Filipina Services* had vanished because they didn't want their story told. But who was the one trying to tell the story? He was. If *Filipina Services* didn't exist, how the hell was he going to do that? "Oh Christ!" he said to himself, "now what the fuck are you going to do?"

"Now what the fuck are you going to do?" Jonathan said.

"No need to swear, Jonathan," Gerry said, "it's not my fault. And speak up can you? This is a lousy line."

"But this is the story Pryce wants and we can't even prove the agency exists."

"There's a contract."

"I know and I'm about to be in breach of it."

"Not between you and Channel Four, idiot, I mean between me and Filipina Services, for a baby. It's of no legal value but it's evidence of the organisation's existence."

"And you've got it? Thank God for that."

"No I haven't."

"What do you mean you haven't?

"I signed my copy for Rizal. But before we could exchange he passed out. He'd got concussion falling off our bed while he was examining the spy camera."

"Do you want to repeat that?"

"No. All you need to know is he passed out and I didn't see him again until the following day and I didn't want to bring the subject of the girls up with him in case he found out I hadn't inseminated them and he'd want me to go through it all again. So I never asked for my copy of the contract. That make sense?"

"In a surreal kind of way but where's all this leading?"

"I could ask for my copy of the contract."

"There's no-one to ask. You've just told me they've all vanished."

"I'll ask Rizal. It's a risk, but..."

"You'd go back?"

"Olivia's going back. It's only natural I'd go with her as her husband."

"What about Damien?"

"We'll by-pass him. Olivia doesn't want him taking over her story anyway. He's out of town again. By the time he gets back we'll have taken his crew and gone. Did you see her story by the way?"

"No but everyone's talking about it. The PM even answered a question in the House today. Promised that his government would do everything in its power to protect 'these magnificent people'.

"He'd seen it then?"

"Shouldn't think so for a minute. No, just one of those toady questions from his own side, 'I'm sure the prime minister would agree with me that the Sandula tribe…something, something'…. you know how it works. Someone in number ten sees something pure and uncorrupted and thinks *bandwagon*, jump on it quick. Are they really that nice by the way?"

"Far as I could see. They laugh a lot."

"They seem to be a potent symbol. All this Garden of Eden stuff, mankind before the Fall. Listen to this," Gerry heard a shuffle of papers at the other end, "here it is, *a paradigm against which the world is judged and found wanting*, that's a *Times* editorial. How did she come across this story anyway? How come you didn't get it?"

"She was the one with the camcorder. It just fell into her lap really. Espinoza showed her the tribe, explained the problem with the loggers. She suggested publicity… and… presto, it seems we have a *Times* leader."

"But if Espinoza's such a sleazebag why's he interested in mankind in a state of grace. Isn't he seriously into sin?"

"He's a complex character, delusional. If he sees himself having a part in this production it won't be the serpent…..more like the role of God. That's what worries me."

"What worries me is Olivia. You say she doesn't want Damien taking over her story but surely she's got no option. They both work for *Worldweek*. You don't. She's going to *have* to go back there with him."

"Don't worry Jonathan, I've thought of everything, trust me."

"*She* can't trust you, why should I?"

If Gerry's guilt at betraying Olivia had become an obstacle to having sex with her, it was one he'd bravely overcome. They lay on top of the bedsheet, naked and sleepy now, feeling the caress of the ceiling fan's breeze. She lay on her side facing him, a film of perspiration lending a sheen to her olive skin. He traced a finger down the profile of her body from the shoulder down to the valley of the waist and up over the hip. The Sandula were doing themselves a disservice, he thought; the excitement aroused by nudity is in inverse proportion to the frequency with which it's seen.

"You know they think we're married?" Olivia said.

"Who?

"London. Damien told them. He got it from the hotel after we'd left."

"You've disillusioned them?"

"Why would you want me to do that? Don't you want to be married to me Gerry?"

"But you *have* told them?"

"No actually."

"Why ever not?"

Olivia smiled and kissed him. "It's what every girl dreams of, isn't it, darling, marriage?" She fluttered her eyelashes. "You're part of my cover remember Gerry. I've got to go back to South Cotabato. I don't want any doubts being sown about who I really am, people ringing up here asking for Olivia Denning-Smith. It would get back to Espinoza. He *is* the owner of most things."

"But you're going back on your own anyway."

"No I'm not. I'm going there with Damien. I have to, it's my job. Besides the set-up has to look convincing to Espinoza. Damien has been sent by the BBC in response to my contacts with the media back home; that's what Espinoza will think. As the intermediary it's perfectly reasonable that I should come along to make the introductions. I'll tell Espinoza you've been called back to London – some big-time account-ancy job."

"Very funny. And what about Father Ambrose?"

"What about Father Ambrose?"

"Think about it Olivia. When he sees Damien, indeed when he sees Damien with you in tow, don't you imagine he's going to recall a certain visit to Hackney?"

Olivia sat bolt upright and clapped both her hands to her cheeks. "Oh my God, I never thought of that. That'll blow everything. Gerry what are we going to do? Gerry you've got to help me."

"I don't see that I can."

"Gerry you must."

"Well I mean I've got my own job...."

"Gerry *please*..."

Gerry sat up and put an arm round Olivia. He shook his head and let out a long breath. "You make it very difficult for me Olivia."

"*Please* Gerry."

Gerry sighed. "Oh well if you insist, there is a way round it, I suppose. If we get in there first we can shoot the film without Damien. That's what you'd like anyway isn't it? You can tell London he didn't show in time and you needed to get in before the world's press arrived. At the same time you can tell Espinoza that London have asked you to step into the breach. After all your amateur video was such a triumph. When Damien gets back here we'll already be there."

"We?"

"I don't imagine you'd want to go alone."

"Gerry you're a saint." Olivia clapped his head in her hands and kissed him.

"Phone's ringing," he said, "you answer it."

Olivia stretched back across the bed and grabbed the phone. "Okay," she said into the receiver, "thank-you," and then to Gerry, "they're here, the crew…it's the two Daves."

"T'boli country," the guide said, pointing ahead. Across a wide, shallow river, wispy cloud crept down a mountainside. From beneath the carpet of trees, trails of blue smoke rose from hidden habitations; below, knee-deep in the middle of the river, a lone prospector panned for gold.

"What's T'boli?" Damien asked. He'd forgotten the guide's name and, like a too-long delayed thank-you letter which can no longer be sent, it seemed somehow improper to ask now.

"Highlanders," Mister Street, "hill tribe."

"Muslims?"

"No, they worship their own spirits. A few are Christians; there is a mission in the mountains."

"Where are the Muslims then?"

"All around, they are the majority in these parts. They call it Moroland. They call us Christians *settlers*. But you can't tell them apart; we all look the same, we are all Filipinos." The guide sat down, took his shoes off and rolled up his trousers. Damien followed suit. Then he put his shoes into his backpack and followed the guide into the water. Ahead they could hear the rumble of distant thunder; by the time they reached the other side, the descending cloud had all but enveloped them.

They climbed steadily, frequently changing direction to avoid coming into contact with people, either in the *baranguays*, the little hamlets which dotted the mountainside, or in the still-forested valleys which echoed from time to time with the whine of a chainsaw. They climbed up a thermal stream, whose hot water ran over boulders like steps, steaming in the already damp air. They came to an old mine-working, a wild-west shaft running horizontally into the side of the ravine. They rested here to wait out the coming storm. From the mouth of the shaft Damien watched the raindrops arrive in a spontaneous deluge. Tiny rivulets suddenly appeared on the slopes of the ravine, translated quickly into waterfalls and cascaded into the stream below, swelling it before his eyes into a torrent. For a moment lightning and thunder synchronised and both men flinched like children. Then, just as quickly as it had begun, the storm passed on. When the rain had stopped they moved out beneath the dripping trees. The temperature seemed cooler now, as if the downpour had washed the air of its humidity, but the going had become doubly difficult. The paths were awash with water and Damien found his feet caked with heavy mud. He kept his eyes firmly on the ground immediately ahead and, for quite some time, had no sight of his guide. It was only when he slipped and slithered some way down a bank that he realised the error of this, for when he grasped the hand which came to his assistance, he looked up and saw that it belonged to another. In an instant he knew just how serious an error it had been, not from his rescuer's unfamiliar face, but from the object the man carried in his free hand.

"If I'm not mistaken," he said, bravely affecting his Sean Connery impersonation, "I'd say that was a Kalashnikov."

The man wore a khaki shirt and ragged trousers, each of a different shade. The gun and the colour of the clothes both said *soldier* but there was little else military about him. He grinned and seemed excited at his find. He pulled Damien to his feet then stepped back quickly, pointing the rifle at him, as if suddenly conscious that the difference in their heights created an imbalance that the Kalashnikov would need to correct. Without taking his eyes off his prisoner he shouted a few words in his own language. Damien heard the movement of branches behind him, and the cracking of twigs beneath feet. In a moment he was surrounded.

The absurdity of the situation struck him. For a day and a half he'd tried not to be seen. Now he'd not only stumbled on a rebel camp but fallen at the very feet of its sentry. Unasked he raised both hands. "Damien Street.... I'm from England... um....over here ...um....on holiday...." He heard his own voice trail into silence.

One of the men stepped forward. He wore camouflage fatigues and a webbing belt with a pistol in a holster. A watch with a steel bracelet hung loosely on his skinny wrist. The man eyed him, looking up in a superior manner, albeit from an inferior angle. "Lieutenant Mai," he said, pronouncing lieutenant in the American manner *lootenant*, "M.I.L.F."

Damien lowered his arms very slowly, watching for trigger fingers. "Right," he said, "Okay....right then...M.I.L.F. That would be the Moro Islamic Liberation Front.... as opposed to the Moro *National* Liberation Front, would I be right?"

"You're very knowledgeable for a tourist, Mr. Street."

"You're very good at English, lieutenant."

"That's fortunate for both of us, Mr. Street. It will make interrogation so much easier."

Bond would have had an answer for that, Damien thought, some banal, punning repartee. How was it his own mouth had gone quite dry? Panic. That's how. It was easy for Bond. He never panicked because he knew he'd be alive in the final reel, ready to star in the sequel. But this story may not have a sequel. Peter Neville's story had no sequel and that had climaxed in almost identical circumstances. They led him the through the trees to a small clearing ringed by makeshift shelters of bamboo and leaves. Wet clothes hung on branches. A sheet of plastic, stretched between trees, drained rainwater into a jerrycan. A fire smoked feebly, its glow all but extinguished by the recent downpour.

But it was the cage which caught Damien's eye. A construction of bamboo poles lashed with rattan, it hung by some sort of vine from a branch high above the fire. That was odd enough, but more disconcerting was its size. He couldn't help thinking it was too big for any native species of animal.

"So," the lieutenant said, observing him, "you see we have some spare accommodation. Fortunately for you, you can have vacant possession. Its last tenant sadly died."

"Died?" Damien said, swallowing hard, "what of?"

"I think you would call it heat exhaustion. Pity, such a brave man too, a member of the armed forces. Unfortunately he was also a spy."

"I'll tell you anything you want to know," Damien said, shrilly.

The lieutenant looked at him without expression. "Papers," he said, holding out a hand.

Damien's felt his knees go weak. "Look I know this is going to sound strange but someone took my passport... I mean I lost it... I mean... "

The lieutenant glanced up at the cage and back to Damien.

"Look, I'm a journalist," Damien said, his voice a register higher now, "I am, really....with the BBC, you know *This is Lon-don. Rum tiddy tum ti, rum tiddy tum....*" But the jaunty signature tune was received impassively. Damien's voice faded to a stop. "It's called *Lilliburlero*," he added helplessly.

"And you are here to report on the liberation struggle of the Moros?"

Damien stopped himself in time from saying no. Why not? Of course that's what he was here to do. And he'd be on their side too, course he would. Brilliant idea. "Yes actually, that's exactly what I'm here to do."

A knee came up into his groin and he doubled over, crumpling to the ground. A boot struck him in the chest. "Liar," the lieutenant said.

"Okay I'm a liar," Damien gasped through the pain, "Okay, Okay, I'm really here to find my colleague, Peter Neville. He disappeared somewhere hereabouts ....last year. Perhaps you know what happened to him. I was on my way to see Ferdinand Espinoza when you found me..."

The lieutenant's boot, about to make contact again, froze in mid air and came to rest on the ground. He squatted down beside Damien pulling his head back by the hair so that they were face to face. "Espinoza? You know Espinoza?"

Damien nodded. "He has my passport."

"You are friends, like Peter Neville?"

For a moment Damien just stared at him. "What do you know about Peter Neville?"

"This is an interrogation Mr. Street. I am the interrogator. I ask questions, you give me answers, truthful answers. You are friends?"

"We know one another. He gave me money once. That's the truth."

The lieutenant stood up and indicated to one of his men that he should help Damien to his feet. To another he issued an order. Damien heard the name Espinoza.

"I hope you are telling me the truth, Mr. Street. I'm sending someone to check your story. In the meantime you remain with us. Please do not attempt to escape, that would be foolish." He glanced up at the cage, swaying slightly now above a thin column of smoke. "Heat exhaustion is such a risk in this climate. Smoking too. Both very bad for the health."

They'd taken the doors off the helicopter so that Dave, the cameraman, could film the aerials. His feet rested on the skids outside with the camera mounted on bungees secured to the doorframe.

"Lower," he shouted to Olivia, "I need to get lower."

Olivia passed the message to the pilot through the headset "He wants to go lower, so he can see the loggers at work."

"Too dangerous," the pilot said, "they have guns, they'll shoot at us."

"Why?"

The pilot shrugged, "because they have guns, because we are a helicopter, because this is Mindanao. They won't have a permit for what they're doing, so they won't trust us."

"They're armed," Olivia shouted to Dave, "they could shoot at us."

"Oh, I see, want me to do a wobbly then?"

"A what?"

Dave swung his legs back into the cabin and leant forward to shout into Olivia's ear. "A wobbly, you know, one minute the lens is pointing at the ground, the next you're looking at the roof of the chopper. Stick the sound of gunfire over it and, wow, we've just been shot at."

"Isn't that dishonest?"

Dave shrugged, "suit yourself. Why isn't Gerry along for the ride by the way? That's his stock in trade, getting shot at. You see his Bosnia piece?"

Olivia nodded. "Wasn't room in the chopper for him. Besides he says he's seen the Sandula already. What did you think of them by the way?"

"Pretty amazing actually. It was great that scene when we first got there and there they all were, beautifully lit and everything. It was like some sort of tableau, that kid standing there on top of the waterfall."

"Yes it was, wasn't it," Olivia said, more to herself than to Dave, "even when you've seen it before....."

They'd ferried everyone out to the forest in relays, Espinoza and Rizal in the first flight, Olivia and the crew in the second. Gerry had waved them off and retired to the house to contemplate larceny. He'd baulked at the last moment at asking Rizal outright for his copy of the contract. If Rizal, whatever his reason, had chosen not to bring up the subject of the girls then why should *he*? Why invite inquiry as to what had really gone on? Burglary was a safer bet.

Except for the servants, he had the house to himself. He waited till the afternoon heat had sent everyone to their beds, then took off his shoes and walked silently down the stairs. He'd seen Espinoza come and go through double doors at the end of the verandah but when he tried these discreetly, they turned out to be locked. He examined the louvres, which were unglazed, and found he could swivel them by hand into a horizontal position. Starting at chest height and working downwards, he slipped the fingers of one hand between the slats where the doors met at the centre. At the twelfth attempt he touched a key with his fingertips. In this position it was impossible to turn but he could at least grip its shaft between the first two fingers. With his eyes closed in concentration he withdrew it slowly from the hole and out through the louvre. He took a deep breath and let himself in.

As his eyes adjusted to the darkness he realised that his actions, probably for the first time in his life, were beyond excuse. It was a nerve-wracking thought. If you were late for a meeting or you'd forgotten some piece of work or even if you were caught speeding you could always invent an excuse, a lie, a mitigating factor. But to be caught here didn't bear thinking about; the only possible explanation for his presence in this room was the true one. Perhaps that's why burglars were reputed to have said 'it's a fair cop, guv'; there was nothing else you *could* say.

The room was a study with a carved teak desk in its centre and another of the throne-like chairs. There were filing cabinets and a sofa and easy chairs, their outlines confused by slats of sunlight, like a dance-floor beneath a strobe. The walls were adorned with photographs, pictures of the two Espinozas: The Espinoza he knew, Espinoza the tribal philanthropist, Espinoza in ethnic clothes with his adoring peoples, Espinoza with young girls in a mountain village; and the other Espinoza: Espinoza the socialite, Espinoza in a white tuxedo, dancing in a Manila nightclub, Espinoza shaking hands with the president, Espinoza with his arm round Michael Jackson.

On the wall behind the desk hung a painting of the rainforest and, below it, a bookshelf with incongruous works by Margaret Mead and Joseph Conrad, *Lord Jim, Coming of age in Samoa, Heart of Darkness*. On the lower shelf he found row upon row of camcorder videotapes, each labelled only with a girl's Christian name: *Magdalena, Carmen, Christina, Julia*. He stood up, a queasy feeling in his stomach. He was sweating profusely now, from the heat, the humidity, probably the adrenalin. But it was more. The room corrupted him, not simply because it involved him in a criminal act, but because it expressed so much of Espinoza's distorted personality that he felt sullied by it, as if he were caught going through someone else's linen basket. He needed to get the job done and get out. Quickly was the word.

Very few people have illegally searched someone else's office, yet Gerry, in common with the whole world, knew exactly what happened when you did. The private detective finds the document he's looking for in the third drawer down, having spent no more than eight seconds examining the contents of the first two. Gerry was to discover that life does not imitate cinema. In order to conclude that a document is not the one you're looking for you have to read at least a part of it before you can discard it. That takes time. And then there are the documents which you read because they attract your attention. Which was exactly how Gerry came across the press cutting. It was in a pile of clippings, mostly from the Manila society columns – reports of functions which Espinoza had attended and at which he'd been photographed. It was quite a small photograph and Gerry might not have recognised the figure in the dinner jacket had not the caption virtually leapt off the page at him. For a long time he just stared at it in disbelief, hardly hearing the warning throb of the distant helicopter. Above the photograph was the strap *MANILA YACHT CLUB DINNER* and below, the caption: *Seated at the table enjoying the evening's entertainment, left to right: Mr. and Mrs Frederick Cuangco, Mrs. Ann Oppenheimer, Mr. Ferdinand Espinoza, Mr. Peter Neville, Miss Juanita Sison.*

He was mesmerised. He knew the helicopter was closing in but for a moment was unable to move. "Mister....Peter.....Neville," he could hear himself repeating, "Mister....Peter....bloody....Neville." Then the whole house vibrated violently as the chopper rattled overhead and he came suddenly to his senses. He pushed the cutting into his pocket, hurriedly closed the filing cabinet drawers and made his exit, locking the door behind him. There was no time to work the key back into the keyhole so he just dropped it back through the louvre, hoping Espinoza would think some maid responsible. By the time the helicopter came down on the landing stage its sole passenger could see him leaning casually on the railing of the verandah. He waved. It was only then that he realised he hadn't actually found what he was looking for.

It was Espinoza himself who had returned alone. He came bounding up the staircase calling out to Gerry. "You must get ready Gerry, you're coming with me, Olivia needs you there, it's so exciting."

"What is?"

"They've gone back to the caves. One of the Sandula women has gone into labour. Olivia's going to record the birth so the whole world can see. I've come to get camping equipment, food. This kind of thing can take a long time."

You'd know that of course, Gerry thought. He watched as Espinoza gave orders and people obeyed. Servants appeared bearing tarpaulins and boxes which they loaded onto the helicopter. Gerry found himself obeying too and boarded the aircraft without further discussion. Somehow with Espinoza you always felt you were a character in someone else's plot.

It was the first time they had been alone together, side by side in the back of the helicopter. They wore headsets with lip mikes. Espinoza wore dark glasses, concealing his expression. For a long time neither spoke then Espinoza, looking out of his own side of the aircraft, flicked the switch on the cable in his hand, opening the intercom: "Tell me Gerry, do you and Olivia fuck?"

Gerry was speechless. He shot an appalled glance in the direction of the pilot.

"It's okay," Espinoza said, holding up the switch, "he can't hear. You can answer the question, just man to man, you understand. You fuck?"

"We're married."

"Not the same thing. I know, I was married. Listen, you come here to get babies so there's a problem."

"Not that kind of a problem."

"Problem with you maybe. You only like it some special way; Mrs. Harris doesn't. What did you do to Rizal's girls?"

" I fulfilled my part of the contract."

"They ran away."

Gerry turned and looked out of the open side of the aircraft, allowing the rush of air to hit his face. He gave himself a moment to think. This was an interrogation; worse it was being carried out five hundred feet above a wilderness. He took a moment to reply. "I didn't know that."

"Why do you suppose they ran away?"

"I really have no idea. I expect Mr. Rizal would know."

"Mr. Rizal was unconscious. Did you strike him?"

Gerry turned back to face Espinoza. "Is that what he says?"

"He doesn't remember. So did you fuck the girls or what?"

"I said I fulfilled my part of the contract."

"Your part of the contract was only to pay the money."

"Mr. Espinoza…. you're not expecting me to go into detail? Frankly this line of questioning borders on the…"

Espinoza burst out laughing. "It's okay, it's okay…" he said, snatching off the dark glasses, his face a broad grin, "just teasing…..just having a little fun. Isn't that right Captain Romero, you understand me, yes?"

"Sure Mr. Espinoza," the pilot said, turning round, "you're a real joker."

Gerry let out a whistle and forced the complaisant smile required of the victim of a practical joke. Except that it wasn't a joke. That was the real Espinoza he'd just been talking to and he wasn't funny at all.

The conversation had been precisely the one he'd avoided holding with Rizal; they both wanted to know what had gone on with the girls. Still, he'd learnt something to his advantage. The girls had run away saying nothing, which made things a whole lot easier. He flicked the switch in his hand: "That reminds me... Ferdinand... the contract.... I didn't collect my copy. Do you think you could find it for me when I get back?"

Espinoza put the dark glasses on again quickly. "Why? You don't need it. It's of no value."

"But it's our agreement."

Espinoza shrugged his shoulders. "It's still of no value. It's a contract for an illegal transaction. Lawyers have a word for it. They call it an 'immoral' contract."

Gerry could imagine Espinoza's eyes shifting behind the shades. "Then why have one at all?"

"Our overseas customers need to know they're dealing with someone. They like it in writing; it's a matter of trust for them. You came here in person. So you know you can trust us. You do don't you Gerry? You're surely not questioning that trust....?

Gerry was outmanoeuvred. He forced another smile and shook his head. "Course not," he said, "course I'm not."

They flew on in silence, through a shower of rain, which came in through the open door, soaking Gerry's left side. When they emerged into the sunshine again the pilot took the helicopter down and skimmed the forest canopy, slowing imperceptibly into a hover. "We're here, gentlemen," he announced suddenly. Gerry looked down expecting to see the clearing but saw instead just the canopy. Then, to his amazement, the helicopter crabbed sideways to reveal a raft of bamboo poles, seemingly floating on the treetops. Painted across its surface in white paint, undulating with the shape of the bamboo, was a large letter H.

"What on earth's that?" he said to Espinoza.

"Helicopter pad. Some of my men built it. It doesn't take the helicopter's weight you understand. He just hovers and you step out. There's a rope ladder to the forest floor."

"What's it for?"

"We're only minutes from the caves here. We couldn't disturb the

Sandula by making a clearing. This will be better for our visitors."

"Visitors? What visitors?"

"Oh there's been interest from all over. We're in discussions with *National Geographic* – front cover if we're lucky. Then there's the big US networks – *NBC, CBS – Süddeutsche Rundfunk*.

"Don't you think… all this might be just a little obtrusive?"

Espinoza removed his glasses for a second time and stared at Gerry with a frown of utter incomprehension. "Why would this be intrusive?"

"Well I mean, the Garden of Eden… it didn't have a car park."

At the foot of the rope ladder a number of boys of the tribe stood gazing up, mesmerised by the great thundering dragonfly, which debouched alternative humans onto the roof of their universe. Gerry wondered, as he climbed down, if he had not already been deified. Wasn't there a tribe in the South seas who worshipped aeroplanes, one even who worshipped Prince Philip? So why not a television reporter?

Rizal was there already, marshalling the enthusiastic boys to assist the visitors, encouraging them by gesture and monosyllable to carry the supplies back to the caves. The party made its way through the forest glade, empty now, and up the rock face to the ledge by the caves. Most of the tribe seemed to have gathered here to watch events unfold. Gerry saw a camera mounted on a low tripod with Olivia squatting next to it. A Sandula man sat facing her and, next to him, Galan the hunter. Above the man's head a large sausage-like microphone hung suspended from a boom. Olivia was leafing through handwritten notes. "Okay," she said to Galan, "let's try again. Ask him what he does each day."

Galan spoke a few words to the Sandula man who smiled and replied in a monosyllable. Galan translated. "He say – *I am.*"

Olivia ran a hand through her hair in exasperation. "I asked him what he *does.* Are you telling me he doesn't *do*, he only *is*?"

"They have no word for *do*, only for *things* they do."

Olivia sighed, "Okay then, look… ask him… I don't know….what he likes to eat."

Galan asked the man. The words sounded much the same. "He say

— I eat. The Sandula have no word for *like*."

Olivia caught sight of Gerry and rolled her eyes upwards. "Gerry, you're used to doing interviews. How do you ask questions of people whose only abstract concept is *being*?"

"You mean: *I give interviews therefore I am.* It's a problem."

"According to Galan they don't have abstract words. They don't seem to have any need for them."

"Make a virtue of it. If they have no word for *like* then they can have no word for *dislike*. Presumably they have no word for *television* either. Therefore they have no *concept* of television; ergo they're uninterviewable, surely a virtue."

"Please don't be flippant, Gerry, it's not been easy believe me. I'm not even sure Galan really knows their language. He could be making it up for all I know. As for Rizal he just wants to be a bloody director the whole time. Every time I find a natural sequence he wades in and starts drilling them like extras. At least he's kept away from Sula."

"Sula?"

"The one having the baby. She's in the cave back there with two women. The sisterhood's closed ranks. No men allowed."

"So how are you going to film it?"

"I've absolutely no idea. That's why I asked you to come. I'll admit I'm out of my depth, Gerry."

Gerry thought for a moment. "If you can't get the camera to the baby, you bring the baby to the camera."

"You think they'd let me?"

"How soon's it going to be?"

"I'm no midwife but the contractions don't seem to be coming any more often. Could be all night."

"Then we take watches, you, me, the two Daves. Whoever hears the first cry wakes the others. You go in, come out with baby. Go all gooey on camera; few choice words: 'Unto us a child is born…' that sort of thing. Not a dry eye in the house."

"Oh yeah, and how are we going to catch the first cry? We can't leave the camera running all night."

Gerry frowned. "You're being naïve, Olivia. You leave that to the dubbing theatre, you know, sound effects, they'll have a disc: *track seven — baby's first cry*. If you're lucky they'll even have *midwife's first bottom slap*."

"Oh," Olivia said, "I see."

As dusk fell, the men lit fires and the tribe gathered round. The absence of sun and the altitude had brought a chill. Rizal brought up sleeping bags for the visitors. Gerry and Olivia sat side by side in theirs and watched while Dave-on-camera took cutaways of the tranquil Sandula faces flickering in the firelight and Dave-on-sound pointed his directional mike towards the mouth of the cave and the increasingly violent cries from within.

"You know we don't know who the father is, don't you?" Olivia said.

"Single parent family eh?"

"Multiple more like. Seems they share children…and partners."

"Now there's a quandary for Boyle."

"How do you mean?"

"Tabloid editor's nightmare. Sex is what sells, but this story's all about purity, innocence, the PM's family values. You can have free love or you can have family values but you can't have both. If it were down to me I'd go for the sex every time."

"God you're a cynic Gerry. Don't you think this atmosphere's just amazing? Doesn't it get to you at all? Look they're just sitting there in total silence listening for evidence that may mean their own survival or extinction. Aren't you moved by that?"

"I feel a piece-to-camera coming on."

"That you being cynical?"

"No, no, I'm serious; milk it while you can. You're not going to get much in the way of interviews are you?"

"Okay then, just give me a moment." They moved a little way from the group and set up the camera so that the Sandula were a moody flickering background to Olivia's close up.

"Ready?" Gerry asked.

Olivia nodded.

"Turn over then."

"Running!"

In a move which recalled Peter Neville's last ever piece-to-camera she turned first to look at the tribe then swung back to face the lens:

"Silent, tranquil, hopeful, fearful," she began, *"we cannot imagine how*

these gentle people are feeling as they listen to the pained cries of one of their own. But in the suffering of Sula lies the hope of all of them. With numbers this small, each birth, each tiny cry, may mean the difference between survival or eventual extinction. Our hearts lie with the Sandula in these tense moments."

"Bravo!" Gerry said.

"Was I all right? I'm not sure about the last line. Perhaps I should have said "we pray for the Sandula in these tense moments."

"You'd sound like an American president. Stick with 'our hearts lie…'."

Hours passed yet no-one slept. The tribe kept its vigil at the fireside, the visitors lay, mostly in silence, in their sleeping bags, mentally timing the intervals between the bouts of moaning, embarrassed, ashamed even to be an audience for someone else's pain. Everyone knew when the moment came – the sudden uncontrolled shrieks and the exhortations of the midwives; then the final elongated grunt, followed by a chilling silence. The Daves switched their equipment on. Olivia got up and walked to the mouth of the cave. A cold blue dawn light outlined a huddle of figures inside. She went in. Outside, the tribe stood in silence. Everyone counted seconds. After half a minute Rizal looked at Gerry, shrugged and shook his head. More silence. And then the sound. One short, tiny shriek at first, piercing like a cat whose tail has been trodden on, then another, then repetition upon repetition of tiny persecuted cries. The tribe began to embrace one another in silence. Gradually the crying subsided and Olivia came out walking towards the camera. She looked radiant as a Madonna, her long black hair loose and unkempt around her shoulders, the tranquil smile of the Gioconda on her lips. And in her arms, the naked child, wet and bloodied against her shirt. She looked at the camera, then looked at the child and ran her hand over its head. "Unto us a child is born…."she began and paused.

Oh God, Gerry thought, I didn't mean it literally, Olivia.

"Unto us a son is given…" she broke off, fighting back emotion. Then she took a deep breath and looked at the camera. A tear detached itself from the corner of her eye and ran down her cheek, pausing to gather weight before it plopped onto the infant's belly. She smiled shyly at this and wiped her face with the back of her hand. Her eyes shone and, as she smiled, her perfect white teeth glistened in the dawn light. "And his name shall be called 'wonderful'..." She paused again then held the tiny baby towards the camera, allowing the child, oblivious of his audience, to blink obligingly through its lens at what would, in time, become nearly half the world's population. "....The prince of peace...," her voice had dropped now almost to a whisper. She raised the child's forehead to her lips and kissed it. Then, still smiling, she turned and carried him back to his mother in the cave.

"Phew!" Gerry muttered out loud, wiping a damp corner of his own eye, "powerful stuff."

"Impressive," Dave said. He detached the camera from the tripod and began to follow the line of men and women now entering the cave. Gerry held back. He'd surprised himself. She'd accused him of being a cynic and she'd been right. But what he felt now was something more than just an emotion she'd managed to touch; it was something...well, dare he say it.... almost spiritual. He felt a tug at his belt and turned to find a boy standing with his hand outstretched. He was perhaps ten or twelve – the long hair and the nakedness somehow made judging ages difficult. Gerry smiled at him, suffused as he was with an unaccustomed feeling of goodwill to all men. "What is it?" he asked.

The boy looked at him nervously, as if coming to some final decision whether or not to press his case. There was an expression in his eyes Gerry had not seen amongst the Sandula before, not just an expression an *attitude*. Here in the forest he couldn't pin it down, though somehow he knew he'd seen it the world over. Only in retrospect, when he was back in the context in which it belonged, was he able to put a name to it... *street-wise*. The boy pushed his open palm toward Gerry again. "Money," he said at last, "you give me money."

From the top of the wooden steps, Gerry watched and deliberated and came to no decision. On the pontoon below, the small figures of Olivia and the crew were loading their equipment onto the helicopter. Even at this distance her movements betrayed a state of seemingly perpetual excitement. Eight hours on, after a sleepless night, she was still exhilarated, emotional, talkative, high on the brilliance of her achievement. But Gerry knew the truth and the truth could destroy her.

"No room for you, then?"

Gerry looked up and saw Espinoza standing over him. He got up and dusted down his trousers. "No, Olivia wants the crew to go with her, which means taking the equipment and everything..... she needs them for the technical side. They're going to try and send the stuff by satellite from the TV station in Davao. That way it'll make the programme tonight, London time. That's in about thirteen hours."

"Never mind, we'll run you down by jeep first thing in the morning. You can join me for dinner. We'll have a little celebration."

Gerry could think of nothing worse. "That's very kind of you Ferdinand but with no sleep last night I'm afraid I need an early bed. But thanks anyway." He made his excuses and went inside. At the bedroom window he stood and watched Olivia again, chatting enthusiastically now with the pilot, with anyone who'd listen, her hands gesticulating, pointing, winding a piece of hair behind her ear. He'd have to tell her. He'd have to. It was the truth. *I've eaten of the fruit of the tree of knowledge, Olivia, and am no longer blind to our nakedness.* He watched as the pilot climbed into the helicopter and began his cockpit checks. There were only minutes left. He went into the bathroom and retrieved the cassette tape from the soap dish in his sponge bag. He looked at it, deliberated and came to a decision.

"We need to talk," he said.

"What is it darling?" She put her arms around his neck, "I'm sorry you've got to stay behind, but you can have a nice intimate dinner with Ferdinand." She giggled.

Gerry unwound her arms and drew her away from the others to the edge of the pontoon. "This is serious," he said. "Look, I want you to have this." He gave her the cassette.

"What is it?"

"It's the *Filipina Services* tape. The stuff I shot of the beauty parade and the interview with the girl."

"But I've already got it."

Gerry shook his head. "I substituted a blank."

In a moment Olivia had lost all her ebullience. She stared at him, suddenly tired, struggling to avoid conclusions she didn't want to reach. "You were going to keep this?"

Gerry nodded.

"Then what were you… why are you…?" Her eyes scanned his face.

"I was keeping it to myself. You didn't want it. Now you need it."

"Now I need it. What are you talking about?"

"It's the story you came to get."

"We've been through all this, Gerry. The story I've *got* is the Sandula, get it?" She was angry now.

Gerry shook his head. "You haven't got a story. It doesn't stand up. You'll need this one."

"Don't be ridiculous. What are you talking about?"

"It doesn't stand up. The Sandula aren't a stone-age tribe. They're a fraud."

"A what!?"

"Keep your voice down. A fraud, a hoax. You've been hoaxed, we've all been hoaxed."

"Gerry you're talking absolute bullshit. You're just jealous of my story. This is absurd…. ."

She turned to walk away. Gerry grabbed her by the arm. "There was a boy in the forest, just after the birth. He asked me for money, in English."

Olivia stared at him. "Well…. somebody'd obviously taught him…. Rizal…. one of his men."

Gerry shook his head. "He'd done it before, you could tell, held his palm out. When he realised he'd blown his cover he clapped his hand over his mouth the way children do. It was a dead giveaway. Then he ran off."

"I don't believe you Gerry. You're just trying to sabotage my story."

"Why would I do that? Think about it Olivia. Isn't it all just too good to be true? They don't even kill animals for God's sake. What forest tribe wouldn't eat meat if they had the chance? And didn't you notice how, every time somebody shows up, there they all are like some tableau, exactly like the photograph Espinoza first showed me?" Olivia looked away. "There's even a child standing on top of the waterfall each time. Isn't there? Don't pretend you haven't noticed. It's the way they rehearsed it. Why else do you think Galan has to go ahead and warn them?"

"This is nonsense Gerry. Let go of my arm."

"Not till you listen to me. "Who first came up with the Garden of Eden line?"

"I did, thank you very much."

"Espinoza described them as mankind before the Fall. He fed you the idea. Don't you see?"

"No I do not."

"And how does he know they have no word for *war*? They have to know *your* word for *war* before you can ask if *they* have one. It's absurd."

She pulled herself away. Behind them the pilot fired the engine in the helicopter and the turbine began to whine, its pitch mounting slowly to a scream. "Gerry, I'm not listening to any more of this crap," she shouted, "you're just doing this out of spite. And you know what you can do with this, don't you?" She held out the tape cassette, "just watch me," and with an uncoordinated female throw, neither quite underarm nor quite overarm, she hurled the small plastic box out over the lake. By a fluke it spun as it left her fingers and, being flat, bounced as it touched the still water. For this reason it continued still further, bouncing four or five more times, the frequency of the bounces increasing in inverse proportion to the distance between them, until finally it came to rest. For a moment it bobbed on the surface while the box filled with water. Then it tipped on one end and sank.

They both stared after it. Olivia wiped her eyes with the fingertips of both hands and suppressed an urge to cry.

"I guess that means divorce then," Gerry said.

Olivia nodded, not looking at him. Then she turned, walked stooping towards the helicopter and climbed in beside the pilot.

Gerry lay on the bed and poked his tongue at the camera in the ceiling. He was tempted to unzip his fly and do something rude, but the possibility that his potential audience might actually get some enjoyment from this deterred him. He thought of Olivia. She'd thrown away the best story he'd ever found and, amazingly, he didn't begrudge her. His guilt was assuaged, that's why. He'd tried to steal it from her and he'd fallen in love with her instead. At least he wouldn't betray her now. It hurt him more that she was sticking by the Sandula story. She'd be humiliated if the truth were ever known. It was odd how Espinoza seemed to have come out best in all of this. The pregnancy trade had evaporated into thin air – no *Filipina Services*, no girls, no tape, no proof. Instead the philanthropic Filipino millionaire presented himself to the world as the saviour of something beautiful and pure and innocent. Except it was a lie. It was all a lie. He closed his eyes and tried to sleep. Outside, an outboard puttered on the lake. He rolled off the bed and went to close the window then realised it held no glass. He glanced down through the shutters. The motorboat drew into the landing stage and cut the engine. Its passenger climbed out then reached down to take a rifle handed up to him by the boatman. He wore camouflage fatigues; a new character for the plot, Gerry thought. He wondered for a moment where this military-looking figure might fit in, decided he no longer cared and lay down on the bed again. Espinoza manipulated everyone, that's all you needed to know. The Sandula had been only players under his direction. It was Espinoza who wrote the script, Espinoza who directed and starred in his own produc-tions. He manipulated everyone. Gerry turned onto one elbow and felt for the plastic duty-free whisky bottle on the floor. Everyone. He unscrewed the cap and took a swig. The liquid was warm and burning, a ridiculous choice in this climate but all he had. Everyone. Think about that. Suppose everyone included himself....and Olivia. Would it all make sense then? He screwed the cap onto the bottle, dropped it onto the floor again and lay back. If Espinoza was the director, then what did that make Olivia? He stared at the lens in the ceiling for a long time then finally addressed it out loud. "Your impresario, that's what. You made her your impresario, didn't you, and she innocently obliged by giving you the whole damn world for a stage. Fuck me, Ferdinand Espinoza, if you haven't known who we were all along."

"Who've we got?" Boyle asked.

"For the studio discussion you mean?" Julian said. "We've got Friends of the Earth, the Oxford anthropologist Ballinger, the Philippine ambassador and the Bishop of Middlesex...."

"What happened to the Archbishop?"

"Too short notice I'm afraid, but the bishop's good value. He's the one who wrote to the *Telegraph* after Olivia's last report, complaining about the misappropriation of the Garden of Eden myth. With any luck he'll go spare when he hears her nativity pitch."

"Do you think we should show them the film before the show?"

"No, better they react to it live. More of a ding-dong that way. Friends of the Earth and ambassador *for*, bishop and anthropologist *against*."

"What's this Ballinger's beef?"

"Thinks it's a disgrace. Should be a proper anthropological team in there, not a meddling television crew. He's going to hate Olivia holding the baby. It'll be great."

"She was brilliant, just brilliant," Boyle said, "girl's a star. Have you seen the promos going out right now? The whole nation's going to be tuning in. Mind you we can't afford to lose momentum. Any ideas how we're going to be able to develop this thing?"

"We thought a portable satellite system, like they use on News," Julian said, "that way Olivia can broadcast next time live from the rainforest directly into the programme. Luckily it's six am there when we go on air so it's just getting light."

"Could we combine it with a phone-in this end? You know, viewers get to put their questions directly to the Sandula."

"Could we think about that Doug? The Sandula aren't actually into sound-bites just yet."

"Okay, but I want ideas. Call a meeting for tomorrow. Everyone. I want this thing brainstormed. Oh and get onto sales. The whole fucking world's going to want to buy this, the whole fucking world."

In opposition to medical opinion Gerry believed that whisky clarifies the mental process. Now that he'd drunk a quarter of a bottle, his faculties were razor sharp. It also gave him the courage he would need. He stared at the crumpled press cutting, folded it and put it in his wallet. Although it was late, he'd heard Espinoza's voice on the verandah and knew he was still up. He took a last swig from the bottle and went out.

Espinoza was leaning on the railing outside his office, laughing with two young girls. At Gerry's approach he pushed them away with a pat on their backsides. The girls took the meaning and disappeared. He turned to Gerry. "Well Gerry, can't sleep after all?"

"Harris to you," Gerry said firmly, "people who know me as a television reporter know me as Gerry Harris."

Espinoza's eyes registered a momentary flicker. "A television reporter? But Olivia told me you were an account…"

"We're not playing any more, Mr. Espinoza. You know who I am; you've always known."

"Shall we go inside?"

They went into the office and Espinoza closed the doors behind him. He flicked on a table lamp and motioned to Gerry to take an armchair.

"I'd rather stand," Gerry said.

"Going to be confrontational are we?"

"That's the intention. Do you want to send for Rizal?"

"Only if you intend violence. Have you been drinking, Harris?"

"How did you find out who we were? Was it Father Ambrose? He'd seen me on television in London I suppose?"

"No, though he did recognise Olivia from the London office. But by that time I'd told him who you both were anyway. No, it was your friend Damien Street. He showed a remarkable aptitude for betrayal."

"Where is he?"

"I couldn't say exactly – out there somewhere. He's a guest of the M.I.L.F. I've only just heard tonight. It seems he gave my name as a reference."

"Is he in danger?"

"Depends what answer I give them. '*Yes he is my friend….*' they turn him over to me. '*No he isn't my friend….*'" Espinoza shrugged.

"Did he say why he was here?"

"He was trying to find out what happened to his colleague, a man called Neville. Your colleague too I believe."

"That's the reason *I'm* here."

"I thought you were interested in babies."

"I'll come to that in a minute." Gerry took the press cutting from his wallet and smoothed it out. "He's a friend of yours and I think you know where he is." He held up the picture.

"Where did you get this?"

"Research."

Espinoza walked over to the filing cabinet and took out the folder of clippings. He riffled through them. "Doesn't seem to be here. Should I be surprised?"

"You can have this one if you like."

"Don't make me angry, Harris. You're not exactly safe here. What makes you so confident you can get out of this in one piece?"

"Because Olivia knows I'm your guest. Because a lot of people know I'm here. And because if anything happens to me I've left instructions for the tape to be viewed."

"The tape?"

Gerry looked Espinoza in the eye and prepared himself for the big lie. "…of Rizal parading the girls for our selection, of Susanna telling me she wants to go to England to have my baby. I sent it home from Davao on our last visit."

Espinoza laughed. "Don't be a fool, Harris, you know perfectly well that's insufficient to make an accusation. We'd crucify you in the courts. All you've got is a perfectly innocent clip of an amateur beauty parade and an uncorroborated allegation by some anonymous girl in a bedroom. We'd just say you paid her. You won't find *her* and you won't find *Filipina Services* either."

"Who said it's uncorroborated?"

Espinoza was silent. He moved closer to Gerry. "What do you mean?"

Gerry had never felt so alone in his life. He craved a glass of whisky like an addict. "While I've been out here my producer's been following up leads in London. Father Ambrose shut up shop in Hackney in a hurry. There were still girls out there, well one at least we know of, who'd yet to come in. Am I right? (*Please say I am, please God*) Well one of them showed up there, pregnant of course, looking for *Innocents Abroad*, your 'London Office' as you call it. When she couldn't find it, someone directed her upstairs to the refuge, you know the one; the woman there's called Joan Little. She telephoned my producer. The girl gave him an interview, told him everything."

Espinoza stared at Gerry for a moment then walked to the door and threw it open. "Rizal!" he shouted. Rizal looked up sleepily from a sofa, got to his feet and shuffled into the room. "The tape. You told me you'd stolen the tape from their camera. Did you watch it?"

Rizal's eyes wandered, avoiding Espinoza's gaze.

"Well did you?"

"It wouldn't play," Rizal said, sulkily.

"What do you mean it wouldn't play?"

"I tried it in the machine, the one you watch the girls on. It wouldn't play."

"That's because it's the wrong format," Gerry interjected, "it's a mini DV. Yours is probably an old VHS. Still, if you want to have a look, fetch the camera from my room. You won't see anything. It's a blank. The one you want's in London."

Espinoza turned to Gerry. "Congratulations are in order Mr. Harris. It seems you have your story. In which case all I can say is you'd better leave. You'll have to find your own way back of course. You can hardly expect me to give you a lift under the circumstances. It's a pity it's rather dangerous out there."

"I thought that could be part of the negotiation." Gerry said.

"Negotiation? You have your story, Harris, what is there to negotiate?"

"I have *a* story, it's not the one I want. What do you suppose the *Filipina Services* story is worth? With the amount of material we've got you're probably talking ten minutes on the Sunday current affairs show. We could do that of course, *will* do that if we have to; but I was sent here to find Peter Neville. That's the big story. If I brought that one back I'd be Stanley to Neville's Livingstone. That's why I'm prepared to trade."

"Trade?"

"You get me to Neville, I drop the *Filipina Services* story."

Espinoza laughed. How do I know you'll keep your word?"

"You don't. You have to trust me."

"Mr. Harris, so far you have demonstrated yourself to be a spy and a thief. Why should I trust you?"

"You have everything to gain and nothing to lose. If I don't make it back safely the story *will* be broadcast. If I do make it back I'm in a position to drop it. I promise you I will."

"Perhaps you overestimate the damage a broadcast will do me. I can easily buy my way out of trouble in Manila you know."

"Maybe so but what about your reputation? And I don't just mean in Manila. What will the rest of the world think when it discovers that the saviour of the Sandula sells babies for profit? Don't you think it might look more closely at the tribe's authenticity?"

Espinoza's eyes narrowed visibly. "What do you mean by that?"

"That it's a fake, a hoax. Can't say exactly why you've done it but there are precedents, Piltdown man, scientists who make up their results."

A tic appeared in Espinoza's cheek. "Go on."

"When I realised you knew who we were, I thought at first you'd done it just to distract us from the baby story; it certainly had that effect on Olivia. Keeping us here would give you time as well, wouldn't it, to cover your tracks back in Davao and try and get hold of my tape? But then I thought you couldn't possibly have organised the tribe at such short notice. A lot of rehearsal must have gone in there. No, the Sandula were ready and waiting to be presented to the world. I think you killed two birds with one stone, Espinoza. I think you used the Sandula to stop the BBC's investigation and at the same time used the BBC to launch the Sandula. You must have thought it was fate, such a renowned broadcaster turning up on your doorstep."

"And what is my motive for this supposed fake?"

"It's my guess they're your fantasy. All the local cultures are adulterated in some way aren't they.....Western influences and so on? You wanted purity, perfection, a people at one with nature. You *wanted* a tribe like the Sandula to exist but, inconveniently, it didn't. So you invented one You created the rich man's ultimate plaything, his very own Garden of Eden."

Espinoza's expression remained impassive save for the tic which now began to pulse with a regular frequency. "I don't wish to hear any more, Mr. Harris. You have your deal. We'll meet in the morning."

"Bishop?"

"Blasphemous!" In the studio gallery the bishop's silver cross flashed simultaneously on twenty monitors.

The studio presenter turned to his left, "Dr. Ballinger?" The twenty monitors flashed twenty new clones, this time of the pullovered academic. "God's got sod all to do with it, bishop. This is a matter for rational debate and scientific enquiry. I really don't know why these media people feel it necessary to lower the level of discussion by inviting along you chaps in frocks to talk about someone who doesn't exist. It demeans intellectual debate in this country. But that's the media for you."

"Go for it," Boyle said from the seclusion of the gallery.

"May I remind you," the bishop said, "that you've just accepted an invitation to appear on the media yourself and that whilst you may not believe in God, there are countless people out there who will have taken considerable offence at that young woman's taking the words of the Lord in vain."

"I don't think she meant it literally," said the woman from Friends of the Earth, "she was just using the symbolism. It's not as if she's saying 'this is the Messiah' or anything. I found it very emotional to be honest."

"Ha!" Ballinger said, "Exactly, emotional. Here we have a major scientific discovery, a resource of incalculable value to the anthropological community and all your pretty young presenter can do is cry. Frankly these people need saving as much from the BBC as they do from the loggers. We need scientists in there, social scientists, linguists not some dolly bird with legs."

"What's a dolly bird?" the vision mixer whispered.

"Sixties term," said the P.A. "means he fancies her like hell."

"So do I," said the director.

"Can I bring in His Excellency Mr. Luis Tadeo, who's the Philippine ambassador to London." The ambassador appeared in a frame on a large screen in the studio. The presenter swung round in his chair. "Mr. Tadeo, can I ask you, what's the Philippine government's position on this now you've seen our second report?"

"We support the position of Dr. Ballinger," the ambassador said.

"What!" Boyle said, "he can't do! He's meant to be on the other side. Friends of the Earth and Ambassador *for.* That's what you said Julian."

"Shit," said Julian.

"In what respect?" the presenter asked.

"Respect is a good word," the ambassador said. "It is my government's opinion that while we are grateful to the BBC for drawing attention to the danger logging poses to the survival of this group of people, insufficient respect has been shown to them either as a social entity or as a subject for intellectual and academic study. They have, in short, been exploited for the purpose of entertainment, as indeed has the Christian religion."

"Quite right," the bishop nodded, "blasphemy."

"And what will you be doing about it ambassador?"

"The logging will be brought to an end, of course, but we also plan to close the area to visitors. In future, permission will have to be sought from the Department of Anthropology at the University of the Philippines."

"Right on," said Dr. Ballinger.

"What?" Boyle shrieked, pacing the gallery, following the ambassador's image from monitor to monitor, "He can't do that! He just can't do that. We've got the portable satellite going in, the live broadcast." He flicked the talkback switch to the presenter. "Tell him he can't do that." he shouted. "Tell him we've got copyright, intellectual property rights, tell him we'll sue, tell him anything."

"So it looks like that's the last we'll be seeing of the Sandula for some time," the presenter said, discreetly removing the shrieking earpiece and turning back to the camera.

"Standby VT 7," the PA called.

"And that's also the last from us for tonight. My thanks to my guests and to all of you for watching. We'll be back at the same time next Friday but for now, from the Garden of Eden and from everyone in the studio here, goodnight."

"Roll music and credits," said the PA

"Good show everybody, well done," said the director.

"I want that man fired," said Boyle.

Fear and sleep are poor bedfellows, and whether it was the sound of the door opening or the lamp being switched on, Gerry was awake in an instant. There was someone else in the room, first a shadow, then a silhouette, then, after a long pause while Gerry eased himself up against the bedhead, a voice.

"Did you know," the voice said cooly, "that Fidel Castro would keep foreign journalists waiting for weeks on end then suddenly burst into their hotel rooms at two in the morning to be interviewed? Happened to James Cameron, last of the great drinkers." The figure moved round and sat at the foot of the bed, moving the empty whisky bottle out of the way. "Cameron gets this fantastic exclusive with the great revolutionary, you see. They talk for three hours, stories about CIA assassination attempts, insights into Soviet foreign policy, the Cuban missile crisis from the inside. But Cameron's gone to bed pissed, hasn't he? When he wakes up in the morning he thinks to himself: Good God, Fidel Castro was right here in my room, sitting at the foot of my bed. What an exclusive. Now what the fuck did he say?"

"You've told that story before, Peter." Gerry said.

"You disappoint me, Gerry. I thought you'd say, 'Peter Neville, I presume'. Ever the one for the cliché as I remember."

Gerry said nothing. His mouth was dry and whisky-tasting and his eyes burned. "Give me a moment," he said. He went into the bathroom, splashed water on his face and drank half a litre.

"Hope I'm not disturbing you?" Neville called from the bedroom. When Gerry got back he was already lying out on the bed, hands behind head, shirt unbuttoned to the waist. He wore no shoes or socks, the brown feet boasting of a change of lifestyle.

"Look Peter," Gerry said, "I understand the tactic and it's nothing to do with Fidel Castro's habits. It's *policemen* who wake people up in the night to be interviewed and the more secret the policeman, the worse the hour. The name *Gestapo* comes to mind. Couldn't we just talk in the morning?"

"You're the one with the tactics, dear boy. Admirable. You walk right into the lion's den with a clever little tactic to get you right out again. Which is why I'm here. What do you want with me? You've got poor Ferdinand's knickers in a right twist."

"Didn't he say?

"He said you wanted to see me."

"It's a little more than that. I want the world to see you. To use your own conceit, I need to show them I've found Dr. Livingstone. It's the story they want….. you know, the cliché."

"And if I don't play, you'll blow the gaffe on my enterprise. Is that right?"

"*Your* enterprise?"

"You know what I'm talking about. *Pregnancies for Profit.* I expect that's what you'd call your piece, wouldn't you? "Tonight from the Philippine island of Mindanao, Gerry Harris reports on a shocking trade in human babies…etc. etc."

"You….?" Gerry closed his eyes then opened them again. He picked up the whisky bottle, held it up to the light and stared through the clear plastic. The room beyond blurred. He placed the bottle against his forehead hoping vainly to cool his skull. "You mean ….I mean …..you *do* mean don't you? It was *you* set the whole thing up, is that what you're saying? I thought it was Espinoza."

"Think of Espinoza as the venture capitalist behind the enterprise. Me, I'm more chairman and chief executive."

Gerry allowed the empty whisky bottle to slip through his fingers and fall to the floor. "Look, is there anywhere in this house I can get a drink?"

Neville swung his legs off the bed. "Follow me." Gerry followed the silent barefoot steps down the corridor and out onto the rear balcony. In the blackness, only a soundtrack of insects, white noise, betrayed the presence of the forest. At the far end of the balcony a light came from beneath a door.

"This where you live?" Gerry asked.

"No, I have a house behind the village. This is where I work."

"But this is the room…." Gerry stopped mid-sentence.

"Yes? This is the room what?"

"Nothing."

Neville pushed the door open. They went in. The room was sparsely furnished – an unmade double bed, a dresser, a chair. A door at the back led into a bathroom.

"Doesn't look much like an office," Gerry said.

"I don't use it for office work. Take a seat."

Gerry sat down in the chair and looked at the bed. "What other jobs are there? I thought Rizal handled this end and Ambrose the other."

"True enough. And don't forget the girls themselves. But that still leaves one position unfilled, doesn't it? Now what do you suppose that would be?"

"I'm not sure I want to know the answer to that question."

"Come on Gerry, what's the missing ingredient? What else does the product require in its manufacture? Let me get you that drink." Neville went into the bathroom and ran a tap. When he returned he held a glass of whisky and a jug of water. He put them on the dresser. "Help yourself."

Gerry poured water into the whisky and took a slug.

"So what's the answer Gerry?"

"I imagine you're trying to tell me that you're more than just Chairman and Chief Executive."

"Go on."

"That you're the father of these babies, that you're the one who inseminates the girls."

"Very properly put, if I may say so, Gerry. Others less perceptive than yourself might imagine I am seeking personal gratification. Not at all. I *inseminate*, I plant my seed, my investment in the business if you will."

Gerry closed his eyes and shook his head from side to side. "Tell me I'm not awake, someone."

Neville smoothed the bedsheet then lay back on it, staring up at the ceiling fan. "Don't you want to ask me how it all came about?"

Gerry shrugged. "I imagine you're going to tell me anyway."

"Like most things in life it started by accident. Friends of mine in London wanted to adopt. Some dinner party chat about me and the Philippines. I said I'd ask people I knew. Ferdinand found a T'boli girl with an unwanted child. Well, the adoptive parents came out here thinking they could just take the baby back, like people were already doing in Colombia, Romania. They were astonished to find the emigration authorities wouldn't allow the child out without proper adoption papers. The baby was returned to its mother. So we put our heads together and came up with this scheme using Rizal's domestic service agency to send a pregnant girl by a roundabout route to London. It was originally just a one off, favour to friends. But word got about in their circle that you could adopt this way and......things just took off."

"And you, why did you come here? Why do you stay here?"

"There are people, Gerry, quite a lot of them in fact, who leave a pile of clothes on a beach, people who set off for work in the morning and never arrive. We are the disappearers; if you're not one of us you won't understand. We have a compulsion to draw a line under one life and begin another. I was a public figure. I couldn't disappear quietly. I was always going to be recognised. But not in Mindanao. Ever since I first saw this lake and the village, I imagined one day I'd escape here, my very own Shangri-la – no wives, no debts, no income tax, no morning meetings, no viewers' letters, no television. Just peace and tranquillity in the most beautiful place on earth."

"And a prosperous business."

"If you like. That's what made it all possible, you see – a source of income. What better job could a man ask for?"

"If a woman did it she'd be a whore."

"Tut, tut, Gerry. How very prim of you. You must remember the oldest profession is still a profession. Anyway, somebody had to do it. With demand growing it was difficult to find enough girls willing to give up their babies. So we decided to recruit girls who weren't pregnant and do a deal with them. It's surprising what money can buy."

"And do they have to be Espinoza's 'companions' first?"

"Not necessarily, but it helps. Gets them in the right frame of mind."

"Would you be surprised if I said I was revolted?"

"Of course not. You're utterly predictable, Gerry. However, I can promise they're all of age when they come to me."

"But not virgins."

"None of your business. You know Gerry, there's a fine line between prudishness and prurience."

"Why you then? Why do you have to be the father?"

"Genes, dear boy. I'm tall, I'm white with a high IQ. The customers are happier with a Eurasian mix than pure oriental. Children don't stand out as much."

Gerry got up and wandered out onto the balcony. "And to think I thought it was Father Ambrose."

"Father Ambrose what?"

"In here, the other night. I saw a girl come out of this door. When I saw him the following day I put two and two together and made five."

"Not an unreasonable assumption."

"Meaning?"

"Meaning that the good father wasn't made for the celibate life. Unfortunately, he shares Ferdinand's tastes. It's what got him sent into the wilderness in the first place, out of sight, if not out of harm's way."

For a long time neither spoke. Gerry returned to the room and stood at the foot of the bed. Neville's hands were behind his head, his knees up, bare feet spread, a body language of self regard and disdain. Gerry knew he was being challenged to take up a moral position, to enter some squalid debate about moral relativity, about living in the 'real world'. There was no point. It would just be self-justification on Neville's part, an attempt to clear his conscience, to win Gerry's approval by persuading him he was some kind of ethical wimp if he failed to collude. He knocked back the whisky glass. "And is that the whole story then? Is there anything else I ought to know?"

"Frankly I don't think you *ought* to know any of it. You'd better tell me just what it is you're proposing to film. If you're dropping your investigation as you promise, you can hardly show what I'm up to, not that I'd let you for one moment."

Gerry shook his head. "I don't know, to be honest. I hadn't the slightest idea when I made that promise that you had anything to do with the pregnancies story."

"I trust you're not planning to renege."

"No, no, a promise is a promise," (easy enough to keep, he thought, when he had no story to trade in the first place), "but I'll need to prove I've found you."

"So I'll need a storyline to account for my disappearance."

"You mean a lie?"

"Offend your journalistic principles does it Gerry? Your friend Olivia seemed quite happy with hers."

"The Sandula, you mean. She didn't know it was a lie."

"But you told her, I bet, and she went ahead anyway. Why let the facts get in the way of a good story eh? You know, I told Ferdinand that lot would never stand up to scrutiny for long."

"Who were they really, the Sandula?"

"Some were villagers from the fringes of the forest, fairly primitive to start with – knew how to make fire from rubbing sticks together, that kind of thing, even if they did wear T-shirts and jeans. Some of the children were orphans of the fighting he'd picked up in town, street kids, anyone as long as they had long hair and looked nice.

He's been rehearsing them for months. I expect he pays better than the Equity minimum."

"Why did he do it?"

Neville shrugged. "He wanted to fool National Geographic. He wanted to be a celebrity. He wanted to be a world-famous anthropologist. You tell me."

"I told him I thought he *needed* a tribe like that to exist and when they didn't, he invented them."

"Rich men expect to get their way."

"You approve of that?"

"I like rich people. Money really can buy you everything, you know."

"He uses his money to buy off the Moros doesn't he? He told me they're holding Damien and that it's down to him, Espinoza, what his fate is to be."

"So I hear. You don't sound very concerned."

"Probably because I can't tell fact from fiction any longer. You were supposedly taken prisoner by the Moros and here you are."

"Here I am indeed – that's a fact." Neville looked thoughtful for a moment then sat up abruptly, swinging his legs off the bed. "In which case….how's this for a fiction? Let's suppose I *was* taken prisoner by the MILF. Suppose I was kept in their jungle re-education centre. Suppose…," Neville smiled to himself, "…..suppose I'd decided to join them."

"That's ridiculous. No-one would ever believe you."

"Why not? People will assume I've been brainwashed. In an interview with you I will insist, with considerable clarity and forcefulness, that my conversion to the cause of Moro independence is genuine and that I intend to fight on as a guerilla, sacrificing my life if necessary, should the struggle so demand. In the subsequent studio interview a psychologist will lend conviction to the story by comparing my case with that of Patti Hearst, the American heiress who joined forces with the urban terrorists who kidnapped her. What d'you say?"

"What about Damien? Have you forgotten him?"

"Not at all. I use my position with the armed forces of the Moro Islamic Liberation Front to intercede on behalf of my former colleague. He is released into your safe keeping, on camera of course, and you can return to London with, dare I say it, a scoop."

"It's a pack of lies."

"It's a pack of half-truths."

"It's half a pack of lies then. I suppose you could argue that Damien's capture was real. So would his release be."

"That's the way to look at it." Neville took Gerry's glass and withdrew into the bathroom. When he returned he held two glasses of whisky. "Shall we drink to it then?"

Gerry stared at the glass. His vision was becoming blurred, he felt unsteady, he was exhausted – talk about brainwashing, how could he be expected to make any kind of choice in this state, let alone an ethical one? He just wanted out now, away from the whole sordid, corrupt business. And that was what he was being offered wasn't it, a simple exit from which he would emerge with credit? Clever. It was a lie, of course, well half a lie. But no-one would ever know that. Nobody would come looking for Peter Neville again. He raised his glass......

It was from the moment of the messenger's return that Damien's situation changed. There was a lot of discussion with the lieutenant, during which the man repeatedly formed a circle with his thumb and forefinger, put it to his eye, and panned his head from left to right. The lieutenant checked his watch, tapping its glass. He gave an order and two men ran across the clearing to the tree supporting the cage. They untied the vine and lowered the cage to the ground, where a small cloud of ash rose from the extinct fire. Damien's heartbeat accelerated into three figures. The same two men came and pulled him to his feet. They pointed to the cage, offering him the chance to go voluntarily. How could Espinoza do this to him? The monster. He'd disowned him, knowing what his fate would be. The men prodded him to make a move but he couldn't, so they dragged him by his lashed wrists and manhandled him through the cage door. Then they tied the door on and began hoisting. Two more men came to help; others approached carrying firewood.

Gerry and Neville left the jeep and set off into the undergrowth. A guide from the village went ahead clearing the path with a bolo. Neville wore camouflage fatigues and a khaki forage cap and cartridge belts slung diagonally from each shoulder. Gerry had thought this touch a little OTT but conceded Neville had looked quite impressive

206

during the interview. Neville, never one to downgrade his own importance, had given himself the rank of Major. They walked for more than an hour until the guide suddenly stopped and whispered something in T'Boli.

"Start filming," Neville said to Gerry, "he thinks we're there."

"Won't it look suspicious if we arrive filming? I mean they're not supposed to know we're coming. Wouldn't they just confiscate the camera if we were for real?"

"You give the viewer too much credit for intelligence. Besides you're with me. I'm a major; I outrank the lieutenant. If I say you film, you film."

A sentry appeared on the path ahead, his rifle pointed at the party. Neville pushed to the front and the man saluted. Neville returned the salute in a languid, officerly way, while Gerry filmed it all with the cam-corder. The light was poor beneath the trees but that probably didn't matter. Channel 4 were into amateurishness nowadays; grainy and wobbly equalled gritty reality.

As Damien moved to get a better view, the cage began to sway. He grabbed onto a bar with his tied hands and hoisted himself onto his knees. Newcomers were arriving below, some sort of superior officer the lieutenant was saluting and a man with a camera. God they'd come to witness his execution, his slow death, smoked like a haddock while they recorded it with their video. The obscenity of it. He began to shake violently, the movement transmitting itself to the cage which began to wobble. One of the men below pointed at him and laughed.

The man with the camera set up a tripod and began to film the scene – the two officers talking and looking at Damien, the rebel soldiers stacking the firewood. From the mounting pyre, the cameraman tilted the camera up towards the cage then back down again. Then he pointed the lens at Damien, who in an involuntary reaction he would later regret (Gerry had zoomed in by now) was seen to mouth the words 'Help, Mummy'.

Schadenfreude, Gerry thought. He really shouldn't be enjoying this but if anyone deserved his comeuppance it was Damien. He adjusted the lens to a wide angle and stepped round in front of the camera. Just as he seemed about to speak he turned and looked up at Damien. Their eyes met in a brief moment of recognition. Gerry winked, turned back to the camera and began to speak:

"It's pretty clear what the guerillas have in store for the BBC's Damien Street. I'm here under safe conduct but his life now lies in the hands of his erstwhile colleague, Peter Neville, who was himself captured by this same faction just over a year ago. Neville of course converted to their cause and intends to use all his influence to try and persuade the officer here to release Damien, though he's told me privately that he's none too confident. For everyone concerned it's a tense moment."

Damien slumped to the bottom of the cage. Gerry Harris had just winked at him. He was about to be executed and Gerry Harris had arrived to do a piece to camera for Channel 4. He slapped his face. It was a nightmare, he'd wake up. Then the cage lurched and began to move. He was going down. It was a dream, it had to be a dream, because there was Peter Neville now, disguised as a guerilla, talking to the lieutenant and pointing. The cage had begun to revolve, spinning on its rope, so that the world moved in a blur first from left to right, then from right to left. He closed his eyes to stop himself from feeling sick He took deeper and deeper breaths, faster and faster. He had to escape. The way you got out of a nightmare was to wake up, he had to wake up, he had to wake up......

He opened his eyes as the water hit his face. A man stood over him holding a dripping gourd. Other faces peered down from behind.

"Gerry is that you?"

"It is," Gerry said, "you're free to go. We've transport waiting. Quite a walk I'm afraid. You up to it?"

"Is this real?"

Gerry nodded.

"And Peter Neville, I thought I saw Peter Neville. Was he real too?"

"He's one of them now. He saved your life."

"Where is he?"

"He's gone. You won't be seeing him again."

"You were filming. Why were you filming?"

"It's my story, the big story, the one you came to get, remember?"

"Best man won and all that."

"Magnanimous of you."

Gerry reached down and pulled Damien to his feet. Damien brushed himself down then looked at Gerry. "Look Gerry, I don't know quite how to say this but...."

"Don't say it then, you'll just embarrass us both."

"No it's just that you're going to be showing this scene, of course, I can't stop you but......"

"Well?"

"You will make me look good won't you?"

At the *Oscar* ceremony there are cameras dedicated to each of the nominees in a given category. Thus the viewer will see a screen split into four, in each quarter of which a would-be winner is seen feigning calm, while simultaneously both preparing for disappointment and rehearsing the acceptance speech. And when the winner is announced he or she pretends utter astonishment in one corner while the other three applaud and pretend not to be in the least surprised in theirs. At the Royal Television Society's annual journalism awards this was not the case. Only one camera patrolled the floor of the Grosvenor House Hotel, transmitting its pictures not to the wider public but to a large screen at one end of the ballroom. As the audience watched the clips of the nominated programmes, the camera positioned itself at the table of the winner, ready to transmit the delighted reaction the moment the guest celebrity read out '*And the winner is...*' So it was that Gerry, watching the camera track towards Boyle's table, knew already that it was to be Olivia's evening and not his. He poured himself another glass of wine.

She rose to the occasion as he would have expected, looking about her in 'what me?' bewilderment, weaving her way shyly through the tables, holding up the hem of her evening gown as she mounted the stage, wiping back an emotional tear before delivering a perfectly rehearsed off-the-cuff speech in which she thanked everybody who mattered and many more who didn't. She thanked the two Daves (who were only doing their job). She thanked Boyle and Julian for having faith in her. She thanked all those who put pressure on the Philippine government to stop the logging. She thanked the Philippine government for stopping the logging. She thanked the Sandula themselves just for being themselves. And then she thanked Gerry.

When he heard her, he sat up, spilling wine on the tablecloth. "There's someone else who deserves my extra special thanks," she was saying, "I'm not going to give you his name. There's a reason for that. He knows who he is and he knows why I'm so grateful to him." She faltered for a moment, looked down at the ground then wound a loose strand of hair behind her ear. "I can't thank you enough…I'm really sorry about everything." Then she turned and shook the celebrity's hand, grabbed the acrylic block which sealed the golden award and swept off the stage to dutiful applause.

"Bad luck Boyo," Pryce said to Gerry at their table, "still think you should have won though. There you go braving wild mountain tribesmen, loyal only to their weapons; you track down your man *and* you rescue your colleague from the jaws of death. All she has to do is hold up a baby and she walks off with the prize. Better looking than you, mind."

"You know what, Northrop?" Gerry said, "You're a facile prick." He pushed his chair back abruptly and got up. "I'm off to do the congratulations bit." From across the room, Olivia saw him approach and signalled to him to stay where he was. She picked up her evening bag and excused herself from Boyle's table.

"Didn't want to talk in front of them," she said as they met. Her eyes looked past him.

"Congratulations," Gerry said.

"I'm sorry, I didn't expect to be in competition with you."

"Nothing to be embarrassed about – best man wins."

"I think we should go somewhere quieter." She turned and led the way out into the foyer. He followed her, his eyes fixed on her bare shoulders and the smooth indentation of her spine. She'd put her hair up and he realised he'd never seen how slender her neck was. It was like a discovery and he wanted to be the first to kiss it.

"You know it was you I was thanking?" she said when they stopped.

He nodded.

"And you know why?"

"Dunno, good sex?"

She relaxed her expression at this and tried a smile. "For not

210

betraying me, Gerry, for not telling the world I was living a lie, for allowing me to enjoy all this when all the time I knew it was a hoax. When I heard you were up for the same award I was convinced you'd blow the whistle. Why didn't you?"

Gerry shrugged. "One, because no-one was ever going to see the Sandula again, least of all the University of the Philippines Department of Anthropology. Two, because the pot shouldn't call the kettle black. Three, because I'm madly in love with you. Any more reasons?"

"What did you just say?"

"Three, because I'm madly in love with you."

"Before that."

"Oh! Two, because the pot shouldn't call the kettle black."

"What do you mean by that?"

"I mean that my film was a hoax too. Peter Neville isn't a major in the Moro Islamic Liberation Front, he's *Filipina Services'* in-house procreator. He fathers the children for the adoption scam."

"Gerry! I don't believe it!"

"True."

"How on earth did you find out?"

"When you threw away the tape, I realised I had no story. So I went back to the film I'd gone there to make, 'Desperately Seeking Peter.' I was looking for Peter Neville, you see. Then I found evidence that Neville had known Espinoza...."

"Wait a minute, Gerry, you told me the film you'd come to make was about pineapple pickers, that you specifically *weren't* doing Peter Neville."

"I lied."

"Oh great! First you're a thief, now you're a liar."

"Blackmailer too. I told Espinoza I wouldn't broadcast the tape if Neville would appear on camera, if I could be the one to find him."

"You just said you didn't have the tape. I'd thrown it away."

"That was the *big* lie. You'd have been proud of me. Anyway they fell for it and Neville came up with this cover story as to how he'd disappeared. And I....well....went along with it. I needed a story didn't I? At least Damien's capture was genuine enough."

"So that makes it all right, does it? One truth cancels out one lie?"

"Who's talking now?"

"Would you believe me if I said I still believe the Sandula were inspirational even if they weren't real?"

"No."

"Can't a painting be beautiful even if it's a forgery?"

"Shall I tell you something Neville told me? That childbirth – one of the women in the cave was a trained midwife. Espinoza was taking no chances. Still beautiful?"

"So we're both guilty."

"'Fraid so. I wouldn't be too concerned about it though. How much do you think the Boyles and Pryces of this world really care? If you went to them and said, sorry it was all a fib, what do you think they'd say? 'Great story, why go spoiling it?' Ever wondered why journalists use the word *story* when it's another word for *fiction*?"

"I don't think you're as unprincipled as you make out. You can still redeem yourself you know."

"Redeem myself?"

"We both came back with false stories and left the true one, the Big Story, out there. You could have another go."

"Impossible. *Filipina Services* has gone to ground. The Davao operation's shut up shop, so has Hackney."

"I know. But remember the woman there I told you about, Joan Little? I went to see her last week. It may be nothing, but she has this contact, some sort of hostel in south London. Her friend there tells her there've been a few Filipina girls turning up there lately – and she thinks they might be pregnant."

Gerry shook his head. "It's no good, Olivia. Without the Mindanao connection we can't prove a thing. And we'd never get near Espinoza again in a million years. I'm not blaming you, under the circumstances, but I'm afraid all the evidence is at the bottom of that lake."

Olivia shook her head. "Wrong." She snapped opened the clip of her evening bag, pushed two fingers into it and pulled out a small plastic box.

Gerry stared, open-mouthed.

"Say something Gerry."

"You mean that's.....?"

Olivia nodded. "It was pure chance, that time we'd gone back to

Davao. The chambermaids were doing the room and they'd taken all the used soap to be replaced. I needed some there and then, so I rummaged in your spongebag. And what did I find in the soap dish? A video cassette. Aha, I thought, this doesn't belong here. So I played it didn't I? Mad as hell at first but then I thought, don't get mad, get even. So I substituted a blank. You were supposed to find out when you got back to London, your comeuppance. Then when you gave it to me by the lake….."

"I was being kind."

"Sod you, Gerry, you were giving me back what you thought you'd stolen from me."

"And you threw it away knowing full well I'd believe it was the real tape. That wasn't very nice."

"You'd just tried to destroy my story."

"I was only telling the truth."

"Oh, yes, the truth, of course." She bit her lip and smiled at him all at the same time. "Well, here's the truth in this little box. It's yours, take it, show it to Northrop Pryce, whatever you like. It's my thank-you." She reached up and kissed him, slipping the tape into his breast pocket. "One other thing Gerry, when you say you're madly in love with me is that the truth?"

"Of course."

"Good. Just as well then." She smiled, turned away and began to make her way back towards the ballroom.

Gerry caught her arm. "Olivia what do you mean, just as well?"

"I mean, Gerry, it's just as well that the father of my child should be in love with its mother."

For a moment Gerry stood there confused, his brain taking time to substitute appropriate names for 'father' and 'mother'. "What are you saying Olivia?"

"I'm pregnant, Gerry."

"And it's mine?"

Olivia nodded.

"And you're going through with it?"

She nodded again and smiled radiantly. "Listen to that. The band's started. Why don't you and I have a dance? Oh, and Gerry, one last thing: before you even think of it, just don't mention the word *adoption*."

213

Homepage of the South Cotabato Christian Human Rights Association
Hosted by Francisco Lopino

January Newsletter

Welcome to our first on-line newsletter, courtesy of the new <u>WWL telephone system</u> which has at last reached Koronodal. Although our communications have at last entered the 21st century, sadly no-one round here is talking much about a bright new future. <u>Unauthorised logging</u> continues unchecked in the island, displacing many tribal minorities and there have been disturbing reports of mercury pollution by <u>gold prospectors</u>.

On the political front we have cause only for further pessimism with kidnapping continuing to cast its fearful shadow. Latest victim is Mr. Ferdinand Espinoza, a member of the wealthy Manila family, who was taken from his mountaintop retreat in South Cotabato by forces believed to be those of the MILF. The rebels are said to be demanding a ransom of several million US dollars. Sources in Manila say a demand of this size is unlikely to be met.

Espinoza recently achieved international prominence with his discovery of the Sandula, a stone-age tribe living in isolation in the rainforest. Following brief worldwide exposure, the tribe has not reappeared. Two separate expeditions by anthropologists from the University of the Philippines have been unable to find any trace.

On the night of the kidnap, inhabitants of Koronodal were witness to an intense glow on the horizon. The conflagration marked the razing of Espinoza's mountain-top mansion, believed to be the action of local tribespeople. One man died in the blaze. While the remains are beyond identification, their stature indicates the likelihood that the deceased was a foreigner. Villagers report that a man who lived amongst them, thought to be an Englishman, is now missing.